SHELTERING INSTINCT

CERBERUS TACTICAL K9 TEAM CHARLIE
BOOK 2

FIONA QUINN

FIONA QUINN, LLC.

SHELTERING INSTINCT

Cerberus Tactical K9

TEAM CHARLIE

BY

FIONA QUINN

THE WORLD OF INIQUUS

Ubicumque, Quoties. Quidquid

Iniquus - /i'ni/kwus/ our strength is unequalled, our tactics unfair – we stretch the law to its breaking point. We do whatever is necessary to bring the enemy down.

THE LYNX SERIES

Weakest Lynx

Missing Lynx

Chain Lynx

Cuff Lynx

Gulf Lynx

Hyper Lynx

Marriage Lynx

STRIKE FORCE

In Too DEEP

JACK Be Quick

InstiGATOR

Fear The REAPER

Striker

UNCOMMON ENEMIES

Wasp

Relic

Deadlock

Thorn

FBI JOINT TASK FORCE

Open Secret

Cold Red

Even Odds

KATE HAMILTON MYSTERIES

Mine

Yours

Ours

CERBERUS TACTICAL K9 TEAM ALPHA

Survival Instinct

Protective Instinct

Defender's Instinct

Delta Force Echo

Danger Signs

Danger Zone

Danger Close

Cerberus Tactical K9 Team Bravo

Warrior's Instinct

Rescue Instinct

Hero's Instinct

Cerberus Tactical K9 Team Charlie

Guardian's Instinct

Sheltering Instinct

Shielding Instinct

Certified Cerberus Tactical K9

Beowolf

CIA Color Code

Red Line

This list was created in 2024. For an up-to-date list, please visit www.FionaQuinnBooks.com

If you prefer to read the Iniquus World in chronological order you will find a full list at the end

of this book.

DEDICATION

This book is dedicated to the wonderful people I met in Namibia.
Your grace, warmth, and humor make treasured memories.

ANGOLA
ZAMBIA
LUSAKA
MALAWI
LILONGWE
HARARE
ZIMBABWE
MOZAMBI
NAMIBIA
WINDHOEK
BOTSWANA
GABORONE
PRETORIA
MBABANE
SWAZILAND
MAPUTO
SOUTH
LESOTHO
Bloemfontein
MASERU
AFRICA
Cape Town

PLAYERS I

Ya Family
Mama Ya
Abraham
Moses
Tess Dagomba - WorldCares

Cerberus Tactical K9
Levi Elliot – handler, Team Charlie
Reaper Hamilton - lead trainer
Goose - Team Alpha veterinarian
Noah (K9 Hairyman) – Team Alpha tactical coordinator
Halo (K9 Max) – handler, Team Charlie
Hailey Sterling – Iniquus Logistics

PLAYERS II

Etosha

Enrico – K9 trainer

Kimba – military K9 handler

Josef - Commander

The Metz Family

Gwen – WorldCares

Iris – mother

Craig - father

PROLOGUE

"Tess, I love you," Abraham's voice, usually a rich baritone, came through the phone as dry and raspy. "I would be honored if you would accept my hand in marriage."

Tess stared straight ahead; her eyes held wide.

In the silence that fell between them, Abraham stammered, "I know what I'm asking of you," Abraham cleared his throat, then whispered, "And I think you understand that my asking you to accept my hand in marriage is a complex commitment."

Her day had been so banal. She was reading from her pile of scientific journals, munching from a bowl of cold popcorn. She wasn't ready for this call or for life to change in the blink of an eye.

It had happened to her before. She'd been living through a normal day when she'd been, quite literally, slung into a new reality. All one could do was hold on tight and go along for the ride.

Tess glanced around and saw the worried look on her roommate Shanti's face.

She felt bloodless as her whole body trembled.

As a child, Tess learned that shivering was the only way to express big emotions and stay safe.

She wasn't a child anymore.

Adults face the world squarely on. Tess tried to roll her shoulders back, to stand erect like a soldier, to borrow some bravery from the rigidity of the stance. "Do you need me to come to you?" were the words that showed up.

Marry Abraham.

She was going to say yes, of course she was. She just hadn't worked the words up to her lips yet.

"I think Ghana, for me, would not be optimal in this situation. I would prefer to come to you."

"Yes, of course."

"Does that mean?" For the first time through this conversation, there was energy in Abraham's words. His vowels fluttered with hope.

"Yes, I'll marry you. And as soon as we can. The sooner, the better."

"Thank you, Tess. There are probably some things that need arranging on your end." In Tess's imagination, she saw Abraham's words glow a warm, golden, relief-filled color. "And there are things for me to do here. I will most likely come at the beginning of June."

"A June wedding will be beautiful." She felt her throat close around those words and hold them back, if even for a moment more. "I'm going to hang up now. I need to figure out what hoops we need to jump through."

"Thank you, Tess. The children and I love you. We will be a good family."

Abraham needed her. With stage three cancer and two young, motherless children, he needed her.

And Tess *needed* to do this.

"Yes. Yes. It will be good. I love you, too. I'll see you soon."

Shanti was on her feet, running in place, her hands tightly clasped and held to her chest. The jubilation that she reined in until Tess swiped the phone closed bubbled out with a whoop and joyous laughter.

Tess struggled to lift her head to catch Shanti's gaze.

"You're in shock!" She ran over and grabbed Tess's arms, which hung heavily at her sides like she was a beanbag doll. "Snap out of it!" Shanti jumped up and down, grinning ear to ear. "You just got engaged to Levi! We need to celebrate."

Shanti probably interpreted Tess's silent tears, slithering, fat and salty, down her cheeks as happiness.

But these tears were shed for the ramifications of that phone call. And all the people who would feel the effects.

For Abraham's plight, she shed tears of heartache.

For what she was giving up, there were tears of grief.

She couldn't believe how this had unfolded. In a snap, the life she had projected out in front of her vanished like the hologram she'd always had the inkling it was. Some things were too good to be true.

But mostly, Tess's tears fell because of what she was about to do to Levi.

She pressed against the wall for stability.

Shanti was no longer dancing and clapping. A look of confusion tightened her features. "What's happening right now?"

"I'm getting married," was Tess's monotone answer.

"Why do you look like that? Like you're seeing a ghost. You should be joyful! You love Levi. You're going to have such a wonderful life together."

Tess licked her lips and scraped them between her teeth to keep her mouth from quivering as she shook her head.

Uncertainty waivered Shanti's words. "That was Levi, right?"

"No," Tess didn't move her lips as she spoke. "That was Abraham."

"Do I know Abraham?" Shanti thrust back, scowling. "Who is Abraham? What do you mean you love Abraham? You love Levi," Shanti's voice flashed to anger and disbelief. "Levi is the man you said lives in your bones. Levi is the man you said fills your dreams with hope and contentment. Levi is the one you pray for every day, and it's his photo you kiss every night. *Levi* is the one you're going to marry. Everyone knows that."

Shanti's thinking that things worked out for the best, that love conquered all, came from a place of privilege, and was sandpaper scratching at Tess's nerves; she wanted to shut this down. "Levi and I are not engaged. I'm engaged to Abraham. You've never met him. He lives in Ghana."

There was a long pause before Shanti pulled her brows tight, making deep lines across her forehead. "Your dad was from Ghana, right?"

"Yes, I've known Abraham almost all my life. And I love him very deeply. It will be an honor to be his wife." Tess's body was made of cotton batting that was rolled tight enough to keep her upright despite her feeling boneless. The thickness padded her emotions to the point that Tess found herself without any sensation.

But quickly, the batting fibers gave way, and Tess collapsed to the floor.

Her tears hadn't stopped rolling down her cheeks. They burned her.

Shanti sat down in the hallway facing Tess. "Hey." And when Tess didn't look up, she reached a hand to Tess's knee. "Hey." Shanti waited for Tess to look her in the eyes. "Can you tell me what's happening right now?" When Tess didn't answer,

Shanti raised her voice and commanded, "What's happening? Is this a seizure? Tess," she gripped Tess's shoulders and spoke slowly and clearly, "Are you having a seizure? Why are you shaking like this?"

Tess scooted back until she could feel the cold surface of the wall through her sweatshirt.

She pulled her feet in toward her hips and wrapped her arms around her shins, lowering her head to her knees to contain the trembling in her limbs.

She remembered this sensation.

She was right back in the terror of life.

Shanti ran to her bedroom and came back with a blanket, wrapping Tess in its warmth. "I don't know what's happening right now. I need some words. I need you to tell me so I know what to do. Should I call 911? Do you need a hospital?"

Tess held her hand out, and Shanti grasped it. Kneeling next to Tess, Shanti changed her tone to the cooing sound someone might use to coax a puppy from under the shrubs. "When you can."

"Abraham," Tess managed.

"The man on the phone that asked you to marry him. Who is he? Is he threatening you?"

"No. No. I have known Abraham since I was a child. Eight. When I lived in Ghana. And I do love him deeply and decidedly. I would do anything for him. Of course, I would." Life was a vortex. As the centrifugal force of today dragged her away from her center, she was smashed against the sides of her reality.

"You *lived* in Ghana?" Shanti shook her head. "Wait, what?"

"My parents met at university. I was a surprise that didn't stop them from pursuing their academic research. When they received a study grant, we moved to northern Ghana, where they were gathering data. We moved there when I was five."

"For how long?" Shanti curled like Tess, her hands gripping her shins, her cheek resting on her knee.

"Until I was about to turn eleven. I have dual citizenship. My dad was Ghanaian, and my mom was American. They met at university and … I already said that."

Shanti sipped air audibly into her nostrils and, even more quietly than before, whispered, "What happened in Ghana? Why do you love Abraham enough that you would do anything for him well over a decade later?"

Tess could hear in Shanti's words the battle of wants—the want to help in this situation and the want not to know what had happened to bring this day about. She was brave to ask the question.

A friend who can sit with you when you're in pain was precious and rare.

Usually, Tess shielded this story from everyone. Levi knew. She had to explain why she had night terrors when she slept with him. She pushed off telling him for as long as she could. But her thrashing and swallowed screams abraded his senses. He told her how he wanted to protect her, and he felt he was failing because she didn't feel safe in his arms.

Tess had to explain that he couldn't protect her from her past.

The past was a roaring monster that she fought to exhaustion.

"What happened in Ghana, Tess?" Shanti asked in a whisper.

Tess pursed her lips, then exhaled. It was hard to tell this story aloud. But Tess needed Shanti's friendship and support. In Shanti's eyes, Tess was doing the most disloyal and self-destructive thing imaginable, throwing away her wonderful relationship with Levi and their hopes and dreams. If Shanti didn't learn the why, she'd see Tess as an unfaithful and undependable person. Tess knew she'd lose her friend.

The story needed to be told.

"I was eight. My family went to the market to buy food and listen to music. We liked going there together to explore. I remember it as lively and fun." Past a clenched jaw, she muttered, "Until it wasn't."

Tess rested her gaze on the wall painted flat white with grey scuff marks from the tires where they leaned their bikes to get them out of the weather on wet days. She pictured her green bike there. The spokes. The meditation of riding to campus. And while those images did bring her a modicum of relief, Tess couldn't hold the corners of her mouth in a straight line. Her lips seemed to melt down the sides of her face, rivulets of lava that would soon harden into a permanent lament.

It took her a long time. And some failed efforts at inhaling before she closed her eyes. Her heavy lids would not open again, but she found her voice. "Yes, eight years old. We were at the market. I remember every detail of that day. Every color, line, and dot. Every sound and every smell. That day and what happened next."

Tess heard Shanti push herself around until they were side by side.

Shanti wrapped an arm around Tess and pulled until Tess rested her head on Shanti's lap. After tucking the blanket tightly around Tess, Shanti rhythmically stroked Tess's hair.

"At the market, a fight broke out over the cost of a Guinea fowl. My father had been standing next to the man who argued that the cost was too much and that the vendor was trying to take advantage of people. Two tribes had been antagonistic towards each other. It seemed to be a low boil until it wasn't. When the fight broke out that day, the men must have thought my dad was involved. They attacked, punching Dad over and over until he collapsed to the ground. My mother was screaming. She had a hold of my wrist, and with a great heave, I was flying up in the air like the games parents play with their kids when they are walking between two adults, letting their kids' feet swing high. Up, up, I sailed, higher than I've ever swung before. Mom called, 'Abraham!' I didn't recognize her voice and couldn't tell why she sounded like that. But now, as an adult, I recognize it as the sound of terror."

"Your dad," Shanti whispered. "This was over the price of a chicken?"

"It wasn't a simple argument about the price of a hen but a dispute between two tribes over land. And that day, in that market, with my parents standing too close to the epicenter, the horrors that shook the entire region began. But, of course, no one understood that at the time. The Guinea Fowl War."

"The Guinea Fowl War," Shanti repeated. The rhythmic combing fingers dragging through Tess's curls had a hypnotic effect.

Tess felt like she'd left her body and was watching herself tell this story from the end of the hall. "Mom swung me up. And as I flew into the air, my mom screamed, 'Save her! Run!' She was telling this stranger to save me. He did. He turned and ran, trapping me to his chest like a sleepy toddler. My arms looped around his neck. My legs wrapped his waist. He was very tall and strong. I thought he was an adult, but he was only sixteen. I later learned he was one of the advanced students that Mom tutored in the evenings. That's how she knew him, knew him well enough to trust him."

"This is Abraham."

"Abraham," Tess said, and his name buzzed her lips. "As he wove through the crowd, I saw my mom fighting to get to my dad. My dad was fighting to get up and get to Mom. And then, the machetes raised high in the air. I saw the blade— They were killed." That last sentence sounded so matter-of-fact.

It *was* a matter of fact.

Facts that couldn't change or be gentled.

That event was an emotion that was so big that Tess had never found a word for it. It was inexplicable. A deep guttural sound vibrated in her bones as if looking for a way to seep out and escape.

But that sound was imprisoned in her marrow forever.

Tess clamped a hand over her mouth in case it wanted to crawl out at this telling. But it didn't. It had lived in her for so long, set up house, and put up its feet. There was nothing that would pry this thing out. Not in this lifetime.

Shanti's thighs under Tess's head trembled as if she were freezing cold and trying to generate her own warmth. After a moment, Shanti's hand, stiffer and less rhythmic, began to comb Tess's curls again.

Tess bet that Shanti wished she hadn't asked.

But now that she'd turned the faucet on, the story continued to trickle out. Not the details, just the broad sweeps. Enough that when she told Levi, he understood her night terrors and how he couldn't stop them.

Tess hoped that Shanti would understand this personal earthquake, too.

"When Abraham returned to his village, he set me on the floor by the doorway in his hut. I remember that I couldn't make my eyes blink. My eyeballs were dry and painful. In their language, which I couldn't understand, Abraham quickly passed the information on to his mom. She—Mama Ya— unfolded three blankets and laid them on the ground. She gestured wildly to Abraham, and he ran out, leaving me alone with the frenzied activities in their hut. With incredible purpose, Mama Ya gathered things, placing them in the center of the blankets. Her son Moses, who was thirteen at the time—helped. I didn't know what to do other than stand there and pee down my leg."

"Oh, Tess."

"I watched Mama Ya making difficult choices about what went into the center of the blankets. Each got a cooking bowl, food, bottles of water, and matches. Each got a couple changes of clothes. When Abraham returned, Mama Ya was busy folding the blankets into packages and then tied them with rope. Abraham had a purple blanket packet on his head."

Tess remembered him standing in the doorway of the dark hut, the sunlight shining behind him silhouetted there.

"I recognized that purple blanket from off my bed. That packet was mine." Tess licked her lips and swallowed, wondering how long she would be given the respite of being out of her body. This was a familiar trick she'd used as a child when things turned from scary to terrifying. It was a useful skill for her soul to be able to sit off to the side as an observer.

But she couldn't beckon this skill; the ability came to her at times of great necessity.

At times when she was suffering existential threat.

"We put the bundles on our heads and left the hut. The chickens clucked and pecked in the yard. The coals glowed in the fire pit with its ring of flat stones. We were walking fast. Abraham had a tight hold of my hand. As we left the village, Mama Ya took the time to tell the people we passed. They ran back to their own homes. The wind carried the news like a banshee's cry. Danger sizzled. I remember thinking it was like bacon, the sound. I can't tell you why I had that impression."

Shanti sharply inhaled with the sudden illumination. "You hate it when I cook bacon."

"I absolutely do."

"So you got out, and you were safe," Shanti whispered as if she was closing the book and the bad was over, the tale told.

Tess needed Shanti to understand that, no, it wasn't it. And because that wasn't it, she would give up anything, *do* anything for Abraham. *Anything.*

Tess bit her lower lip, then scraped it free. "Mama Ya thought in a day or so we could go back. We hid in the forest. We ate our food. We drank our water. And we listened to the screams. When our provisions ran out, decisions needed to be made. Abraham snuck back to the village to see what was happening. The only thing left of the village was piles of ash. The chickens were gone, and so were all the vegetables in the Ya family's patch. That night, when the screams came from pockets of forest around us, Mama Ya said they were hunting for the people hiding. She decided to go west toward the village where she had family. We ran for days with nothing to eat. No water. We ran as the fighting spread. Huts burned. It was as though the earth heaved and threw people into the air. Then they landed to be thrown again."

"Shit," Shanti exhaled. She really regretted asking. It was in her voice that she wanted to backpedal to the time when she didn't know.

"We got to Mama Ya's cousins' village and begged for safety. They were from a neutral tribe and were afraid of retaliation for harboring the light-skinned child—me. Mom was white. They allowed me to stay in the hut but not be seen. They hid me behind their tallest baskets. It was the dry season. There was no extra food for people to share. We ate bugs from the trees and worms we dug up."

"Oh."

"Mama Ya treated Abraham like he was an adult and understood that he'd made a covenant when he accepted me into his arms at the market. My mother's dying plea was that Abraham keep me safe. And he lived up to that promise no matter what happened next. He made sure that I ate first, even when it meant he would go without. Our stomachs were so pinched … When the war reached the cousin's village, the people were heaved again. And again. And again. This went on for two years. Then came peace."

"How … How did you get to America?"

"After the unrest quieted enough that Mama Ya felt safe to travel to Accra, we walked to the American Embassy. There at the gate, Mama Ya handed the guard two things that Abraham had the foresight to bring: my parents' picture with their names on the back and their address book. My aunt and uncle flew to Ghana to pick me up."

"To go home to a country you probably couldn't remember. Your family must have been so grateful to the Ya family."

"They were. But how do you pay back that kind of moral debt?"

"You marry Abraham?"

Tess wasn't willing to come forward in her timeline quite yet. "My aunt gave Mama Ya some money. I know it was enough money for Mama Ya to have a small house. For her to furnish it. To buy some clothes. Some food stores. And have something in the bank for the dry seasons. That sounds like a lot of money. But in Ghana, a little money goes far. Mama Ya didn't save me in the hopes of a reward." Tess shook her head. "That would have been too distant a thought. We were struggling from moment to moment for survival. And yes, it would have been so much easier on her had I not been with them. She saved me because her heart was golden."

"Yes. Yes. Obviously. But there are different kinds of love. Your love for Levi is not the same love you feel for Abraham." Shanti argued.

"I am not a heroine in one of your novels, Shanti. My life

isn't the way I would have designed it or even what I thought was bearable. I only live because of Abraham. There is no question here. There is no choice. If you watched your parents' murders, and you ran for your life, eating bugs and begging for safety, you wouldn't try to force a happily-ever-after on me. Abraham has cancer and needs Western medicine. If he dies, his children will need a mother. A mother that they met while their father was still here. A mother they believe is their family."

"Wait. Wait. Hold on there." Shanti shook her head and held up her hands. Every part of her body language yelled, "No, stop!"

Tess was starting to feel combative, angry that she had to explain her determination to be there for Abraham. She was back in her body again.

Pressing herself away from Shanti's lap, Tess sat, her legs crossing in front of her. She waited for the blood in her head to settle into its normal rhythm. "Abraham didn't give up his food or shield me with his body for some distant prize. He did it because his heart is pure."

"You've kept in touch since you came back to the States? Have you seen him over the years?

"I went to Mama Ya's funeral. I met Abraham's wife. She was pregnant with their third child. And tragically, she died in labor. Both she and the child passed."

Shanti's hand grasped the cloth over her heart. "My god, the tragedy of that."

"Her passing has been a terrible ache in Abraham. He isn't interested in loving anybody other than his wife. Not in this lifetime. That's not who he is."

"But he proposed."

"It means he needs me. It means I have an opportunity to keep him safe."

"From what?"

"From what comes next. Abraham's village was destroyed, his people dispersed, and his family killed."

"What about his brother?"

"Moses? He died in a car accident. I am the only family Abraham has left. He needs his children to be safe, and that's what this is about. It would be the biggest honor of my life to shield his children from whatever is on the horizon." She looked at her lap. "I have to believe that someday Levi will at least understand my decision. He's been to war. He knows the atrocity, the deprivation, and the fear."

"And he knows all about Abraham?"

"Yes, they've met. He went with me to Ghana to the funeral. Levi knows what the Ya family means to me. Abraham," Tess met Shanti's gaze, "I *love* Abraham. And Levi will eventually conclude that just like he has an ethos that he lives by, I have one, too."

Shanti's voice was deflated as she said, "You know if you do this to him, Levi will never forgive you."

Tess went completely blank. "I'd never ask him to."

1

————

Levi

Present Day

   Texas

Dressed in khaki tactical from head to booted foot, a Beast Mode logo taking up center mass on his company T-shirt, the man stretched out a confident hand, shifting it between Levi, Reaper, and Goose.

He wanted to shake the boss-man's hand first, but he was unsure of the hierarchy, so there he stood, hand extended, waiting for the superior to reach out.

It made more sense than it would in a normal first greeting. Cerberus Tactical K9 wasn't public-facing. There was no way to research in advance to figure out the corporate hierarchy or to match a photographed face to a name.

Reaper was the chief K9 trainer at Iniquus's Cerberus Tactical. Goose was one of the veterinarians. But the teammates were here looking for a tactical K9 for Levi. All three men were considered teammates, and Levi wasn't in their chain of command. Still, Levi hesitated for a split second because he was the new hire.

Since neither of his teammates twitched, Levi extended his hand. "Levi Elliot."

"Conroy Dexter, I'm one of the partners here."

After releasing Conroy's grip, Levi indicated with a bladed hand. "Our trainer, Reaper. Our vet, Goose."

"Welcome. Welcome. Glad to have you." Conroy reached up and adjusted the bill of his ballcap to cast a shadow across his eyes.

Reaper pointed to Conroy's shirt. "Beast Mode, you come up with that name?"

"Ah, we all threw names in the pot. It's the one we could agree on. And I'm not saying that we hadn't worked that out over a few beers." He chuckled good-naturedly. "So I have the names of both dogs you're thinking about, Casper and Diabla. Since you've seen videos of their skillsets and already have a good rundown on their health from the paperwork I sent with the inquiry, I think we're going to have a mighty fine day today. Casper and Diabla are amazing athletes."

"Looking forward to it," Reaper said. "I'd like it if you could take us on a tour of the kennels while you share more granular details about your training process."

Conroy looked wary. "Yeah, we have a policy against kennel tours and sharing details." He rocked back on his heels and shoved his hands into his pockets. "Now, what I can do is I can teach you how to command the dog and show you their work in action, but our training process is proprietary."

"There's a rationale behind that?" Reaper asked. The slow smile and back tilt of his head was a move that Levi, even in his brief time at Iniquus, recognized. Reaper had his bullshit sensor out.

"There is." Conroy pulled his phone from his pocket, pressed a button, said, "Cerberus Tactical is here," then slid the phone back away. "We produce highly trained beasts that bring top dollar and deserve every penny of that money. Our pups are sourced out of Europe—the Czech Republic and Belgium for the most part. You all know this—it takes years of work to fine-tune the skills they need to perform the tactical duties that save lives." He lifted his brows and then dropped them with emphasis. "How we get to that finished product is our secret sauce. If we share it, our dogs lose value."

"I see." Reaper was casting his gaze around the complex before refocusing on Conroy. "So maybe you'd share an outline of your training philosophy?"

"Our training philosophy is to find out what the dog likes to do best and hone that down to a sharpened tool."

Reaper gave a slow nod. "Okay, then we'd like to tour your facilities and training grounds."

"Yep. How about we go around back?" Conroy turned to Levi as they set off walking. "Levi, you're the one looking for a K9 partner, right? Or are you all looking to expand the Cerberus kennel?" He swung his gaze back to Reaper and Goose. "If you like what you see today—"

"I'm looking for the right partner," Levi cut the guy off.

Conroy had the hungry look of someone who thought he might have a big fish on his line, and supper was all but assured.

What Reaper and Goose decided was none of Levi's business.

Levi was hard-focused on making the right partner choice.

The dog by his side was going to be one of the most significant relationships of his life—a battle buddy to go through everything headed their way.

In the field, a K9 made up for Levi's human deficits with

the ability to sniff out dangers, use its keen hearing and eyesight, and the ability to bring to bear around two hundred and forty pounds of bite strength that launched when the bad guy made the wrong twitch.

And that K9 had better be trained to know just what that twitch looked like.

Beyond the training, Levi was looking for a dog of his heart, one where they could be of one mind, a buddy system of mutual support and care.

Everyone on the Cerberus team said that Levi would know when he found the right dog just like he'd know when he found the right girl.

Unfortunately, Levi had found the right girl, Tess. He knew they were meant for each other the first time he looked across the park and saw her with her hand out, seeming to gather the air, then rubbing her fingers with her eyes looking skyward. There was something magical about that moment. About her.

Levi had asked her out, and from the get-go, they fit together like hand in glove. With Tess, Levi had felt seen and loved in a way that was so deep and held so much conviction that it lived in his cells.

Tess was his everything all the way up to the Dear John letter that was handed to him while he was deployed.

"I'm engaged to marry Abraham. I'm so sorry."

Levi must have read that one sentence over a thousand times, trying to get it to make sense.

That Tess would love Abraham was a no-brainer. Levi would have found it odd for her not to. When Tess and he went to Ghana for Mama Ya's, Levi met Abraham and extended his gratitude. When they were together, Levi hadn't been jealous or concerned. He had no sense that Abraham was competition. Back then, Levi had only felt gratitude toward a man who had, at great peril and sacrifice, saved Tess.

That Tess ended up married to Abraham instead of him was unfathomable. He still couldn't believe it after all these years.

Given his history, Levi was a might cautious about trusting his gut when it came to a connection.

Physical strain and bodily pain from doing his job felt good in Levi's system.

The emotional kind? Not so much.

Thoughts of Tess brought back a picture of her that he'd long treasured. Tess was looking over her shoulder, smiling, with her eyes soft with love for him.

Ah, there was the sharp stab of her hook still caught in his chest.

There was the drag that he always felt when she came to mind.

Levi never gave in to that sensation; he wouldn't stalk her social media, wouldn't ring her up out of the blue, but it sure would be nice if he could cut that cord.

It was a great miracle that he'd experienced a woman like that in his life.

And she was the sole reason he'd never let himself get into a situation like that again.

Yeah, except for the brotherhood he formed on the Teams, Levi found keeping emotional enmeshment at arm's length was best. That strategy kept his head in the game. Kept him pointed in the right direction without distractions.

Brothers, brewskies, doggos, and maybe a good conversation and laugh or two with an interesting woman. That would have to be enough for him.

2

———

Levi

Conroy strode toward the end of the building. "I think you're going to like Casper. A dog so stealthy he's like a ghost."

Goose leaned toward Levi and said under his breath, "Isn't Casper a friendly ghost who likes to show himself?"

Levi tipped his head down to hide his grin.

Conroy glanced over his shoulder, "Casper is a Malinois out of the Czech Republic."

"You got him as a pup, or you bought him once he'd finished his first round of training?" Goose asked as he moved up to walk side by side with Conroy.

"We get them as soon as they're done nursing. Our program begins at the beginning."

"The paperwork didn't indicate which command language they learn," Levi said.

"All American. We only speak American at Beast Mode."

The group circled the outside of a steel building that reminded Levi of a municipal airport hangar.

Conroy stopped at the back corner.

From the layout, the field stretching out in front of them was designed for bitework exercises.

Here, next to the building, was a path of thick mats. Conroy pointed up toward the roofline, some two stories overhead, where a bar extended, a rope dangled, and a hot pink tennis ball hung from that rope. Conroy pulled his finger down to direct the group's attention to the horizon.

Beast Mode obviously set this up to open with a bang. Some kind of show was heading their way. But right now, nothing was out there but a line of green grass touching blue sky.

"Levi," Conroy said. "Tell me your capacity handling dogs before you signed on with Cerberus."

"SEALs." Levi didn't need to sell himself. That he worked for Iniquus's Cerberus Tactical K9 was credential enough. He understood the need to prove he wasn't a newbie or a wannabe when it came to a trained working dog. These K9s had lethal potential by nature and nurture. If you didn't know what you were doing, it was a liability.

And while Levi didn't know the laws around it, it seemed to him that if Beast Mode sold a weapons-ready K9 to Joe down the street, there was the potential for bad outcomes and lawsuits.

Heck, even with exquisite control, military-trained K9s—well, any K9—could act out.

The training was supposed to mitigate that problem.

Unfortunately, Conroy wasn't willing to divulge that training. And that was a concern.

"SEALs, huh?" Conroy squinted into the distance, then pulled his phone from his pocket to check for a message. There didn't seem to be one waiting for him.

Levi stood wide-legged with his arms crossed over his chest. "That's right."

"How'd you land with Iniquus?" Conroy slipped his phone into his pocket, then gave it a pat.

"I heard from friends who worked there that a new K9 team was spooling up." Levi was leaving Navy ranks at a golden moment. Openings with Iniquus were few and far between. While they hired their operators from the lists of retired special forces, just having those credentials on a resume didn't mean much. It was invitation-only for a chance to sit down with Iniquus Command and show that you made the grade.

Levi had served alongside a handful of former SEALs who had joined Iniquus after leaving the Navy earlier than he had, each for their own reasons.

His brothers had talked about Iniquus' ethos and integrity, how they coalesced as a family that all watched out for each other.

Those who were used to the adrenaline and push of an operator's world often had a tough time adapting to the normal pace of life once they left the service. So, the familiar structure and ongoing training of similar tactical skills made for a soft landing when moving from the military to the civilian world.

His brothers who were now at Iniquus had honored Levi by submitting his name.

And now, he was at the beginning of this new life.

Conroy had been shuffling his feet as though he was trying to come up with a topic of conversation.

When he'd brought his finger down from the pink ball, Levi imagined Conroy had expected Casper and a handler to come charging toward them. But with the field still empty, he was stuck with, "Reaper said a nose and a bite." Conroy squinted at the horizon. "I know your team picked Casper and Diabla to see today. But I'm not sure why you all landed on those two dogs. If I knew a bit more about your needs out in the field, I might be able to make a suggestion."

Just like Conroy wanted to hold his cards to his chest about Beast Mode training, so did Cerberus.

What did they do? Anything required to keep their client safe. Saving kidnap victims, close protection, pulling people out of mudslides or from under earthquake wreckage, Levi's job was basically SEAL-shit but for non-military client needs.

"It can run the gamut," Reaper answered Conroy. "If they have a keen nose and a strong bite, if they can work off lead following commands, my training team can work on specifics."

Conroy's phone beeped, and he checked the readout. "Pete's bringing Casper around now. I think you're going to like him." Conroy lifted a bladed hand and looked past the sun to a field. "They were out for his morning jog. They're coming up now." Conroy seemed relieved he didn't have to make any more small talk.

Some folks were like that; they just preferred to keep to themselves.

Standing shoulder to shoulder, the Cerberus team watched as Pete and Casper pounded toward them.

Slender with a marathoner's body, Pete's black hair was damp with sweat. His T-shirt had more wet spots than dry. He looked like he'd been pushing hard.

Casper looked like he was just getting started.

It was curious that they had Casper running before the inspection.

Levi thought that didn't bode well.

From this setup, he'd guess that Casper was hyperdrive instead of the high drive they were looking for.

While Levi was willing to change his mind, and he was

giving Beast Mode the benefit of the doubt, this didn't sit right with him.

A long, hard run could wear out a dog enough that it could stay on task and make a good presentation.

Levi bet that if they showed up tomorrow, Casper would be running before they got there.

In Afghanistan, Levi had been the recipient of that trick at the military kennels. When Levi arrived, he thought he was signing out an easy-going doggo, but as soon as the K9 got a bit of rest, he turned into a maniac.

If Reaper and Goose ended up liking Casper, Levi would insist the team drop by unannounced and see how Casper performed his skills.

With a hand signal from Pete, Casper sat and stayed as his trainer walked slowly over to the group, showing that Casper could follow the orders to stay in place.

Beautiful dog, Levi thought, but he wouldn't say anything out loud that might send signals, positive or otherwise, of how he felt. An unemotional face was part and parcel of his special forces training and one of the reasons he'd had to learn body language subtleties in others.

As soon as Pete came to the mat, he nodded a greeting to the Cerberus team, then turned to Casper. Pointing at the suspended ball, he called out, "Get it," then he turned and scrambled to the top of the mat, where he bent in half, squatting to lower his profile. With an arm fixed on the wall to support himself, Pete formed a launch pad with his back. Extending the leg closest to Casper out like a tripod, Pete braced his body against the force of nature pelting his way.

This was the posture Levi took when he needed to get his dog over a wall.

Casper flew over the space.

Power rippled his muscles, making his fur seem liquid. Five

feet out from his trainer, the front paws came up for the leap, landing on Pete's hip. The back legs tucked under, and Pete pressed himself up to catapult Casper.

Front paws on the side of the building, Casper took two vertical strides before arching back like an Olympian on the high dive. Now horizontal, belly to the air, Casper stretched to his full length, mouth wide, as he pulled his legs over his head in a back flip, ball clasped between his teeth. With his paws pointed toward the ground, he floated down into Pete's arms.

They both collapsed onto the padding as Pete broke Casper's fall and kept him from injury.

It was a feat of athleticism that brushed goosebumps over Levi's skin.

Damned impressive.

Goose and Reaper took hard stands, maintaining a poker face while Pete played tug with the ball, giving Casper his reward for a job beautifully executed.

Conroy grinned widely. He knew that had made an impression. And first impressions were sticky. For the rest of their inspection, if Casper made a mistake, there would be a psychological effect that would tempt the team into making excuses for Casper and tamp down the concerns.

Pete stood tall with a big old grin brightening his face; he extended his hand for a shake, then quickly pulled back. "Sweat and slobber, gentlemen. I'll have to make do with a howdy."

Conroy introduced Reaper first; he'd obviously concluded Reaper was the most important member of the decision-making team. Then came Goose, deemed second-most important since he was the vet who would give a thumbs up or down on Casper's health.

These were hundred-thousand-dollar decisions.

There was no way Cerberus could take on a dog that wasn't in prime shape.

Lastly, Conroy introduced Levi, though Command had told Levi that he was the ultimate decider. If Levi were anything other than an all-systems go, the sale wouldn't take place.

Levi didn't mind being relegated to a position of least importance. It meant that no one would pander to him, and he'd have more space and focus to come to a decision.

Sitting beside Pete, Casper eagerly waited for his next task.

Casper only had eyes for Pete and never scanned the men in the conversation circle. His nose didn't twitch with the new scents. He had no curiosity.

Levi clocked that and would bring it up when the team sat down that night to share their impressions.

In the SEALs' kennels, they trained the dogs to think. That meant they were always aware, looking, planning, and ready to execute.

Yeah, that Casper was so hyper-focused on Pete was concerning. But from Pete's face and posture, he thought that Casper was performing to perfection.

His pride wasn't ill-placed. Casper was magnificent.

It was just a concern Levi added to the pros and cons list.

"We thought that since you're out here," Pete said, "I'd suit up, and we can do a takedown simulation."

"How far was your jog before we got here?" Reaper asked Pete.

Pete dropped a hand to Casper's head. "Ten miles."

"How far does Casper typically run in a day?" Reaper asked.

"Fifteen in all. Some with me, some on the treadmill. Casper prefers to be outside. He gets bored on the machine, so I try to get the run in."

"Do you run with any of the other dogs?" Reaper slid his hands into his pockets.

"Right now, Casper is my running buddy. He's getting me ready for the New York Marathon."

Reaper responded with a nod.

Levi lifted his chin. "Hey, Pete, back when I was in the Navy, my team didn't have a dedicated K9 assigned just for me. I'd choose a dog from the kennel who had the skillset that best fit our operational needs. When I picked up a new dog at the kennels, I always insisted on wearing the bite suit. Hope you don't mind, but it gives me a chance to know, up close and personal, how things might go down in the field."

Conroy turned to Pete, and a silent conversation passed between them.

"You know what they say," Reaper added, "don't trust a gun you haven't shot yourself."

"Yup," Conroy said, lifting a hand toward a picnic table with a dark pile resting on top. "That's what they say."

The men wandered over.

"Casper's about fifty-five pounds?" Goose asked.

"That's right." Pete put a hand on Casper's head.

Suited up from head to foot in the protective gear that would shield Levi to some extent, Levi moved to midfield, then signaled he was ready.

When he got the go-ahead from Pete, Levi took off running.

Goose was filming so their team could assess the event in slow motion that night at their hotel.

Levi didn't hear Pete's attack command, but after years of this kind of work, Levi could sense the disturbance in the atmosphere as the K9 thundered toward him.

Casper launched himself into the air, and as he flew by, he lowered his jaw to bite down on Levi's arm. The points of Casper's teeth punctured Levi's skin even through the heavy padding. The velocity spun Levi around, throwing him off balance.

Casper got him down.

With jaws clamped into place, Casper violently shook his head while leaning back onto his haunches. With that steady forward drag, it was hard for Levi to scramble his feet underneath him. Finally able to stand, Casper dangled from Levi's forearm.

Jaws locked, Casper's powerful neck twisted back and forth.

Levi could feel the muscles in his shoulder lock up to stabilize that arm.

Fifty pounds of dog. Two hundred plus pounds of man. It wasn't a fair fight. Not even close.

That doggo was a beast.

Levi lifted the training baton in his free hand and simulated what a target might do if they defended themselves.

Casper was undaunted.

Levi had waited to see how long Casper would go before he gave up. But time passed, and nothing changed in their fight dynamic other than Levi's face-planting a second time and the ensuing Casper drag and shake.

Next test: What would happen if Levi changed things up and went from aggressor to capitulation?

Levi pressed his face protectively into the grass. He lay there rock-still as Casper continued the assault.

Pete called Casper off, and Casper was having none of it.

From the way his arm was getting jerked backward, Levi surmised that Casper was being dragged bodily away.

Casper's full focus was on demolishing Levi's arm.

Levi thought if he weren't in this suit, he'd lose the limb.

In the field, the target wouldn't have protection. Did they want the person mauled? Maybe, on a rare occasion, but for most of the Cerberus assignments, nah.

And did they want a dog that wasn't under voice command? Absolutely not.

Still face down, Levi heard the sizzling zap of electricity. Some trainers use a shock to catch the dog's attention and refocus them on commands. Although, there was always the risk that the dog would turn his prey drive onto the unprotected trainer.

A moment later, Casper released.

Levi rolled slowly, making sure Pete had a hand in Casper's collar before he exposed his face. Tomorrow, he'd be bruised and sore.

Reaper reached out a hand to help hoist Levi back on his feet. "I think we can move on to Diabla now. I've seen what I need to from Casper. An amazing athlete, just not a good fit for our needs."

Levi caught Reaper's gaze, and Reaper lifted a questioning brow. Did Levi agree?

Panting heavily from the exertion of that fight, Levi offered a thumbs up as Pete and Casper moved back over the horizon where they'd first appeared.

Conroy indicated the picnic table. "Levi, leave the suit out here, and we'll put it away later." With a gesture toward the building, he set off walking. "Good to get a better read on what you boys are after. You've seen a bite. How about we start Diabla at the wall? You can see how well she can search out a scent. I'll take you to the observation room for starters. And then, if you'd like, we can hide you out in the woods so she can track you from a scent source."

As Levi pulled the gear off, he knew that Diabla was going to be a fail.

What Levi needed was a K9 trained by someone he knew and trusted with the job. It was then that Levi thought about his friend Enrico, who was down in southern Africa training dogs to help stop rhino poaching. Enrico was a master at the craft of tactical K9 training.

And in their last conversation, he'd said something about needing to sell his favorite dog, Mojo.

Levi would give Enrico a call when he got back to the hotel to ask why Mojo had to leave his job at the game preserve.

Who knew? If not Mojo, maybe Enrico had a line on a dog that would be a good fit for Levi.

3

Tess

Namib-Naukluft National Park, Namibia

Cocooned in the puffy warmth of her sleeping bag, face fresh in the cold desert night air, Tess had been blissfully in the void of sleep when a phone ping blinked her awake.

Rubbing the heels of her palms against her lids, she turned toward the rustling of her friend, pulling herself up to sit. "Gwen," Tess whispered, "what time is it?" The night had been too short, and the green walls of the tent hadn't brightened with the rising sun.

"Three fifteen. It's not time to get up yet. Our team channel … hang on, I can't find my glasses."

Whatever thoughts one of their fellow tourists had in the middle of the night could, honestly, have been a "note to self" and posted in the morning when people rose to the new day. As Tess squirmed deeper into her bag, hoping to plunge back into the wonderful nothingness of perfect sleep, Gwen reached out and patted Tess's thigh. "Got your GPS handy?"

"Why?" Her hand stretched into the cold air, feeling for her grab-and-go bag with the ten survival essentials she kept within arm's reach when in the field—be it for work or, like right now, for play. Pulling her headlamp into place, clicking it on, and adjusting the light to green so she could see red map lines and not affect her night vision, Tess dug her backup, handheld GPS unit from the bottom of the pack. Wi-Fi was non-existent out here in the desert. Even basic phone connectivity had wide swaths of dead zones, and this was one of them. Where Tess didn't get the ping, her friend and colleague Gwen did. It was all carrier-dependent, and, luckily, Gwen had her Namibian phone with her.

"Mandy went to the bathroom and got lost on the way back," Gwen spoke in an undertone that would keep their conversation in their tent, letting the other happy tourists sleep on.

"Lost?" The communal bathhouse was only about fifty yards away.

"Lights are out. She was using her phone flashlight." Gwen tugged on a pair of fleece-lined tactical pants. The days out here were uncomfortably hot, and the desert nights were bitterly cold.

After searching the GPS for "gas" and finding the station, Tess pulled warm clothes over her pajamas.

The mating calls of jackals rode the breeze. Their howls were reminiscent of a wolf, only high-pitched and short-lived. "Eerie as hell. I bet Mandy was scared to death alone in the dark with a cellphone light and the jackals," Tess murmured. "I would be."

The sweater Gwen pulled over her head muffled her voice. "I texted Mandy to sit tight. We're coming for her. I bet she'll feel better now that she knows the cavalry is coming."

Tess scooted on her butt down the bag to grab her boots,

"Check them for scorpions." Gwen tugged on a wool sock.

"Yup." Tess unzipped the door and held her boot upside down for a good shake and tap before putting them on and lacing up. If a scorpion had found its way to the toe of her boot, she didn't want to release it in the tent. She still had hopes of getting a few more hours of shut-eye after this impromptu adventure.

"I bet you Mandy isn't wearing boots. She was walking around camp last night in flip-flops."

"Okay, what's the danger?" Tess asked.

"Never walk barefoot or without a flashlight at night in Namibia as a rule. Some snakes are active after sunset, and slow-moving snakes are easy to step on. The puff adder, for instance. Highly venomous."

"And the closest hospital is five hours away. That seems like a dangerous distance." Tess scanned her light over the area immediately in front of her. "Are there puff adders here in the desert?"

"Usually not. I was just using that as an example."

"Wonderful. Well, just so you know, I downloaded the Namibian snake app before I came."

"Of course you did," Gwen said, grabbing her bag.

Once Tess had cleared the door, she waited for Gwen to follow.

Aiming her light toward the ground, Tess pointed out the jackal tracks that had circled their tent at some point that night. But they must have scampered out of their campsite because Tess didn't catch glowing eyes in her green light. She scanned along the group's designated area, ringed with a wall of stones. That wall might have provided some buffer from the blowing desert sand, but it did nothing to separate the campers from the wild.

Seven of their group's ten tourists slept in tents; three had decided—at their guide's suggestion—to sleep under the stars as he did. Of course, the tourists with no wilding experience were on the ground with the desert animals, and the guide slept high and protected on the flat roof of their off-roading vehicle.

Tess stopped at Mandy's tent and unzipped the door. She reached in and grabbed up Mandy's boots. Pulling out socks that Mandy had shoved in the tops, she held them at arm's length and gave them a vigorous shake. Sticking the socks under her arm, Tess turned the boots over to do the scorpion tap, put the socks back in, tied the laces together, and draped them over her neck before zipping the tent shut.

No one needed a surprise jackal curled on their sleeping bag.

"Thorough," Gwen said, pulling her arms through the straps of her safety-ten pack.

"Absolutely," Tess whispered, "I'd feel better if she had these."

"I hear you."

With her GPS on her palm, Tess dropped a pin to indicate their tent's location. That way, she and Gwen wouldn't be wandering the desert as lost as Mandy—more lost; Mandy was at the gas station just outside the camp gates. Eventually, the workers would show up, and Mandy would be sitting at one of the picnic tables in her jammies and flip-flops.

Tess glanced toward the tour vehicle and saw that the soup pot from dinner was resting on the fold-out table. "Five bucks says he tries to feed that to us for breakfast."

Meals were part of this excursion's fee. When the driver, Otto, skipped over lunch yesterday, everyone was too polite to ask when they'd get to eat, but this also made them hangry with a side of carsick.

It had been a visually exciting but hot and unpleasant five-hour car ride from Namibia's capital city of Windhoek. The trip had been two hours longer than anticipated because of the stop to change a flat tire and another when the engine decided to conk out for no apparent reason.

Along the route, dotted across the powdery earth, termite mounds towered as high as Tess's head.

Baboon families lounged by the side of the road.

An occasional giraffe or springbuck would make everyone point and gasp.

And then there were more termite mounds. And more termite mounds. And more.

Tess liked them. She held a sense of awe that tiny termites could make their own skyscrapers. She'd love to see one of the mounds cut in half to discover the interior architecture. But, given that they were full of termites, Tess was equally glad Otto didn't offer to chop one open—for everyone's sake, including the termites.

It was all magical and amazing.

The only problem was that Tess wasn't great without food. Since she was sitting next to Otto, she took up the subject with him, making sure the guy knew she was displeased and that they expected to be fed properly throughout. Maybe her tone wasn't as diplomatic as she'd wished, but Tess succumbed to the effects of hangry like any other human.

Tess got it. Namibian jobs were sparse. With a twenty percent unemployment rate, people were willing to work for meager wages. Tess had concluded along the drive that Otto was probably pocketing the designated food money to fatten his wallet. That was understandable, especially since he'd told Tess he was divorced with a child support check going to Botswana.

But still, Tess knew from her lean-pocketed grad school days as a single parent that there were plenty of creative ways to feed a crowd. Otto could skim a little off the top without someone posting bad reviews for future tourists to read, causing them to click over a different tour operator's page. Seemed to Tess like that was biting off your nose to spite your face.

As Tess stumbled along following the GPS red arrow on her rescue hunt for Mandy, Tess realized from her inner dialogue that her hangry hadn't been appeased since yesterday, and she needed calories to let go of her inner grumbling.

A missed lunch wouldn't have been that big a deal, except she'd skipped breakfast for their early departure and then arrived at the campfire to find a dinner unfit for consumption.

Not just unpalatable but inedible.

They'd all been starving, and—after Otto's bragging about his gourmet camp cooking skills—the travelers had high expectations and growling stomachs.

When the group gathered in a line to dish up their share of food from a pot in the fire pit, they discovered that Otto offered them a dinner of half-cooked rice. The chicken wings he'd thrown into the pot, with white, gelatinous-looking skin, floated to the top. Some vegetables that had been green and leafy were now cooked to strings. But the combination of soggy everything and the crunch of the uncooked rice made this stuff not just visually off-putting but a top candidate for causing a bad case of travelers' sickness.

Tess and Gwen pulled out the meal replacement bars they'd left in the vehicle, keeping them safely away from their tent where the enticing chocolate scent might lure scavenging jackals.

That's what they ate for supper. And now the friends were out of options. Tess needed to think about something other than her empty stomach. "I'm not a fan of being out here with the jackals."

With her headlamp in her teeth, Gwen wound her long black hair into a messy bun at the nape of her neck. Tugging her lamp back into place, she said, "They're out here looking for a quick snack and maybe a willing female for a little midnight lovin'. You're not a small animal, and you're not furry enough to make them consider you for a girlfriend."

Tess pulled a tissue from her pocket and blew her nose in a wet and satisfying way. "I don't know about that. I haven't shaved in a couple of weeks."

"TMI, my friend."

"Right." Looking around, Tess could understand Mandy's disorientation. Every camp looked almost identical—tents, numbers, and vehicles— all the tourist groups were like theirs. "Over there." Tess pointed at the activity to her right. "Turning my head with my headlamp on and seeing the jackals humping is just kind of rude on my part, wouldn't you say?"

Gwen chuckled as they stumbled forward through the deep desert sand.

It didn't take long to get to Mandy. There she sat with her arms wrapping herself, shivering.

Gwen called out, "We're here."

"Oh, thank goodness it's you. I didn't know who was behind those lights and whether I should be relieved or scared." Grabbing first Tess, then Gwen into a tight hug, Mandy stuttered through chattering teeth, "I thought I was going to freeze. I can't tell you how much I appreciate this."

Mandy sat to get her boots on. "And thank you for boots and socks. Flip-flops in thirty-some-odd degrees aren't great."

While she waited, Tess pulled a tissue from her pocket and blew her nose again.

"Did you come down with something?" Mandy asked. "You keep fussing your nose."

"Strangest sensation. I'm so dry I'm getting nosebleeds." She slid the tissue away and then used the hand sanitizer she kept in her jacket pocket.

"Is your nose bleeding now?" Gwen tensed up. "Are you chumming the air for predators? Maybe take a step to the side."

"Are you kidding?" Mandy's voice ratcheted up. "Is that a thing?"

"It's not a bloody nose this time," Tess said. "Something in the desert gives me an allergic reaction. It was the same in Arizona." Tess reached out her hand as if she could catch hold of the air and roll it through her fingers.

"Every time I come here, I have the same problem," Gwen said. "I call it a Namibian facial when I've rubbed my nose raw. Two percent humidity isn't my comfort zone."

With Mandy shivering in her flannel pjs, Tess felt badly that she'd thought of boots but not a jacket.

As they retraced their path to the tents, Tess slid an arm around Mandy to help keep her warm. "It's just up ahead. I can see our tent configuration."

Tess was actually enjoying this side adventure.

Walking in the crisp temperature, the satiny darkness of the sky was made spectacular with shooting stars. Under the glittering riot of the Milky Way, Tess felt like she was part of a bigger whole. And that felt good.

The jackal humping and fellow traveler search party just added to the memories Tess was storing away on this week-long vacation from their jobs.

Gwen and Tess were climate scientists for WorldCares NGO. Their job was to watch weather patterns, hoping to accurately forecast where WorldCares should pre-position supplies in advance of a humanitarian crisis.

Their next research project would focus here in Namibia, where a dangerously low rainfall during the last wet season made their dry season calamitous.

The drought was already stressing the production systems in Namibia.

Things had turned dire across the entire country.

Tess suddenly felt self-rebuke flood her system for griping about Otto and the food situation. Then she reminded herself they had paid for all their meals, and the rice was uncooked. If Otto had served the group mopane worms—the caterpillars collected, dried, and cooked as a traditional form of protein—Tess would have loved the adventure of tasting it. She'd read that they were delicacies but hadn't found them on a menu. So it wasn't the food but the preparation, or lack thereof.

Before this tour, she and Gwen had dined on wonderful foods in Windhoek—fresh oysters and ox tail. But that wasn't available for everyone in Namibia.

Here, there was a stratification of haves and have-nots, a remnant of when South Africa ruled and Apartheid enforced strict policies. Those regulations had an enduring effect on where and how the people lived.

Things were often lean in Namibia. It took a daily dose of creativity to survive.

But much more so right now.

After finishing up this adventure tour—something Tess called "wonder-wander"—they were heading to Gwen's parents' vineyard just to the north, outside of Etosha National Park, one of the best animal preserves in Africa.

There, they'd start analyzing the crop and weather data, developing predictions of what was to come in the near future.

WorldCares had just learned that the government was feeding its people from the emergency reserves. Difficult choices lay on the table. So, WorldCares wanted a report on how the communities were adjusting. Could their tribal knowl-edge get them through to the next rain, or were the people succumbing to the weather events?

Lives depended on help arriving on time with the right equipment and supplies. WorldCares had been honing that skill for the seventy years it had worked to relieve suffering.

Both women felt the pressure of getting this right.

Even though Tess wanted to forgive herself for grumbling about the food on this trip, she felt the privilege of knowing she could pull something off her shelf at any time, make a meal, and feel full.

It hadn't always been like that in her life.

She should never forget how life-threatening things could turn in a flash—in the swing of an arm and a plea for help. One minute, things were happy. And the next, she was running for her life.

4

———

Tess

Break of day

Big Daddy Dune, Namibia

A polite line of international travelers stood by the three-sided, last-opportunity, open-air latrine. Gwen held out her packet of wet wipes.

Tess pulled out a sheet. "Thanks. No water out here. What do you think of that decision?"

Gwen tugged a sheet for herself, then slid the packet into her pocket. "I see a lot of tourists dressed for the cold morning desert. I don't think they can fathom how hot it will get when this sand heats. And not knowing that means they didn't come prepared in other ways. Salty snacks."

"I could use something salty right now. I'm still hungry from when we left yesterday."

"Yeah? The packet of instant oatmeal didn't do it for you?" Gwen chuckled. "You are so bad at being hungry."

"I earned that trait honestly. But we've been spoiled by the amazing campfire meals we've had on assignments over the years. I think that's why I'm extra disappointed." Tess gestured to the people in line. "I don't fault these folks. You'd think their guides would, I don't know, guide them? People can't understand the ramifications of something like two percent humidity unless they've experienced it. I mean, you can't think ahead if you have no clue what's on the horizon." Tess lifted her chin. "Did you bring water?"

"I have a liter in my pack." Gwen adjusted her strap as both women stepped forward with the line. "With this heat, that should be enough to cover our time here and get back to the vehicle."

Casting her gaze about, Tess said, "Since this place is tourist only, you'd think there should be at least some kind of vending machine situation, even if it's not cooled. But with solar panels, a cold drink could be available. A water source of some kind seems important, right?"

"You're like Miss Hyper-Prepared. I can't imagine you not having seven scenarios you'd extrapolated and built contingency plans around, except maybe bringing enough meal replacement bars. You're pretty annoying about all that if I were to be perfectly honest."

"Let's not be." Tess slid her sunglasses off, then put them back in place.

"Okay, it's also true that listening to your thoughts of potential doom, while irritating—"

Tess smiled. "A given."

"It's also one of the reasons why I always feel safe around you. You plan, and I coast. Sorry, not sorry." She twitched her knees back and forth. "This is taking forever. What's wrong with these people's systems?"

"Too much half-cooked rice?" Tess offered. "About being

prepared, that's reflexive from my childhood. But as I said earlier, I can't prepare for everything because I don't know everything. Right?"

"Uhm. Nope, I'm not following."

As Tess stepped forward with the line, she said, "Here's an example. I had a scary thing happen simply because I didn't know what I didn't know." She focused back on Gwen. "I was visiting a friend in Midland, Texas, and decided to change my airline ticket, drive to the Grand Canyon, and check some things off my iconic-must-do list. I'd drive over the Hoover Dam, then I'd fly out of the hub in Vegas, which would give me two more checks."

Gwen smirked. "You were unprepared for all of the Elvis interpreters?"

"No. I was unprepared for the nothingness. On the East Coast, you get on the highway, and every thirty minutes or so, there's a gas station and some kind of food and toilet," she gestured toward the latrine as someone rounded out of the facility, and the line took another step forward. "Typically, when traveling, I fill up when my tank dips under half-filled. You never know when an accident or some such will leave you idling on the highway, and you don't want to run out of gas. I was on three-quarters tank this time, but as I drove by a gas station, I thought I'd just top it off and grab a cup of coffee."

"Good decision, I take it." Gwen pulled off her sunglasses, exhaled on the lenses, and polished them with the hem of her T-shirt.

"I drove down the highway, and suddenly, it was the desert. The cute kind with cactus and–"

"Dirt?" Gwen chuckled.

"Yeah, that kind of desert."

"This must have been a while ago if you thought there was cute dirt."

"Undergrad. So I got out and was taking pictures."

"Of the dirt." Gwen grinned broadly, looking thoroughly amused.

"Picturesque dirt."

"You'd have to show me. I can't imagine that." Gwen gestured to the area around them. "This is pretty darned picturesque. I take back my snide comments."

"Thanks. So there I am driving. After about an hour of that, there was no one and nothing. No pull-offs, no houses, no other cars."

"No cell towers to tell someone you were freaking out. Given the fact that you did undergrad a very long time ago, I bet at the time the connection was zilch."

"I had a flip phone, which was useless, and a GPS unit. The GPS said there was no gas for four hours in any direction, of which there were only two, where I'd come from and straight ahead. My car holds about four hours of highway gas miles."

"Ah, I see. You'd already driven over an hour at that point. Not enough gas, what else was lacking?"

"Water for one. If I broke down, there was literally nothing and no one out—I take that back. That's not right. I saw a lone cow that looked like it was lost, and I saw a guy on a bike heading the opposite way than I was. Shorts, shoes, no shirt, no camel bladder of water. Nothing extra on his bike."

"No bells and tassels?" Gwen turned to the front of the line and scowled. "For heaven's sake. What the heck is going on? I need to pee."

"I'm distracting myself with the story. Okay, the guy on the bike should have been prepared with his survival ten and maybe saddlebags with food and water. A water bottle? A shirt and hat? Tire repair kit? I guess, in my mind, only a serial killer would act that crazy." Tess wrinkled her nose. "As I say all this out loud, Namibia rings a lot of those 'What the crap did I get myself into?' bells for me."

"No cows, though. But there were baboons on the side of the road who looked like they'd like to hitch a ride." Gwen scuffed a foot into the sand. "So there you were … "

"Terrified. Squeezing that steering wheel for dear life, telling myself that if anyone popped up in the middle of the road and tried to flag me down, I'd note the coordinates and tell the police."

"But if they also happened to have an ax in their hands? You thought that one through, too." Gwen grinned. "Tell the truth."

"If anyone got in the road, I planned to floor it and drive right over them. I primed myself for that eventuality."

The woman behind Gwen turned to give Tess a long, hard look.

Tess offered up a flat-lipped smile. "About twenty years ago. Everyone's fine," Tess said, and the woman turned back around.

Gwen raised her brow and tucked her chin. "See? You were fine. No need for all that worry."

"Mmm. I think maybe my guardian angel was working overtime that day. There was the unusual compulsion to top off the gas, and then there was the thirty minutes of driving on an empty tank that, to this day, I can't fathom."

"You know this. When it says empty, you still have a bit."

Tess shook her head. "I rolled into the gas station in New Mexico, and when I got to the pump, I couldn't get the top off. I had to ask the guy who was gassing up beside me. He two-handed it and had to lean his weight to get it off. My tank was so empty that it had vacuum sealed."

"And no people until that gas station?" Gwen asked.

"No one and nothing after the cow and the biker."

"Wow." Gwen shook her head.

"Yep. It was definitely wow. And since there wasn't a bar in immediate view—"

"And you weren't of legal drinking age to imbibe—"

"That, too. I soothed myself with fat and sugar."

"Bunuelos?" Gwen lifted her chin. "Your turn in the loo. Please hurry."

Tess handed off her survival ten bag to Gwen. "Bunuelos, yes. You know me so well." She rounded the metal wall to take her turn in the latrine. As she dropped her trail pants to her boots and squatted over the hole in the ground that had ripened to a nauseating smell with the sun's heat, she called out, "What are your thoughts about Big Daddy Dune? Do you want to climb it?"

"It's not a hard climb. Hour up. Five minutes down."

"Yeah. So you want to do that?" Tess held her breath as she pulled up her pants; a few more seconds, and she'd be in less noxious air.

Gwen traded places with Tess, calling out, "To be honest, I think I've climbed my share of dunes. It's lost the novelty for me. I want to see the salt flats and the desiccated trees. They're so beautifully stark against the horizon. I planned to spend my time photographing them."

"Exactly my thoughts."

As Gwen emerged from behind the metal privacy wall, rubbing sanitizer over her hands, Tess draped her arm over her friend's shoulder. "And this is why we get along so well."

Gwen held a hand toward the trail, where tourists followed one behind the other like ants at a picnic. "I can taste an impending adventure. Are you ready?"

5

———

Tess

Hot and thirsty, feeling inspired and happy, the women had filled their cameras with spectacular photos, and the tension of the journey eased into contentment as they traced their way back to the vehicle.

"Latrine?" Gwen asked as they passed by.

"No. I think I sweated out any extra moisture." By habit, Tess reached out and gathered a handful of air, then rubbed her fingers together. It was something that Abraham had done back in their years of flight in Ghana. He taught her how to feel the air not just for changes in weather but for any shifting dangers that vibrated the wind.

Gwen tipped back the last drop from her plastic bottle. "Same. Which is a shame because there are no wait lines like this morning."

Back at their tour vehicle, Otto was nowhere to be seen.

Tess tried the front door. "Locked."

"Rude," Gwen frowned.

"But he was nice enough to park under the only scrap tree in the parking area."

"And right near the latrine. Both handy and unpleasant." Gwen cupped her hands around the sides of her face, shielding her eyes from the glare so she could see into the back window. Slowly, she made her way around the vehicle, looking through each pane. "You're not going to like this."

Tess raised her brows.

"The driver's not the only thing missing." Gwen looked the tree over for camouflaged critters, then sat on the elevated root next to Tess.

"That doesn't sound good. Do I want to know?"

"Water," Gwen said on an exhale. "He didn't bring the gallon-sized water jugs with us."

"Surely you're mistaken." Tess got up to do her own inspection and sat down next to Gwen. "Man! I knew that I was recalling that Texas desert story for a reason. Well, that sucks."

"Little bit sucks for us." Gwen agreed, taking off her boot and holding it upside down. A stream of sand fell to the ground. "Sucks more for our group. The others who climbed Big Daddy had water bottles with them, but they were the little, lunchbox-sized ones." She looked up. "The sun's overhead." Focusing on her boot again, Gwen gave it a vigorous shake.

"As soon as we gather up," Tess said, taking off her own boot, "we need to make a beeline for the ranger's station. Surely, they have an emergency water supply there. I didn't see a gas station or store on the way in." She licked her lips and tried not to think dry thoughts. "Did you know that at a hundred and eighteen degrees, you can die in about two days? It's a pretty gruesome death."

"See how quickly your imagination turns to survival scenarios? Put your mind to rest. There were rangers at the gate coming in here, remember? And there's that little campsite to the right of the entrance. They had a plastic water tower. It's a thirty-minute drive, and we'll have access to some there."

As the group trickled back to the vehicle, they became aware there was no relief for their parched systems. Without the anticipated water, there was little energy among them. It was very quiet as the friends draped themselves over each other and waited for Otto to get back from wherever he'd disappeared to.

Would Tess hang on her friends like that? Opposite. The rule of thumb was to huddle in the cold and let the air move over you in the heat.

Eventually, Otto showed up.

Gwen asked him why he didn't bring water out for a desert hiking excursion.

His answer was a silent look of disdain that he shot in her direction.

Frankly, Tess had become anxious about this man as soon as she scooped dinner into her mess plate the night before. The stories he'd regaled her with on the hours-long trip south had made her think at the time that he was a skilled adventurer. After that meal, Tess realized his stories were braggadocio.

Since the dinner, she no longer trusted him to know how to keep their group safe.

In their work with WorldCares—even though their job had a lot to do with data calculations—it was imperative that she and Gwen get out and see the environments that they were analyzing. They had to see what was happening on the ground with the people. What did they eat? How did they cook? What were the cultural norms that Tess and Gwen couldn't look up in a book?

In all her time putting the dots together in the field, nothing like this had ever happened. Their previous guides were systematic, with a protocol that was rigorously followed and an understanding that the health and welfare of their clients rested on their shoulders.

With Otto? Not so much.

The look Gwen sent her told Tess that her friend had come to the same conclusion. They were with an ego. A blusterer. A self-aggrandizer. Someone who might make a show of skill and yet—forget water on an excursion to the desert with the level of physical effort required of Big Daddy. It was unconscionable and dangerous.

Well, it was only a short time, and they'd be near the ranger station.

As soon as the doors unlocked, Tess piled into her place at the front and encouraged the others to be quick about it. "We should hurry," she cajoled. "The sand is heating up."

The blank faces that met her comment told Tess that these tourists didn't know what they didn't know. Driving on hot sand was dangerous.

Tess and Gwen were both in their early forties. Not quite old enough to be these people's mothers, but it sure felt like the group needed some parental guidance.

Pulling on her seat belt, Tess felt apprehension slide down her spine. She understood what the heated sand meant.

They'd set off that morning in the chill of a still-darkened sky. They aimed to get to a particular spot to catch the sunrise.

The dunes in this area were unique in that they were comprised of sand with a high concentration of iron oxide. With time, the oxides rusted, turning the Namibian dunes a bright copper.

As the sun rose, it shone on the side of the dune, illuminating it in a vibrant orange. On the shadow side of the dune, the sand looked black in contrast.

The stark opposition and the crispness of the demarcation

line between orange and black seemed hyper-pigmented against the bright azure of the cloudless Namibian sky.

It was a stunning visual.

It was absolutely one of the most gasp-worthy natural sights Tess had ever seen.

Driving on, they had entered the park. It had been a bouncing and bobbing ride as they wended their way over the roadless wilderness to get to the parking area.

Tess had felt bad for those in the very back row as they flew up and banged their heads.

But this morning, with the cool temperatures, the grains of sand were tightly packed, sticking together with friction. Now that they were moving into the high heat of the day, those same sand grains would expand, losing what little moisture they'd had. Now, the friction from the wheels would force the grains of sand apart, putting them at risk of getting sand bogged.

And the group had no water.

Water was the second thing in the hierarchy of survivability, right after air.

Too little water could mean heat stroke, which could be deadly unless quickly reversed. Tess had been at other scenes of crisis where there was too much water that was the threat.

No worries about the latter. Not out here.

The sooner they got to the ranger station, the sooner Tess could relax her guard.

They climbed into the vehicle with little energy, found their places, and pulled on their belts. Everyone was already fatigued and dehydrated to the point that they weren't talking much.

Otto backed out of their place, and the bumping and jumping began in earnest as they made their way to the front of the park. Tess had decided to raise the water issue as soon as she saw the wooden entrance gate. But she and Otto were like sandpaper rubbing against each other. He might be able to pull off his 'bushcraft master' guise for the others, but Tess and Gwen had spent too much time with special forces operators and people with real skillsets to be fooled.

Otto knew they knew.

But Tess would be damned if she'd hold her tongue and put everyone in danger.

Those were the thoughts running through her mind when the back wheels started to spin, and the vehicle began to tip upward in the front.

"Everyone out," Otto ordered.

Tess and Gwen got out and moved toward one of the small scrub trees that provided a bit of shade and a patch of packed dirt instead of the sandbox around them. By habit, both women lifted their knees and stomped to warn any critters in the area that they were there. From the relative shade, they watched as Otto let the air out of each tire to gain surface. Okay, that was a good start.

"I'm not particularly comfortable with this scenario," Gwen said under her breath.

Tess widened her eyes so Gwen would share her concerns. They probably aligned with hers.

"Our group has no survival skills nor seemingly any self-preservation instinct," Gwen said. "The sun is high, and while we are one of the first groups out, everyone will be heading for the exit here in the next bit. The tourists in the area aren't used to being in desert heat. Everyone who was going to climb Big Daddy did it as the morning half of their excursion. No one is going to be coming into the park for the rest of the day. That's my calculus."

"And those who are leaving probably drank their water and wouldn't risk slowing their forward momentum to help lest they sink in and get trapped as well," Tess added. "No one's going to stop on the way out."

"Nope." Gwen pressed her lips together. "No one's going to stop."

"Maybe Otto can get us out of this." Tess stepped back out into the scalding reach of the sun as Otto scooped a hand in a come-on motion to rally the troops.

"I need you all to push," he said.

"Taking bets on that, Tess?" Gwen asked as she moved over to the side of the vehicle and put her shoulder to the frame.

On Otto's signal, the group put their body weight and muscle strength to work, trying to push the vehicle forward and getting sandblasted by the spinning tires.

The chances of them pushing this vehicle free were not great, especially if Otto kept using that heavy foot on the gas pedal.

The group had exhausted their energy. The effort under high temperatures was making them sweat.

A tourist tram drove by without looking their way or slowing their speed. Granted, they weren't moving fast, but at least they were moving forward. "Next time one comes by, I'm going to run alongside and beg for water," Tess told Gwen as they returned to their tree.

"Okay, you take the first one. I'll do the second." Gwen lifted her chin as Otto tried letting more air out of the tires. "Hey," Gwen called over, "we've got floor mats in the vehicle. You can dig the sand out around the front of each tire and shove the mat as far under as you can get it. The rubber on the bottom will give you stability, and the friction of the carpet will help grip the tires. You can at least get the vehicle going forward."

"No," Otto said and moved to the next tire.

"It's worked for me in the past," Tess added.

Otto just shot a couple of daggers their way and kept making his round of the tires, letting out a specific amount that he measured with his gauge.

"I'm not feeling confident here," Gwen muttered. "Got any other techniques you've seen work?"

"I have one, but it worked on mud, not sand." Tess reached up and grabbed a branch overhead just to have something to do with her hands. "Hang on, inbound." She pointed at an open-sided safari vehicle heading their way. They could see the moment that the driver recognized the problem and steered toward the more solid-looking ground on the other side of their tree. Tess jogged alongside. "Hey! Does anyone have any extra water? We have no water."

An elderly lady dug in her bag and tossed out a small bottle as they pulled away. "Thank you!" Tess raised her hand in gratitude, then pocketed the water bottle as she made her way back over to Gwen. "Little bottle, but it's something. That was kind."

"Drink it now?" Gwen asked.

"If we rely on Otto, we're going nowhere." She pointed to the other side of the sand trap. "Mandy is out there with her shirt off, working on her tan."

"Crazy."

"Be that as it may," Tess said. "I think this bottle will give everyone enough liquid to take a small sip and swish around their mouths to stop their gums from sticking to their lips. Barring that, it might help someone if they get heat sick, keep it from becoming an emergency. Though to be honest, I'm not feeling generous. I mean, I told them what could happen in this situation and how to mitigate it. Is anyone listening to me?'

"I'm listening because I've learned you're usually right. They don't know that about you, so no, they just think you're a nag."

Tess caught Gwen's eye. "I'm depending on your begging skills to add to our reserves."

"Next steps?" Gwen asked. "If we can't get the vehicle out and no one helps, I'm thinking we'll have to hike out of here."

"That was my conclusion." Tess was glad she had on a good pair of lightweight hiking boots. "As soon as the sun hits the horizon. We both grab our safety packs. We take all the water with us that we begged because we can't save anyone if we go down on the trail."

"And we pray not to get lost," Gwen added. "It's pretty far, and after last night, I'm worried about walking in the dark. It would be easy to get disoriented like Mandy did."

"GPS." Tess reminded her.

"Helpful. You downloaded the maps, though, right?" Gwen asked. "You're not depending on connectivity?"

"I never depend on anything. I did the calculations. It's a seventy-five-minute hike under normal terrain circumstances."

"Of course, you did the calculations. So what?" Gwen looked over to Otto, who was showing off to the others as if he were a bushmaster, and this was a mere inconvenience for him. "We double the time when walking in the sand?"

"Right. So, say we start walking at seven. We could possibly get there while it's light, which I prefer."

"Here comes my shuttle." Gwen ran out and did exactly what Tess had done. "Hey, we're out of water. Do you have any to spare?"

This transport was moving faster than the other, probably hoping that the briefer its wheels pressed into the sand pit, the less he'd sink in.

Two water bottles flew out the sides, and Gwen tracked after them.

"Okay, you're winning two bottles to one. I'll take the next vehicle," Tess said.

"You were telling me about a time you all pulled out of something like this? Mud?" Gwen pocketed a bottle and opened the other one. "If I'm hiking three hours in the sand, we can't be wrung out."

"The others?" Tess asked.

"I'm not a mama bird. Look at them. We said shade. Are they in the shade? No. Do they think this is inconvenient? Yes. Do they understand this could be life-threatening? No. We could share any water we beg from the next vehicle. Maybe."

Tess accepted the bottle and took a drink.

"I'm feeling a bit resentful toward the group, to be honest. But that could be the first stage of dehydration." Gwen accepted the bottle back. "You were telling the story of getting the car out?"

"Yeah. It was the same scenario in that there were no strong trees to use with the winch. Different because it was mud. The guys went forward and dug a hole as deep as they could get it and then a trench between the hole and the front of the vehicle."

"Okay, I have the visual." Gwen pulled off her hat and stuck it between her knees as she dragged the elastic from her bun and gathered her sweaty hair into a ponytail.

"They tied the winch line to our spare tire and put the tire in the hole. The line was in the trench.

"Got it." Gwen put her ball cap back on her head.

"Then they filled in the dirt. They got the three heaviest guys to stand on the ground over the tire. Mmm." Tess paused, trying to remember. "Maybe that's not right. As I say that out loud, that seems too dangerous. Maybe the three heaviest guys happened to be standing close to the area where they buried the tire. Either way, that configuration was enough that they could run the winch and get our tires out of the mud. Took them ten, fifteen minutes?" Tess handed Gwen the bottle. "Otto's calling us over to push again."

"Necessary and dangerous."

"Yup."

The two rejoined the group. The metal on the vehicle, painted a dark olive, was heating up in the sun, and it burned

Tess's hand as she tried to find a good place to turn her effort into forward momentum.

Everyone did. Everyone tried.

The tires spun. That was a no-go.

Tess and Gwen moved back under their tree.

"You know, for such a dry and scrappy tree, the temperature is remarkably different under here." Tess looked up at the sound of a motor. She saw a young couple heading their way. The woman was rolling down her window. The guy was slowing down. "Don't slow down," Tess yelled as she began to run alongside them. The woman leaned out her window, twisting her body to keep Tess in view. "What can we do?"

"Go to the ranger station at the front," Tess yelled. "Tell them we're in real trouble. We have no water. Eleven people. No water. Tell them to send someone. We need help!"

6

———

Levi

Cerberus Tactical Headquarters
Northern Virginia

When Levi and the others pushed through the door at Cerberus headquarters, they found Team Alpha's tactical coordinator, Noah, in the conference room, mapping out possible strategies for a mission they had spooling up.

Multi-colored lists filled the whiteboard behind Hailey, a logistics specialist they'd scooped up from her job at World-Cares when she and a fellow Cerberus team member, Ares, got engaged.

"Ramping up?" Reaper asked, dropping his bag out of the way by the door.

"A tropical storm in the Caribbean is growing in strength. Looking at the spaghetti models, I'm predicting a sizeable hurricane, maybe even a cat five. If that happens, we might be heading out on search and rescue if our clients can't get off the island," Noah said. "Flights are sketchy." He nodded toward Hailey. "There's a scramble to get hold of the few plane tickets still available. Hailey's trying to keep families and pets together."

Hailey sent a welcome home smile toward the three team members coming back from the Beast Mode fiasco in Texas. "The pets' issue is the one that's making this tough."

"People would rather die than leave their animals behind," Goose said, stepping around Reaper to find a seat at the end of the conference table. "It's a given."

"Good flight home?" Hailey asked as she uncapped a pen and turned to add information to the board.

"Good enough." Levi dropped his bag next to Reaper's, then stood with his hands resting on the back of one of the captain's chairs as he looked over the information listed on the board.

All six Team Alpha handlers would deploy to the search and rescue mission on the island to rescue as many as fourteen clients who couldn't get out in time.

Man, he itched to be out there with them. The problem for Levi was that he wouldn't deploy anywhere without a dog.

The process was taking a lot longer than he'd anticipated. The criteria were stringent, as they should be. There was a limited pool from which Command could choose their operators, which was equally true for their dogs.

Levi could admit to being disappointed by their trip to Beast Mode. From the video, Casper had looked like a solid dog with polished skillsets. But that was the magic of editing; you could leave all the ugly parts in the garbage folder.

Noah focused on Levi, leaning back and crossing his arms over his chest. "Still no leash in your hands. I'm guessing things didn't go as well as you'd hoped."

"It was an adventure in futility," Goose said.

"Eye-opening." Reaper dragged a black captain's chair from under the conference table and sat. "We'll cross that vendor off our list. The dogs had a bunch of red flags, and the owners weren't big on ethics."

Levi clapped a hand on Halo's shoulder as he passed behind his teammate to find a seat.

Hired after he retired from the Australian Commandos, Halo was the only member of Cerberus's six-man Team Charlie in the room. Iniquus added Team Charlie to the lineup over the last few months. The new hires were getting their sea legs under them, adjusting to their new positions, and learning to navigate the Iniquus culture.

While Levi wasn't the last hire on the team, he was the only one without a K9. Most of the team had been out of the military long enough that they had time to train their own dogs to their own specs.

Halo and his Malinois, Max, had come on and—within the first days of fieldwork training with Panther Force in Estonia— had already saved a handful of people's lives. Halo's actions were no joke badass, and the bonus was that he met his fiancée when they worked through a series of disasters together. Halo said that if you can trust someone with your life, it was a bloody good base to build a future.

Levi was glad for him. He was a lucky guy.

"So what happened with the dogs? Not a good fit?" Halo pushed his paperwork out of the way so Levi could sit.

. "Not even close." Levi crouched and reached under the table to give Halos' doggo, Max, a scritch. "Worse than needing too much training time to get them up to snuff," Reaper laced his fingers behind his head, his elbows wide, "those dogs would need too much unwinding from Beast Mode training before we could polish their skills."

"That's always three times as long," Halo said. "And you never know when past training will pop out and bite you."

"If it does," Reaper agreed, "it's always at the worst possible time."

"What was the problem?" Noah asked.

"They were healthy, I'll give them that," Goose drummed his fingers on the table. "But that's about all I'd give them. They're not Cerberus quality."

"No?" Noah lifted his brow. "I'm surprised to hear that. Their reputation in the industry is a good one."

"None of the Beast Mode dogs could work off radio collar directions," Reaper said, "or even out of sight of their handler for one."

"And get this," Goose added, "not a one of them had a blood bite."

Halo canted his head. "That's one of the first things I did with Max. I mean, why put in the time and effort to train a military K9 if you aren't sure how he'll respond when they get that taste? I've seen trained dogs become predatory after that part of their brain switched on, and their handlers lost voice control when the dog spotted prey. With dogs bred for tactical work, that's a dangerous situation. I'm sure we all know of a dog that was put down for safety's sake."

"It's unfortunate," Reaper said. "Had I known that from the beginning, we wouldn't have wasted our time. It goes to show you never to assume. But then, they weren't very forthcoming about their methods and procedures. They considered everything proprietary." Reaper pulled his ankle over his knee, resting his hand on his shins as he turned to Levi. "We regularly train our dogs with blood sleeves. In a real-world scenario, either in rescue or tactical work, there will be blood to some extent. The dogs better know how to ignore it and stay task-oriented."

"Who donates the blood?" Levi asked.

"Different slaughterhouses," Reaper said, "so a variety of smells and tastes. Non-human."

"What's your theory on why they didn't let them get that blood bite in?" Noah asked.

Reaper scratched the side of his face. "I've given that some thought. Here's what I came up with—the team sources their dogs out of Europe, right?"

"Usually, a good thing," Goose said. "Cleaner bloodlines."

"But they get the pups as soon as they've weaned," Reaper said.

"Their dogs don't do basic training in a Schutzhund program in Europe?" Noah asked. "They bring them back as puppies? Why? Are they trying to save money?"

Noah's dog, Hairyman, wandered over to sniff Levi, and Levi leaned to the side, giving Hairyman room to crawl under the table and curl up with Max. "Conroy said their training methods begin at the beginning."

"I see," Noah said.

"Do you?" Reaper asked. "Because I don't think that group could have left us anymore in the dark." He made air quotes again. "'Our training methods are proprietary.' It was their drumbeat answer to all my questions." Reaper edged down in his seat until his head rested on the back of the chair. "So my theory: Beast Mode buys these dogs as weaned pups. They take them before they've had their basic training and before they've gone through their adolescence. The price is a fraction of a Schutzhund-trained K9. It's a high gamble, potentially high reward scenario. I think they purposefully don't let their dogs taste blood, or they could lose the money they invested in that dog."

"So Casper," Halo swiveled toward Levi, "I would have laid

wages you would've picked him, mate. On video, he's an amazing athlete."

"Beast Mode was playing games," Levi laced his fingers, pressing his thumbs together as he rested his elbows on the chair arms. "Before Casper came in for our inspection, they ran him ten miles."

Noah let out a low whistle.

"Levi put on the bite suit," Goose said, "and Casper nearly ripped his arm out of the socket. It took both Conroy and Pete and a shock device to get Casper to release."

"That level of prey drive?" Halo asked. "That dog's not safe. I'd imagine after seeing that, you all didn't trust the training."

"It was all smoke and mirrors," Levi said.

"So where do we go from here?" Goose asked.

Levi grinned. "How about Namibia?"

Hailey looked up from her computer.

"That's about a sixteen-hour flight." Reaper pulled his brows together. "Seems far for a joy ride,"

"What's in Namibia?" Hailey asked.

Levi pulled out his phone and scrolled through his video files. "I have a buddy, Enrico. We went through K9 training at the same time. Former SEAL dog handler. He was a lot like Reaper, just a natural feel for how to get a dog to know the job and have fun doing it."

Reaper caught Levi's gaze.

"Hey, man, I'm not trying to butter you up. I'm just trying to make a fair comparison for folks, so you all know Enrico is the opposite of Conroy and Pete." Levi handed his phone to Reaper with a video queued up.

"No flattery taken," Reaper chuckled, accepting the phone and tapping play. "You like his training methods? He produces well-trained dogs?"

"When you were in the SEALs, Reaper, you told me you had a dedicated K9 for your team. But you probably knew some teams, like mine, that picked a dog from the kennel to meet the mission's needs."

"Pros and cons to that scenario," Reaper said, his gaze fixed on the video. He replayed it in slow motion.

"Enrico was in a similar situation to mine. I'm good at what I do when I'm handling a dog, the tactical side of the equation. But I'm not a trainer. Where Enrico, on the other hand, is a natural. When he returned the loaner pooch to the kennel, the K9 had always vastly improved its skillsets." Levi flicked a finger through the air for emphasis. "Two things happened. On the good to interesting end, handlers, me included, tried to figure out which dogs Enrico had just worked so they could choose that one for their next assignment. And—"

"The kennel started steering all the problem dogs Enrico's way." Reaper handed the phone to Goose. "What's that dog's name?"

"That's Mojo. He's Enrico's pride and joy." Levi nodded at the phone. "And you're right. They gave him the troublemakers. Don't get me wrong, Enrico loved the challenge. But it's not great to be out running and gunning with a questionable fur-force when lives are on the line." He watched Goose's face as he tapped pause and zoomed in on some aspect of the video. "I remember one time that the risk put Enrico's team in danger. When he went back, he chewed everyone a new hole. It was a sight to behold. But he was right to do it."

"Why's he in Namibia?" Goose asked, passing the video to Noah.

"Enrico is an animal lover through and through. Everyone knows that about him. He'd wear you out talking about his after-military career plans. Africa was calling him. Enrico has a special kind of anger that runs through him when he talks about poachers. While we were in the sandbox, Enrico was making African contacts, learning what he could from them, and helping the rangers out by solving some of their training issues where he could. A buddy of his at Etosha Park in Namibia called up, saying they were having trouble with their scent training. Would Enrico mind flying over and seeing if he couldn't pinpoint the problem?"

"Did he?" Reaper asked.

"Jumped on the first plane. Two things. First, their trainers were putting the scent source in the training wall while a helper would stand on the other side. When they heard the trainer start his high-pitched praise, the dog's reward of choice—say, a tug toy or a Kong—was tossed over the top. That was supposed to appear to the dog that the scent source itself was providing the reward."

"Why would that be bad?" Hailey asked.

"Couple of things," Levi said. "Let's start with the payment for a good find. In order for the reward to be immediate and look like the scent provided it, the helper would have to stand behind the concealed item. At that point, the dog could hunt the human scent and know that the thing they were looking for was behind one of those doors in the training wall."

"Oh, yeah." Hailey gave a nod. "I get that."

"And because the scent wall divided the room in half and the reward person was behind the wall, it was convenient for the trainer to hide the scent. That's especially true if they were working on the skill over and over again."

"Yup." Hailey nodded. "And the problem with the trainer hiding the scent source?"

"The trainer could very well have some subtle body tell that you and I couldn't see on tape but a dog would pick up on easily. Too long a look, a pointed looking away, anything really.

A dog would pay attention and remember how to get his reward."

"And this scenario is very much like the one we saw in Texas," Goose said. "The second dog we inspected, Diabla, was tuned in to her handler for that very reason. When we set up a double-blind, she couldn't find the scent."

"How do you fix that?" Hailey asked.

"It's not a good practice to give any kind of reward—voice or play—when the dog finds the scent because the dog will stop working after the find," Levi said. "In a real-world scenario, there may be several scent sources in a room that we need to clear. We want the dog to go in, indicate on every last scent that it finds, and when they've found everything and signaled each one for its handler, then go back to an exact spot. It's there that the handler offers a reward."

"It's called DFR, delayed final response," Reaper explained. "A two-person team could still do the job. One person wearing gloves would place the scents and leave through a second door so there was no possible exchange of information in front of the dog. The dog searches the room, finds all the scents, and then goes to his spot to get the praise and games."

"Pretty quick, the dogs in Etosha were up to their real-world tasks," Levi said.

Hailey smiled. "That's so interesting."

"When Enrico was there doing the work, it was everything he'd imagined it to be. He fell in love with the place and took a job. For the last few years, he's been training K9s to support both the rangers, who track animals outside of the park and the military and police forces that protect inside the park. We're talking about developing fearless tactical dogs that fight the bad guys but don't get eaten by the lions." Levi grinned.

"I've been to Etosha. It's an astonishing experience," Hailey said.

"Yeah?" Halo turned to her. "What were you doing down there?"

"A WorldCares friend of mine, Gwen Metz, and I went over to see her parents. Similar to Enrico, her folks were on a bucket list vacation to celebrate their twentieth anniversary. Once they got there, they fell in love with the people and the country and didn't want to leave. So they uprooted, quite literally, and moved there."

"Why quite literally?" Levi asked.

"They're biotechnologists." She shut her laptop lid so she wasn't peering over the screen at everyone. "Their work focuses on developing heat and drought-resistant grape varieties so vineyards can use less water. The Metzes dug up the grape vines they were cultivating and decided to test them out in Namibian conditions. The vineyard is just outside of the national park. I got to lounge around, sipping wine and enjoying the experience. Since it was dry season, the animals would gather at the watering holes at dusk and dawn. We'd go in with one of the Metzes' guide friends to see the animals cluster. Just the trip of a lifetime. It was surreal." She smiled. "It was hard to believe I was there, and an elephant was walking beside our vehicle. Where I had lived in East Africa, we didn't have the Big Five animals."

"Their vineyard is right outside of the park?" Reaper asked.

"You can see the entrance when you're on the top of the hill."

Handing Levi's phone back to him, Noah said, "Tell me about that video."

"Mojo is one of the dogs Enrico trained to work alongside the military. Tough job. Brave people who do that work. Enrico said that just this spring, the soldiers were in a gunfight with a gang of poachers killing rhinos. The poachers would leave the carcasses and take the horns to sell. In that fight, two poachers were killed and one of the soldiers. It was the soldier who handled Mojo that went down. Mojo can't work in the park anymore. Rhinos set him off."

"Off?" Reaper scowled.

"Yeah, he's rhino sour. Enrico says he could probably build Mojo's tolerance back up, but they have to balance how much time and focus that would consume. And like we were saying about retraining the dogs from Beast Mode, you're taking a chance that something could retrigger Mojo. Enrico thinks just getting him a job where there aren't any rhinos is the ticket."

"There aren't any jobs with the rangers outside the park?" Halo asked.

"As to the rhinos, they're out in the wild in the other areas of Namibia," Hailey said. "I understand they've been working on growing the black rhino population in their natural territories."

"Meaning anywhere in Namibia might be problematic for Mojo?" Halo asked.

"Down south in the desert?" Hailey said. "I don't think they'd range down that far. South of the capital, Windhoek, I think that's mostly Oryx and ostriches. Some baboons. Lots of termites."

"Let's get back to the problem with Mojo," Reaper said.

"When he smells rhino, Mojo becomes fiercely protective and uncontrollable by voice command. We saw that play out with Casper. It's a significant concern."

"Except that's the opposite of becoming predatory after tasting blood," Noah said.

"Enrico put it this way: Mojo can't be commanded when a rhino is around," Levi explained. "He's busy guarding and protecting. Enrico put him through his paces outside Etosha without the rhinos, and Mojo was spot on. Enrico figures he needs to sell Mojo to an outfit that won't be around rhinos. So that's a consideration. I'm not sure how often that would come up with Team Charlie if we considered Mojo."

"Good chance it would never come up," Reaper said. "If you were attaching to one of the tactical forces, we'd just make sure that you weren't tapped to go to the zoo." He flicked a finger toward the phone, and Levi opened it and handed it back to Reaper. "Did Enrico get video of the rhino reaction?"

"No video of the reaction. I'm assuming they're too busy making sure that everything stays safe. But there is video comparing Mojo's work before the incident and the same skills outside of the park afterward. He's impressive."

"My worry would be that he'd accumulate a list of situations where he takes the dominant role. That could quickly make him useless in the field," Reaper said.

"Mine, too," Levi agreed. "Enrico said that Mojo has been in life-or-death situations before and after. He thinks Mojo might be blaming himself for allowing his handler to die. Enrico doesn't know I'm looking for a dog, so he's not trying to sell me a Casper."

"So he *is* for sale?" Noah asked. "Beautiful animal. You can see the intelligence in his eyes."

"He's a purebred German shepherd. I've been hearing stories about Mojo and his training since he was a pup. Since they can't use Mojo as a working dog, Enrico figures that with the price for Mojo, he could get a whole litter of pups raised and ready to expand their kennel. They've already lost twenty-something rhinos this year alone. They need more help, and their budget is small."

"Interesting," Reaper said as he watched the video without providing any context. He handed the phone back to Levi. "Okay, let's see if we can't get over to see this Mojo pooch." He turned to Hailey. "That vineyard your friend's parents run, is it dog-friendly?"

"The Etosha trainers do part of their puppy training there. They encourage the guests to play with the puppies so they get used to different people's looks and smells since the dogs work around tourists from all over the world. I bet the Metzes know Enrico."

"Could you reach out to them and see if they have room and board for three with the possibility that Mojo might be spending the night?"

"Since I do Cerberus logistics, I think I can handle that." She smiled. "When are you thinking of going?"

"I have this week," Reaper said, "and then my training schedule is tight."

Hailey scribbled notes on her pad, then looked up. "So, first flight out once Enrico is on board?"

7

Levi

Metz Winery, Namibia

Ever since Levi passed the video of Mojo around the conference table, the team had been forward-leaning. True to her promise, Hailey had them on the first flight out of Reagan. They'd landed in Windhoek, rented a vehicle, and driven north to the Metz Winery, where Hailey had arranged their stay.

There was no moss growing on an Iniquus timeline. They developed a strategy and moved on it.

That dynamic orientation was part and parcel of Levi's time in the military. He'd be sleeping in a tent one minute, and the next, he'd be loading onto a helicopter, winging out on a do-or-die mission.

Levi liked that kind of life. Nothing stagnant. Enough downtime to get basic tasks accomplished and then shots of adrenaline that kept his system running in prime condition. He thought it was good for him both physically and mentally.

And ever since Tess, Levi never had the inclination to put down roots. He couldn't see that in his future, either.

In the military, his call sign was "Tumbleweed." But Levi had been glad to shed that moniker when he left the service. He'd been long enough away from his childhood on the ranch that it didn't feel like a good fit anymore.

Reaper pulled their vehicle up to the front door at the Metz Winery. An older couple stood shoulder to shoulder, waiting for them.

"Looks like you found us just fine," the woman said as they climbed out. "I'm Iris, and this is my husband, Craig. Welcome. Welcome."

After introductions and handshakes, Craig moved around to the hatch. "It's unusual to have availability in the dry season. Luckily, we had a group cancel at the last minute. Sorry, your rooms aren't side by side. But I'm sure you'll make out fine. It's not a big place. Why don't you start by unloading your bags and getting settled? After that, you can move your vehicle around back to park."

Levi was last to reach for his duffle.

"Why don't you two follow me," Craig said to Goose and Reaper. "Iris, you want to take Levi around?"

Iris passed her husband two keys, then stood to the side, waiting for Levi to slam the hatch closed.

With his duffle slung over his shoulder, he turned to follow Iris.

"We're so glad to have you. It was nice to hear from Hailey. It's been a while since she visited, but we've kept in touch over the years. A friend of a friend is a friend of ours."

"Thank you, ma'am." Levi shortened his stride and slowed his gait to match Iris's pace.

"Of course, Hailey came to visit with my daughter Gwen. They worked together at WorldCares. You'll get to meet Gwen tonight. She's bringing another colleague sometime this morning."

They walked along a tiled porch with a latticed roof.

"Does Gwen do logistics?" Levi asked politely.

"Gwen's on a team that keeps an eye on both the weather and the resulting ground conditions. Her focus is on African weather systems and how they affect the continent, then up into Europe and over to the Southeastern United States. Her team hands their long-range predictions off to management. Once an area is deemed at risk, Hailey would get her marching orders and move the right kinds of field support into place. Tents, food, water purification, what have you." She tipped her head back to catch Levi's gaze, then dropped it again as they moved forward. "At the time, Hailey stayed in close communication with Gwen's team so as to streamline getting needs met. You know, getting everything in place without wasting their resources. It's a balancing act. And it's all very imprecise. Weather and people are predictable in their unpredictability. But Hailey changed jobs to work with Iniquus after she got herself engaged to a mighty fine young man. From what Gwen says, Hailey's is a second-chance romance, which makes for a nice story."

"Yes, ma'am. WorldCares loss is Iniquus's gain. Though the same work is going on. Both organizations are out trying to do good in the world, just from a different angle. WorldCares looks farther out, and Iniquus jumps in when there's an emergency."

While Levi's job would run the gamut, Iniquus Command mounted Team Charlie to meet the increased demand, protecting Americans working outside of the United States for both institutional and corporate clients. Sometimes, that could be a kidnap case or a close protection stint. But Iniquus projections predicted there would be a lot more search and rescue missions following volatile weather. Where a rainstorm suddenly becomes a mudslide or flash flood, where hurricane-force winds leveled an area or swept it away in the storm surge, Iniquus would send the teams in to get their clients to safety.

That demand was pushing Team Alpha and Bravo hard. Already, Iniquus Command was taking the operators' recommendations to develop a Team Delta.

They stopped at the corner, and Iris gestured toward a giraffe munching the leaves on a tree. "That's Betty. We found her on the property here as a calf. She was in bad shape from some predator or other. After we nursed her back to health, she was free to move on. We don't pen her or anything. But she seems content to stay. You'll see that all around Namibia. Back in North Carolina, you might take in a stray kitten. Here, we take in animals like Betty."

"She's beautiful." There was a sense of peace watching her. A grace.

After a moment, Iris asked. "You've been with Iniquus a long time, then, Levi?"

"I recently retired from the Navy, ma'am. I'm a new hire."

"That's why you're seeing Enrico about a dog? Were you a SEAL K9 handler like he was? Is that how you know him? He said y'all are old friends."

"Yes, ma'am."

"You know, you don't have to ma'am me. Where're you from?"

"Oklahoma. And I'm afraid that after my upbringing and my time in the military, saying ma'am and sir is a reflex that I won't overcome. I hope you won't be offended."

"Not at all. Coming from North Carolina, I know all about how that gets ingrained."

They walked along the hallway. "You know, my dad was in the military. He handled a K9 in Vietnam by the name of Cheeseball. She was a decorated war hero, got a Medal of

Bravery for charging the enemy in an ambush. Saved my dad's life. When it was time to come home, Cheeseball was considered 'equipment,' and they ordered Dad to leave her behind. Of course, Dad wouldn't entertain the notion. That's not the kind of person my dad is. He and his men devised a plan and snuck her home to live with us." Iris inserted a key into the lock. "Here we are." She pushed the door wide and gestured for Levi to go in. "This is one of the rooms where we put dog people. Some folks have allergies, so we have designated dog areas."

"Thank you, ma'am." Levi moved through the door and took in the rather romantic-looking room with a drape of mosquito netting. Levi could see a couple coming here on their honeymoon to make a lifetime of memories. But it wasn't what he was used to. He went more for the utilitarian and easy to keep up.

"As long as your dog is under voice command, you can come and go without using a leash. Just don't let the dog go into anyone's room that doesn't have a dog symbol on the door or in the communal areas on the rugs. You shouldn't run into much trouble. It's all mostly tile. Things get dusty around here. And in the wet season, there's mud." Iris walked farther into the room. "Look there," she pointed at a picture on the wall. "That's me as a young girl with Cheeseball. I put that photo in all the dog rooms. To this day, I miss that sweet girl."

Levi set his bag down as Iris opened the door to the bathroom. "Lights are here on the wall. Kind of an odd spot." She gestured Levi over. "It takes a minute to get the hot water flowing. We have these buckets out. If you wouldn't mind trapping the cold water instead of letting it run down the drain, we'd appreciate it. The cleaners can empty it for you or just dump it on anything outside that's still alive. We don't waste a drop if we can help it. That's certainly true during most dry seasons, particularly true this year." She moved out of the way so Levi could go in and see the setup.

"From Enrico, I hear you're looking to buy Mojo." She shook her head. "It's going to be hard on that man seeing Mojo go. But you probably know all about that, freshly out of the Navy. It's hard on the handlers to leave and pass off their dog to someone new."

"Fortunately or not," Levi rejoined her in the bedroom. "I didn't have my own dog when I left. But that happened to a SEAL buddy of mine. He had a dog, and they were as close as can be. They went to train out in Arizona, and my buddy, Tripwire's his name, came down with some kind of illness from the dirt in the air."

"Dirt in the air? I've never heard of such a thing. We've got plenty of dirt in the air here. Especially this year. Namibia is usually dry as a bone in what is considered our winter months —which is summer in the United States. But this year? It's like nothing I've ever seen before." She pulled the key from the door and handed it to Levi. "Come on, let me show you around. Your friend, is he okay now?"

Levi locked the door behind himself and pocketed the key. "He's fine enough that he's able to work on Iniquus with our search and rescue team. His lung capacity didn't meet the requirements to do his job as a SEAL, so he left the service. His dog of the heart was assigned to a Delta Force unit." He followed behind Iris as they retraced their steps.

"Can you imagine? He must be just heartbroken."

"It helps that the new handler sends weekly photos and videos, and Tripwire can keep up."

She laid her hand over her heart. "Now, isn't that a kindness?"

"It is, yes, ma'am. And if Mojo and I are a good fit. I'll make sure that Enrico stays part of Mojo's life that same way."

Iris patted Levi's arm. "Here's where we like to have breakfast. We tend to have our biggest meal in the mornings, a European-styled menu. It's comfortable to be out here that time of day, and the landscape is pretty with the sun coming up. Just let the cook know in the evening what you want and what time you want it. Fill out this form with your room number and leave it in this box." She moved toward a set of double doors. "You said you didn't have a dog when you left? I didn't know that was a thing."

Levi reached forward to snag the handle to hold the door for Iris. "Like Enrico, I traded out dogs regularly. No time to bond."

"Oh, now that's not true, is it? I've seen it time and again when we've helped out on the puppy side of Enrico's training." Iris swept her hand to indicate the room. "Our lounge. Games and books on the shelves. Our bar is do-it-yourself and honor system." She pointed at a box near the array of bottles. "Anyway, the soldiers from Etosha come in to get matched with their dog. Enrico watches to see their reactions to each other. He wants the two of them to look at each other and make an instant connection. That's the way it was when I met my husband. He was just standing there in the library. He turned to me, and I thought, 'Oh, there he is.' Yup, he was mine. We were fated to be together." She smiled at Craig as he led Goose and Reaper into the lounge.

Yeah, Levi had that same experience but a very different outcome. Tess. She had been on his mind so much these last few days. He'd been tempted to look her up and just see how her life was unfolding. But he knew that Tess in Abraham's arms with smiling pictures of their anniversary would shoot a hole in his heart. Better to distract himself with finding his dog.

Iris turned to him. "You married, Levi?"

"No, ma'am." He slid his hands into his pockets. "I haven't had that privilege."

"Hmm, well, who knows," she popped her brows, "Gwen and you might catch eyes. I could see you getting along just fine."

Levi didn't offer a response. And Iris didn't seem to need one.

"No smoking on the premises," Craig said as they joined Iris and Levi. "It's the dry season. We don't need a bushfire."

8

———

Levi

Metz Winery, Namibia

Enrico turned the corner and climbed the stairs to the breakfast veranda with a hand in the air as his greeting.

"Good morning," Iris sang out. "Have you had coffee yet? Had breakfast?"

"I could do with both." He smiled.

As Levi rounded the table to greet his friend, Enrico wrapped Iris in a hug, speaking over her shoulder. "I see you met my buddy, Levi. It always shocks me what a small world it truly is."

When Iris stepped out of the way, Levi was grinning ear to ear as he and Enrico wrapped each other in a bear hug. "Aw man, it's been entirely too long. I had no idea how old you were getting."

Enrico released his grasp and clapped a hand on Levi's shoulder. "Who did you bring with you?" He scanned the table.

"Enrico, this is Reaper, our head trainer."

Reaper rose, reaching across the table for a shake.

With a bladed hand, Levi indicated the other end of the table. "Goose, the Cerberus vet for Team Alpha."

Goose raised a hand, then swiped a napkin over his mouth.

"Glad to meet you both." Enrico turned to find Levi looking expectantly toward the door.

"Mojo's here?"

"I thought it would be best if you meet him on the playing field with a bite suit on." Enrico checked his watch. "We don't need to be out there quite yet."

"Sit yourself down," Iris pulled a chair for him. "Craig and I were just getting to know these fine men from Iniquus." She turned her head and called, "Channelle, we have one more for breakfast. It's Enrico, and he's brought his big appetite."

"Yes, ma'am," the voice floated back into the dining room.

Levi held the chair for Iris, then took his own seat.

"We enjoy learning about how people find themselves on the path to our vineyard." Iris pulled her napkin across her lap. "It's never a simple story. To catch you up, Enrico, we just learned that Levi needs a K9 partner because he was hired for the new Team Charlie."

"I'm assuming an Alpha and Bravo," Craig said. "What made Iniquus think to start building a new team?"

"Storm activity," Reaper said. "Alpha and Bravo were getting spread thin, and that runs against Iniquus policies. Our teams need to have time to recover both physically and mentally. That's true for human and K9 alike. We need time to train between events. Our clients deserve top-notch care."

"What kind of clients?" Craig asked.

"It runs the gamut," Reaper said. "We do close protection assignments as well as search and rescue. The earthquake in Morrocco, the flash flood in Spain, the Cat five hurricanes that took a surprise turn in the Caribbean, whenever there's an event that puts our clients in harm's way, we're the boots on the ground that gets them to safety."

"But Mojo is a tactical dog, right, Enrico?" Iris asked. "You've trained him to chase down the bad guys?"

"Yes, ma'am."

Iris swung her gaze to Levi. "And you need that for search and rescue?"

"There are times we need to pull groups out of zones that suddenly turned hot when there's an incursion or terror event," Levi said. "In those cases, the dogs help to guard our group, find munitions if necessary, track a missing person."

"Or let's say that we have our group together with enough food, water, and supplies to get our people out," Reaper added. "That's our contracted duty. These are desperate circumstances, and others might want to take those supplies. A K9 is an extra set of eyes and ears to help us keep track of our surroundings, force multipliers."

"Of course, the people would try to get to those supplies." Iris's mouth pulled into a frown. "They're desperate. Looking back, when I was a young mother, there was nothing that I wouldn't do to keep my child safe."

"Exactly, ma'am," Reaper said. "At Iniquus, we understand that. And we want to help. We're there first to protect our clients. Once they're out and safe, we work with the emergency services to do what we can. With a trained K9 team, we're proud of the lives we save."

"That's not just a humane move," Craig said. "It's pragmatic."

"How do you mean, dear?" Iris asked, taking a nibble of toast.

"These guys work with emergency management all over the world. They get to know the folks in charge, build relationships.

Those relationships serve a good purpose. They can pat each other's backs. You help me, and I help you."

Iris spread more butter onto the toast. "That sounded cynical."

"What I mean is that Iniquus teams are recognized helpers with skills. They'd be welcomed into a hazardous area." Craig pointed toward his wife. "You know this from your sister getting stuck on the side of the mountain."

"My sister lives in western North Carolina," Iris explained. "After the rain made the whole mountain into a mudslide, they had the devil of a time getting food and water up to people. They had rescue teams with mule trains and pack goats. But they were having a time of it, trying to keep the do-gooders at bay."

"Rightly so," Reaper said. "There are things to be done at base camp—cooking, cleaning, supporting. But to get someone untrained out in a disaster multiplies the number of people that need to be rescued. It stretches the resources further."

"Pack goats," Goose lifted his juice glass and took a sip, "now, that's something I'd like to see."

"Maybe Iniquus should consider adding that to your mission capabilities." Enrico grinned.

"Let's get Charlie and Delta up and rolling before we start talking about pack goats," Reaper chuckled.

"Like I was saying," Craig leaned back, crossing his arms over his chest, "you know the authorities at a location, and they know you. You're taking numbers off their search count. You're available to assist if you come across something. The more support you can be to each other is a net positive. Look, that's how you even knew to come and give Mojo a trial. Since Levi and Enrico were SEALs together, Levi can vouch for Enrico's capabilities."

"We've known Enrico since he moved to Namibia," Iris

said. "He stayed with us here at the vineyard as part of his first assignment. It was fixing a problem with scent training, if I'm remembering correctly. One of the military dogs had just had a litter. We host the puppies here at the vineyard to expose them to family life. Eleven puppies in that litter, if you can imagine."

Craig nodded. "Yep, and Mojo was one of them. So we've known Mojo all his life. Enrico picked out three of the pups he thought could do the work in Etosha. I think most of the rest went to various groups that assist people with disabilities, leading the blind and the like."

"Well, yes, but four ended up being pet quality," Enrico said. "They went to families in Windhoek. We need every tactical dog who can do the work to help us. Right now, we have a tiny budget. Most of the money is going to feed the military who work at the park. We're praying for rain. The dry season should be over in a few more weeks. I'm hoping we can hold on that long. Animals and people alike are suffering."

Iris fixed her gaze on Levi. "I know that here in Namibia, the hungrier the population gets, the more conflict we see between humans and the animals. That's the same everywhere, don't you think?" Iris lifted her hands and let them flop back in her lap, "I'm not even sure what I'm asking here."

Levi looked up as Chanelle brought Enrico's breakfast in. "Iniquus believes that the environmental challenges ahead of us are going to be the biggest national security threats of our time. It used to be that we were fighting over the resources of gas and oil so that we had that available to build our economies. But now, all around the world, there is deep insecurity about the drastic changes on the horizon. Water and food are the next pressure points."

"That just sent a shiver down my spine." Iris gripped the edge of the table. "Our Gwen says that her job used to be much more straightforward. Weather patterns are becoming unpredictable, and that makes WorldCares' struggle to be in the right place ahead of the crisis."

"We're really experiencing the unusual weather here in Namibia." Craig picked up his fork, laid it across his plate, and shoved the plate away from him, signaling the staff that he was done. "Our wet season wasn't as wet as it needed to be. There's no food for the wild animals. Then, the wild ones want to come and eat our domestic ones before we do. It's getting prohibitively expensive to feed the domesticated ones."

"Except for Betty." Iris raised an emphatic brow. "Betty gets fed."

"Despite the bounty of this meal—it's delicious, thank you—there's certainly little food available for us humans." Enrico loaded up his fork and let it hover in the air. "Without enough food in the stores or people's gardens, the government had to release some of the emergency food supplies. We've burned through about seventy-five percent of the emergency storage."

"When Gwen gets here, Enrico," Iris said, "she's taking the rest of the week for vacation. But after that, she can sit down and look at the models. I'll bet she can come up with helpful insights for y'all over at Etosha."

Craig turned to Reaper. "So WorldCares developed their models to steer their humanitarian efforts. What do Iniquus models say?"

Reaper's gaze hardened. "To be honest, sir, in our lifetimes, we're going to see increasing global instability. Weather extremes are changing the intensity of worsening water supplies and food supplies. In the United States right now, people are talking about how expensive the food is getting. But as you all know from Iris's sister's experience, we just had storms whip through Florida and up the East Coast. A lot of the groves were destroyed. That's our citrus and peach supply. It'll impact the price of food for years to come. Those financial pressures will be hardest on families with lower incomes, like our disabled communities.

Levi reached for the water carafe and poured himself a glass. "When I was over in Iraq, and some up in Syria, we saw the Syrian civil war had a lot to do with drought. The people from rural areas had to move to the cities. The cities' infrastructures weren't set up to support that many people." He told Craig. "For sure, it's not the only reason why there was conflict. I've just found that when there are existing tensions, a spark can light a fire."

And as he said that, Levi's stomach lurched. He remembered clearly how Tess shivered against his body one night after waking up from one of her night terrors. She whispered her survival story that all started when a fight erupted over a Guinea hen.

The human suffering that followed was incomprehensible.

For Tess, it had been a wound that would probably never heal.

While he was away at war and saw the atrocities, he always thought about how Tess had to navigate that as an orphaned child, and his compassion was immense.

It reminded Levi that at any minute of any day, something as small as standing next to the wrong hen can change your life on a dime.

9

Levi

As the group finished their breakfasts, Enrico checked his watch. "I think it's time we head out for the evolution."

Levi felt anticipation bubble through his system. "Oh yeah! Let's do this, brother."

"Craig and Iris, are you coming with us?" Enrico asked as he pushed his chair under the table.

"Hell yeah, I am." Craig scraped his chair back and stood. "Can't wait to see what you've planned for today."

Iris bustled toward the door. "Let me tell the staff where we'll be and change into boots."

Enrico scooped his hand in a follow-me gesture. "I brought my vehicle. The logos will get us into the training grounds without the high-dollar scrutiny you might get from your rental. It's a ten-minute drive."

Rounding the front of the building, Craig moved to the left side to sit shotgun. The Iniquus men climbed in, each taking a seat, leaving the one by the door free for Iris. Gripping the back of his chair, Craig pulled himself around to see the group. "You know I heard the Iniquus name for the first time a couple of weeks ago. Tidal Force is one of your tactical forces, isn't it? That group was working over in Kenya a bit ago."

"Yes," Levi said. "I was attached with Tidal Force recently. We were providing security for an American corporation's Kenyan retreat."

Iris stepped into the van, and Goose leaned forward to slide the door shut while she reached for her seat belt.

"Yep." Craig nodded. "I read all about it. Iris, I was saying that Iniquus made the newspaper when they saved that woman on safari from the lion attack."

"Lion attack?" Iris asked. "Did you tell me about that?"

"Out of Kenya, Iris. It was a young woman, too. You know, they're saying the lion attacked her because of where the woman was in her cycle. The lioness thought she was competition," Craig said. "The young lady was pointing her camera toward some birds taking a photograph, and just out of nowhere, wham."

"Our lions are pretty shy," Enrico said, starting the engine. "They're usually off in the tree line camouflaging. While the best times to see them are first light or last, it's rare that a wildcat would be anywhere near where a person would come into contact. Even a tourist with binoculars in Etosha." He put the van into drive and rounded back toward the road. "Our guides are amazing at finding any animal in Etosha. They can point them out, and a tourist with a zoom lens can possibly make out the shape of their head, the twitch of an ear. But their cameras can't take a clear photo. To do that successfully, you'd have to have a massive lens or something military-grade. While it's disappointing for tourists who've seen lions lying in the roadway, blocking traffic on social media feeds, I've never heard of that happening in Etosha. Honestly, it's safer that way.

Guides can bring open safari vehicles into the park, but no weapons are allowed. There's no protection."

"Good for jumping out if an elephant is stampeding," Craig said.

"Rare." Enrico reached up and adjusted his mirror.

"Craig, I'm just thinking about what you said, though." Iris leaned closer to her husband. "From a biological point of view, I don't know that I buy that about the woman's cycle."

"Okay, then you might not buy this either," Craig turned forward as they jostled down the main drive. "The Tidal Force men leaped out to save her. Since a weaponless human can't win a fight with a lion, I'm not sure what the heck they were thinking. But the others in their safari group told the journalist that the lioness took a swipe at the woman. She fell from the vehicle. The men sitting around her were out like a flash in the mix."

"Oh, my!" Iris gasped. "They jumped a *lion*? I've never heard of such a thing."

"Perhaps the group's sudden movement startled the lion," Enrico said as he waited at the top of the drive for a truck to rumble past. "It wasn't a smackdown. She'd have mauled the lot."

"Sounds about right. And then those guys got that girl some lifesaving first aid." Craig gestured toward his collar. "The lioness got her in the neck."

Iris pressed a hand to her cheek. "Did that poor girl survive?"

"That's what the paper said." Craig reached up to grab his seat belt and pull it on as Enrico turned from the unpaved vineyard road out onto the highway. "She was hospitalized to get some blood, but she made it through."

"Are there lions that roam Namibia? Or have they moved them all to the park?" Goose asked.

"There've been lion sightings by our rangers," Enrico called over his shoulder. "They're trying to put a number on the population, but, like I said, lions don't really want humans to see them. They definitely aren't lying in the roadways. You won't run into one on your day hikes, even with a dog that might look like a nice snack. Mostly, the rangers are finding them up in the hills."

"Good to know," Levi said with a grin.

"Levi, you were working with Tidal Force in Kenya? Were you there when that happened to that woman?" Iris asked.

"No, ma'am, the team went a few days earlier than I did to do some sightseeing in the area. They wanted to meet with the members of the Maasai, which they did. Their warriors weren't on that safari. I didn't join the team until several days after that. I missed my opportunity to rope a lioness. It's been a while since I did any rodeo sports, so maybe it's for the best." He sent Iris a wink.

Iris tapped Craig's shoulder. "Levi's from Oklahoma."

"Everyone ready?" Enrico asked. "Here's the plan. We're driving over to the field where we set out bite suit equipment. Today, we're practicing chasing down a poacher by low-flying a helicopter in to release Mojo for a takedown. Then Mojo will hold the poacher—that would be you, Levi—until we can get boots on the ground to take over the arrest."

"I see," Levi said. "And how long would you anticipate it taking for those boots to get over and stop me from getting mauled?"

"All depends on you, brother. This is Mojo, not Cujo. You fight, you get the bite. I suggest you lay still."

Levi stood in the powdery earth, watching that he didn't put his foot on the rocks that spotted the area and risk rolling his ankle.

Any grass around him had dried to straw, and Levi wasn't sure how the grazing animals were getting any nutrients from that at all.

"This normal?" he asked, lifting his chin to indicate the tufts of dead vegetation.

"It's dry season. We expect dry," Enrico said. "But this is something you might see on Mars. It's not good, man."

"Lot of rocks out here for a dog take down," Levi observed, "Even with a bite suit on."

"We cleared an area." Enrico pointed. "That tree out there—"

"By tree," Levi asked, "You mean that spot on the horizon?"

"That's the one. You beeline in that direction, and by the time Mojo is on the ground, you'll be in the cleared field. When you hear the helicopter, I'd get to running hard. The wash can throw rocks."

"Good to know." Levi tugged the suit over his arms and pulled up the zipper. He pulled the collar around and attached it in place to protect his carotid. As Levi suited up, he shifted his shoulders around. He was a bit sore still since the last time he'd played this role two days ago in Texas when Casper didn't want to let go.

After pulling up the hood, Levi cinched it down tight and tied the cords. As uncomfortable as it was, Levi had seen a buddy have his ear bitten clean off. That was an experience Levi wanted to avoid.

Off to the side, Levi overheard Enrico talking to Reaper and Goose. "I thought we'd start with a show-stopper. Mostly because it happens to fit in with the equipment we have available to us today, and it was already on our training schedule. But also because I want to impress the heck out of you." Enrico grinned. "Truth is, Mojo is going to be hard for me to part with. I'd feel better about the situation if Mojo was with a brother." He hitched his thumb toward Levi. "One good thing Levi taught me when we were on deployment was his dog policy. When he was going down range with a tactical K9, he always jumped into a bite suit so he'd know how the dog would act in a takedown." Enrico rocked back on his heels. "It's a good policy. It's important to understand the dog's temperament and how best to control the situation. Nothing like being on the receiving end to give you a clear idea."

They could hear the helicopter rotors coming in from the east. "That's for you, Tumbleweed." Enrico chuckled. "Might as well start running now to get your muscles warm and loose so you don't hurt yourself."

Levi took off at a jog. Well, the best he could with the heavy padded suit on. This was an important test to see how Mojo would perform in the field.

His choices here could have life-or-death consequences in the future. As much as Levi loved Enrico and as much as Levi wanted this to work, he had to lead with his head and then check his heart.

Working both search and rescue and tactical support, it was imperative that Levi protect future missions and future lives by only choosing a dog with a focused nose and a weaponized bite. That bite had to be accurate and controlled.

The wash of the helicopter sent debris spray that pinged and pocked Levi's face. But under the suit and hood, he felt nothing. *Yet.*

As the wash of air became loud and heavy, Levi threw his head around to see what was coming his way.

The helicopter was about a hundred yards off, skimming

the ground as it glided slowly forward. A soldier, tethered to the door, leaned out, gripping the handle of Mojo's tactical vest.

Mojo wasn't scrambling. There was no anxiety in his body. On the contrary, Mojo had locked on to the prey, *him.*

Holy heck. That dog was the damned tip of the spear. And that spear was going to be flying at him. Still looking behind him, without any design other than the lizard part of his brain desperately trying to find a rock to hide under, Levi sprinted forward.

Well, sprint-like.

From over where Reaper and Goose stood, he probably looked like a maniac.

Hovering feet from the ground, the soldier released Mojo.

As Mojo hit the dirt, he rolled to disperse the energy of the helicopter's forward momentum. That roll looked practiced and precise.

Good job on that training, Enrico. A broken leg day is a bad day indeed.

Mojo finished the roll, landing on his feet. His body lowered and streamlined; he shot forward in a swirl of caramel and black.

Fur missile launched! Here he came.

Levi turned to face forward. His system heated and sweat-slicked over him. His heart was racing. Something about Mojo set Levi's nervous system on fire. It was like he was back in the Sandbox, racing away from the enemy.

Levi could hear Mojo's breath. Turning his head, they locked eyes.

The K9 took a mighty leap.

With no airtime, no time to think or process, Levi reflexively lifted a defensive arm.

Mojo sank his teeth into the padding of the bite suit.

Dangling in the air, Mojo's velocity was spinning Levi against his will.

And suddenly, there was Levi, flat on his back. He had hit down hard.

Flailing about, simulating a poacher fighting back, Levi could feel every bit of the two-hundred-plus pounds of K9 jaw pressure.

Pushing back into his haunches, Mojo shook his head with a powerful neck.

The sinews in Levi's shoulder were tearing, and he had no desire to keep up this fight.

How far off were those soldiers?

Even though Levi's brain hollered, "Flee!" Levi had trained to bypass the absurd and make clear-minded choices. The only survival choice here was to force his body to lay perfectly still no matter what happened next.

Twisting his head, Levi could see that the helicopter had landed, and there were boots on the ground running toward him.

Levi focused on his tactical breath, holding himself statue still, waiting for the handlers to get on scene.

Even with Levi's submission response, Mojo's mouth still wrapped Levi's arm. While the bite lost its pressure, Mojo hadn't released the padded sleeve. One move, one, and Levi knew the punishment would begin again.

The bite was the easiest part for the dog. What came next would tell everything about the dog's personality and the quality of his training. Man, Levi was praying this wasn't another Casper situation.

Mojo was very clearly having a ball.

How many times would the recall commands need to be issued? Would the handler need to intervene with a bite-release device or a shock? Either would be disqualifying for Iniquus.

"Mojo, release," a soldier commanded.

Mojo inched backward so his mouth no longer encircled Levi's arm. With his legs bunched under him, Mojo was ready to leap forward and trap Levi again if need be.

Levi thought he might like to test that.

As the soldiers approached, Mojo's eyes remained locked with Levi's. The intensity of the strength and intelligence Levi read there was damned impressive.

"Levi?" the soldier called out.

"That's me."

"How are you doing today, sir?" the soldier commanding Mojo asked.

"I'm just going to lie here very still."

"When I command you to, roll to your stomach and spread your legs as wide as you can, then lace your fingers behind your head. If you would like to observe Mojo's behaviors when you roll, face me. Ready?"

"Yes, sir."

The soldier barked out the orders, and Levi followed them precisely.

"Mojo, to me."

From his crouch, Mojo turned and raced to the soldier and sat at his feet looking up for his next command.

"Mojo, flank."

Mojo rounded to the side of the soldier, and together, they walked slowly forward.

"Mojo, en guard." Mojo shifted into fur missile launch position as the soldier patted Levi down.

"Sir, I will now place the handcuffs on your wrists," the soldier said. "We will lower one arm then the other on my command."

"What would happen if I didn't? What would happen if, for

example, I spun and knocked you over, and you didn't give Mojo any commands?"

"Would you like to see, sir?" There was laughter in the soldier's voice.

"I would indeed," Levi said.

"Very well, I would have you do it when both hands are behind you. You might be able to get your hands on the ground. I might be blocking them from Mojo's view. We'll try our best to make your scenario work."

The two men acted their way through the first arm, then as the second came down, Levi twisted, threw the soldier to the ground, then yanked his legs toward his chest, rolling to get himself standing. Before Levi could plant a foot on the ground, he was whipped into a kneeling spin.

Once again, Levi found himself in the dirt before his brain could analyze the situation.

Mojo gave his arm a good shake to remind Levi who was in charge.

It was Mojo. It was definitely Mojo. There were no ifs, ands, or buts.

"This is good enough, sir?" the soldier asked, definitely laughing this time. "Or you would like to continue?"

"Yep. That'll do it," Levi said through gritted teeth. "Could you get that release again, please?"

Mojo responded to his recall with the crisp precision of a soldier on the parade ground.

Enrico took control of Mojo as the soldier ran off to the helicopter and moved on to the next skill they would practice in this evolution. With Mojo in a sit by Enrico's side, Levi pulled off the suit, then sank to the ground, winded.

Mojo's gaze never left Levi.

In other circumstances, like with Casper, Levi might be

worried that the dog would try for another bite while Levi wasn't protected by the suit.

In Mojo's case? No. That was a solid, disciplined K9, exactly what Levi would expect from Enrico's work.

When Enrico looked down, Mojo swung his head, looking expectantly for his next command. Enrico gave him a scrub and high-pitched praise. Then he said, "Go on, Mojo, meet my friend, Levi."

Mojo's gaze followed Enrico's finger over to Levi. Then, with a grin and lolling tongue, Mojo jogged over to tickle Levi with a wet snout, sniffing his ear and neck.

When Mojo rounded to the front, he caught Levi's gaze, then swiped a friendly tongue over Levi's cheek and mouth.

"What do you think, Levi?" Enrico ambled over. "Good bite?"

Mojo curled himself around until he tucked into the nest Levi made with his crossed legs and put his head down on Levi's knee.

"Looks like you made yourself a friend," Reaper called as he and Goose made their way over.

Catching Enrico's eye, Levi said, "Man, that was some beautiful badassery."

Levi's heart was full. If Reaper and Goose weren't around, he thought he might even shed a tear. Damned if Iris wasn't right. He knew. *He just knew.* Mojo was *his* dog.

Again, there was the memory of how he'd experienced a connection like this one other time in his life.

Why had her ghost suddenly reappeared?

All week, she'd been there, brushing through his mind.

Levi tried to quiet that part of his brain that whispered, *Tess.* He hoped it would stop.

10

———————

Tess

Metz Winery, Namibia

When Tess and Gwen showed up earlier than expected at the winery, Gwen's mom greeted them, but her father was still up at the K9 training field with their friend, Enrico, and three of the winery guests from Northern Virginia.

The women stowed their bags in their respective rooms and changed into hiking boots. Gwen wanted to take Tess up to the observation platform so she could see the lay of the land.

Waiting for Gwen to show up, Tess had been daydreaming while watching Betty munch the dried leaves from the tree. "Your snack can't have anything nutritious about it," Tess told Betty. "The Metzes must be filling your belly. You look healthy."

"I'm all set," Gwen called as she approached.

"What other kinds of animals are here on your parent's property?" Tess tipped her head toward Betty. "I can't imagine how amazing it must be to have a giraffe hanging out in the courtyard."

"Besides Betty?" Gwen let her gaze slide across the horizon. "Let's see. My parents have free-range animals to produce the meat they serve in the restaurant. Zebra, wildebeest, and kudu—they're the ones with curly horns and oryx. Oryx is my favorite, maybe kudu. Then, there are the transient wild animals. Dad says they have baboons from time to time. Don't approach them. They've got a nasty bite full of bacteria. Are you up on your rabies shots?"

"Kind of. I need my three-year booster in another couple of months. Better than nothing, I guess. Why? What's going to bite me up there?"

"It's Namibia. Anything. Wild mountain zebras and the Chacma baboons come to mind. They like the hills."

"Wow. Well, I'm not planning on petting any of them. Live and let live, right?"

"Dad's seen black rhinos when he's up there. Sometimes, they come down to the vineyard, especially when they're searching for water. That can cause problems. Of course, as with much of sub-equatorial Africa, we have an impressive catalog of reptiles, spiders, and other creepy crawlies."

"Yeah, you reminded me of that at Big Daddy. But hey, it's the end of winter here. They're all in brumation snoozing, right?"

"Meh. Hibernation, like for northern mammals, and brumation for reptiles in Namibia aren't equivalent. Imagine it more as a snooze than a deep sleep. But I wouldn't worry about it. In all the years my parents have lived here, they've never seen any. Most animals don't want to be seen. They'd rather be left alone."

"Even puff adders at night?" Tess tucked her chin to remind

her friend that that teasing on the save-Mandy hunt wasn't funny.

"You know what?" Gwen held up a set of keys, then pointed toward a pickup truck. "I'm purposefully and decidedly not a Namibian snake expert."

"Same. But I have that snake bite app as a backup."

Gwen turned to Tess. "I remember you mentioning that when we rescued Mandy. But I was too sleepy to care what you said about it." Gwen turned her head to watch her mother approach. "You know, if I were to go through my contacts and pick out the single person most likely to have that app on their phone. I'd pick you."

"I have other apps, too. I have one that will assess you on the trail and help you make choices about going on or turning back. If you're in range, you can tap the button, and it will put you in touch with a doctor who specializes in wilderness medicine. Basically, how to MacGyver an exit. Probably not a good resource for baboon bites, though."

"Maybe not. Like I've said many times before, it's like you scan for every tiny thing that can go wrong, and you build plans and contingency plans, and contingency plans for your contingency plans. Don't get me wrong, I'm not calling you out by saying that. Your vigilance serves our team well."

Tess knew her behavior was sometimes off-putting. But compared to how she once had lived, Tess felt she maintained a reasonable and responsible level of vigilance. There was a time when Gwen was right; all Tess did was scan the horizon for the next big and bad to race her way. "It's probably exhausting to deal with."

"Nah. It's kind of interesting to learn all the ways I can meet my doom. Also, as I said at Big Daddy, one of us needs to be prepared, and I prefer it to be you. Never change."

"There you are." Walking toward them, Iris was drying her hands on a dish towel. "Did you get yourselves settled in?"

"The room is lovely, thank you," Tess said warmly. "We've been sleeping on the ground and sleeping in vehicles, so this will be a luxury."

"Sleeping in vehicles?" Iris swung her head toward Gwen. "What on Earth?"

"It's a whole story, Mom. I'll tell you tonight at dinner so Dad can hear it, too. It has to do with a vineyard, so I think you'll get a kick out of it."

"Oh," Iris reached out to tap Gwen's arm, "that's right. I wanted to tell you two that we're having dinner on the veranda around eight." She turned to Tess. "We get up early to eat while watching the sunrise. Early to bed, early to rise … " She smiled. "So eight tonight instead of seven. I want you to meet the team from the U.S. who are working with Enrico." Iris turned to Gwen. "Our sweet Hailey works with them."

"Hailey? Wow. It's been a while since I talked to her," Tess said. "After she left WorldCares, it hasn't been as easy to stay in touch. I need to reach out."

"If Hailey sent them, this would be an Iniquus team," Gwen said. "What are they doing over here? Seems odd."

"They're looking at one of Enrico's dogs to buy. Mojo is the dog's name. Beautiful. Powerful. Just a magnificent dog. I always enjoyed him when he was here with Enrico, but this morning, I got to see a bit of him in action." She put a hand on her stomach. "It was intimidating, I'll give you that. Anyway," Iris lifted her brow, "I thought you might like to meet them, so I'm arranging a little welcome party."

Gwen turned to Tess with a laugh. "You can hear it in Mom's voice. She's matchmaking."

Iris shrugged, "You never know when the right guy will

walk into view. I'm just saying there's worse to be had than a retired SEAL."

Gwen quirked a lip toward Tess. "SEALs are Mom's type, but she married a lab rat, so there's that. Right, Mom?"

"Well, Gwen, you know, same as I do, that most men you've been dating don't like it that you go into the field for so long and so often. Seems to me that a man in that line of work is in the same boat. If you got along, it might be a happy coincidence that you're here at the same time."

"Okay, Mom, thank you," Gwen said dryly.

Iris smiled at Tess. "Gwen doesn't like it when I interfere." She turned back to her daughter. "But honestly, Gwen, there's one I have my eye on for you. I'm not going to say which because I know how you are. But once you meet him, you'll see what I see in the man. He's solid and steady. Adventuresome and gentlemanly. Someone brought that man up right. It's not always easy to find someone like that in the wilds of greater Washington D.C."

"Well, not one that doesn't come with an ego, that's for sure." Gwen laughed. "Maybe Tess will like him."

"Tess was already married. She doesn't need a push."

"Off a cliff?" Gwen muttered.

"Oh hush," Iris laughed at the face Gwen made. "At any rate, you'll meet him tonight. Now, let's see here, boots and packs. Where are you two headed off to?" Iris asked.

Gwen lifted her strap and adjusted it on her shoulder. "I told Tess about the observation deck Dad built at the top of the hill. We have time to go up, take a look around, and get down before dinner."

"Once you get to the base of the hill, it's forty-five minutes up and an hour to get down. A half hour or so on the deck? That should work," Iris said, scratching the side of her head. "But I'd like it if you girls didn't take much longer than that, so you have time to clean up and put on something pretty. This is a family meal, but it's a guest-family meal. We don't want to show up looking feral. Right, dear?"

Gwen kissed Iris on the cheek. "We'll take the pickup to the trailhead to chop off some of the walk time, so you don't worry about me looking *feral*."

As they started off for the pickup truck, Gwen said, "Tomorrow, Tess and I want to go into Etosha at dawn, as soon as they open, to see the animals drinking at the springs. Just to set your expectations about us at your party tonight, I plan to get to bed right after we eat."

"All right."

Gwen reached around her mom's waist, and they walked arm in arm. This was a bittersweet scene for Tess. At mundane mother-daughter moments like this, Tess felt the loss of the little things.

"How's the food supply, Mom?"

"For the animals? Dire. Here? Fine. We have gardens for vegetables and such. But we're shipping in a lot of our supplies to keep up the standards of the winery. I can't say that's not expensive. But you know, one bad review changes a business's capacity to attract future visitors. Folks traveling to Namibia to see Etosha wouldn't understand our drought situation or take it into consideration as they're typing up their thoughts."

Gwen nodded.

"We're leaning into wild meats. Most of our visitors find that adventurous. But I must say, it's a very bad situation." She turned to Tess. "There are natural springs in the area. The government uses them to make watering holes for the wildlife in the park. That serves two purposes: the guides know where to take the visitors to get their vacation pictures, and they can make sure that the animals aren't dying from lack." Iris lifted her free hand to point over to a concrete building. "That's our solar-powered pump. Sunlight is one thing we have in profusion. We have a spring on the property. That's how we're able to keep the vegetables watered and the grape vines from turning into raisin vines. When we got started, Craig and I laid out a drip system that waters at night. We try not to waste even a drop. But the grape harvest this year is going to be hit or miss. We're not holding out a lot of hope."

"Could you lose your vines?" Gwen's voice was painted with concern. "Or are you talking about the harvest?"

"Yes." Iris stopped and let her gaze sweep over the hillside, striped with vines. "Either or both."

"Then what would happen?" Gwen asked.

"We've been grafting Marula trees from the oldest trees we can find, hoping that since those trees have been through it all, they know how to self-sustain. But they also attract elephants. And elephants know how to do some damage."

"Marula?" Tess asked, opening the pickup door and putting her hiking pack on the seat.

"The fruit makes a Namibian specialty liquor," Gwen said, making her way around to the right-hand driver's side. "It's a delicious, kind of nutty citrussy taste."

"We have some that we produced this year, Iris said. "We'll have it after dinner so you can taste it yourself. All right, girls. I'll see you back in a couple of hours. Have fun!"

The dirt road that took them to the trail Gwen's dad had made for the vineyard guests was a quick drive.

Gwen left the keys in the ignition, and with their packs slung over their shoulders and a check on their water situation, the women began the climb.

The heat of the sun wasn't nearly the scorching fist that beat on her head at Big Daddy. But it was still hot, and Tess knew she'd be exerting hard to get up the craggy trail.

Dressed in boots and hiking shorts, Tess's long-sleeved sun-blocking shirt protected her from the sun's burning rays without needing to apply sunscreen, which she loathed.

Her skin was closer in color to her mother's Austrian ancestry than her father's Ghanaian skin tone. But her dad's genes meant Tess rarely got a sunburn.

Tess remembered—or thought she remembered—her mom complaining about cooking like a lobster under the sun. Tess even had a distant memory of standing behind her mom, slathering on some plant potion to pull the heat out of her mom's bright pink skin, and her mom saying, "You're such a kind helper girl, honey pot."

With their hiking packs on their backs, the women wended onto the trail. The stones were loose and rolled under the thick soles of her boots. The rest of their forty-five-minute trek was silent as the women focused on their foot placement.

They dropped their bags on the observation deck and stood to bask in the swath of land at their feet. Arms held wide to take it all in, Tess tipped back her head and closed her eyes. The breeze whipped away the heat, and the air felt fresh. "It smells like an adventure," she said as she came up right.

Gwen stood at the far corner of the platform, filming a video to describe where she was for her friends who followed her on social media.

When she tapped the camera off, Tess pointed into the distance. "That's the Etosha gate, isn't it? I can't wait to go tomorrow."

"Let's see." She moved over to Tess and squinted in the direction Tess's arm was indicating. "Yes, that's Etosha."

Gwen found a different angle on the platform where the wind whipped her long black hair in a way that looked dynamic but didn't float tendrils into her mouth. With the grape vines in the far distance, Gwen was describing her parents' vineyard.

As Tess reached for her water bottle in the side pocket of

her pack, her phone slipped out of her pocket and clattered down the rocks.

Tess went after it.

Bending to pick it up and dust it off, her foot slipped off the boulder and down between the two rocks. Something bright and painful happened to her calf.

It was a sensation that Tess couldn't place.

It was so painful and unexpected that she screamed as she leaped back toward the breadth of the boulder, discovering through that movement that her boot was caught between two rocks.

Gwen clutched at her chest as she raced forward to check on the problem. "Cripes, Tess, you scared the shit out of me. Did you hurt your ankle?"

"Oh my gosh. Oh shit. It's a snake."

With the video recorder still taping, Gwen swung her lens toward the ground around Tess. "Did you just see it and get startled?" Standing on the flat surface of the platform, Gwen swept her camera slowly over the area. "Did you feel a bite?" Gwen's voice was calm. She always was steady in a crisis, and Tess appreciated that in her friend.

"Yeah. Sharp. Did you see the snake?" Tess's body did what Tess's body always did when she felt endangered—she trembled to disperse the gathering adrenaline storm. "We need that image." She *knew* intellectually what was happening; she just couldn't connect with it as reality.

"No. Where'd it go?" Gwen jumped off the platform to get a different angle.

With her foot stuck between the rocks, Tess could only point as the length of the snake slithered out of sight.

"Okay, good. I caught part of it on video." Gwen stopped, turned off her camera, and slid her phone into the thigh pocket of her hiking shorts. "It looks like it's gone now."

"My foot's stuck." As Gwen moved her way, Tess held up a hand to stop Gwen from coming toward her. "Don't come over here. I don't think it's safe. Don't snakes have nests?"

Gwen stopped and blinked, "Okay. Stay absolutely still." She picked up a rock and started banging on the boulders around Tess to vibrate the area and get the snakes moving.

That was something Abraham had done in Ghana with his walking stick, but Tess had forgotten about it until this very minute. "What kind of snake was it, Gwen?"

"Let's do that next. First, we need to get your foot freed up. I think we need to avoid any tugging or jostling. I'm going to untie your boot and loosen the laces. Then, I want you to hang on to me while you slide your foot out slow and steady. We'll deal with getting the boot in a minute."

With her hand gripping Gwen's shoulder, Tess began to process the implications of what just happened. People the Ya family knew had died of snake bites in Ghana during their years-long flight. With some venomous snake bites, there was nothing to do but say goodbye and wait.

Tess wasn't ready for that. She didn't want to say goodbye. And her step-sons were still in college. She had to see them graduate and settle into their adult lives, fulfilling her promises to Abraham.

Gwen squatted beside her, touching Tess's calf with gentle fingers. "Oh yeah, you've got puncture marks." Gwen twisted and looked up to catch Tess's gaze. "How does it feel?"

"I don't know. The adrenaline flowing through me could light a small city. So whatever I'm feeling is masked. Puncture marks, it was venomous."

"Slow and steady," Gwen modulated her voice to sound solid and bulky, something that Tess could lean on. Tess always liked Gwen's crisis voice. The "we've got this" quality lowered stress levels.

Right now, Tess felt the very opposite. She was the quivering smoke that rose from a candle flame. There was absolutely nothing dependable or solid about her.

"The only move you're going to make is to slide your foot out once I have this loosened and then a couple of steps to the platform to lie down on your back. That way, people have a place to work when they come to rescue you."

"I have to walk down, Gwen," Tess said through chattering teeth. "Who's going to come to rescue me?"

"Your app, right? You call them, and they know what to do." Gwen didn't let go of her, moving slowly to help Tess keep her balance when Tess's whole world seemed to tilt on its axis. "We're right by Etosha," Gwen said. "They've got to have people to help there."

Tess still clutched her phone in her hand from when she'd retrieved it. She swiped it open and tapped the snake app, but her hands were too shaky to read. Tess handed her phone off to Gwen, then sank to the platform and laid herself long as Gwen had instructed.

With her focus on the app, Gwen said, "The first thing that needs to happen—Tess, listen to me, this is very important—you need to stay very still. The sun is on your face. Why don't you throw an arm over your eyes? Good, that's good." Her voice turned sing-songy. "Breathe. Work on your breathing. Calm your system. Sink into meditation. Focus within and bring down your anxiety. The more you can relax, the slower your blood flow, and that's what you want. Nice and slow. Good job. Keep it up. Nice and slow."

With her arm covering her eyes, it was more comfortable than squinting into the descending sun. But it left Tess disoriented. "What are you doing now?"

"I'm looking at the video I took of the snake. According to the app, different snakes have venom that affects the body in different ways. I'm quoting here, 'you must be careful what kind of first aid you render.'"

"Just tap the button and talk to them," Tess muttered. She was doing her job, breathing in for four counts and out for eight, but her lips still buzzed.

Nerves or venom?

"Sweetheart," Gwen said softly, "that app needs connectivity to work. And neither of our phones has any bars."

"Shit."

"We've been in bad spots before. We've figured it out. We'll figure this out, too. Okay? One step, then another. The first step is to identify the snake. I can't access their library. But I can see their list of the most dangerously venomous ones. And the snake in my picture isn't on this list. Small wins. We'll take that."

"But you don't know what it is off the top of your head? Things you've learned from being here all the time?"

"I try very hard to avoid the subject. Okay, generalized first aid," Gwen read. "Most snakebites, even cobra bites, are not fatal. Bites should be treated as a medical emergency."

This was really happening. "It's a medical emergency, Gwen."

"Here's what it says about what we should do next. 'The single most important thing to do is to get to a hospital without any delay. Don't use any local or home remedies. There's only one cure for snakebite, and that's antivenom.' Scanning," Gwen said. "Okay. 'Immobilize the limb that was bitten, but do not apply pressure. Lie still. Keep the victim calm.'"

"Are you kidding me? That's all they've got?"

"Slow your breathing, Tess. The platform looks uncomfortable, but I don't want to put a jacket under your head. It doesn't mention elevating, and I think maybe keeping you as flat and calm as possible is best, so your circulation is as slow as possible."

"Nothing else helpful?" Tess asked.

"It says to make a note of where the bite occurred and the time." After a pause, Gwen added, "Okay, I took a picture with GPS coordinates, and it has a time stamp. Close enough."

"Yup."

"Immobilize. I'm not sure how to do that right now. I say just lay very still."

"Okay. So I guess maybe if you can get to the truck and go get help? Take my phone with you so you have the snake app as soon as you're within cell tower range. You can call and send them the video you have of the snake, and they'll have action plans."

"Tess, I can't do that," Gwen said softly. "This is *Namibia*."

Tess shook her head.

"Stop moving. You're to be perfectly still, regulating your breathing. Namibia has predators. The jackals at the campsite—"

"They're lovers, not fighters." Tess worked to release her frustration. "Time is the enemy here."

"I'm working on it. I'm actively searching for a solution. I have my binoculars up. I'm scanning for someone to help us. So about the jackals humping at the camp. As I understand it, jackals on their own are one thing. A hunting pack is another. There are cheetahs up here and other predatory cats. If I leave you here alone. The bite might be the least of your worries."

Tess opened her mouth to let out an exhale that seemed to come from the tips of her toes, whooshing up her body and out. Abraham had said something very similar to her out in the forest in Ghana. Tess knew this to be true. But sometimes, in life, you have to make tough choices.

"Please go," Tess whined.

"Sorry. I shouldn't have said that. Bottom line, I'm not leaving you. I'm looking through the binoculars and can see a vehicle on the road."

Without thinking, Tess started to push herself up to see, too. But with a hand on Tess's chest, Gwen forced her down again. "Keep your arm over your eyes, Tess. Be still. Breathe. I'm going to try to use my signal mirror to shoot an SOS down and hit them in the window. I've got a second to get myself together. They're not at a good angle yet."

"You think they'll come up here?" In the field, Tess wasn't used to being the victim. She was so much better at managing a crisis.

Like Gwen, when bad things were rocking and rolling, Tess knew what to do and how to do it. But this scene pulled up a long-forgotten memory.

It had been a happy day. The Ya family thought they'd found safety in a quiet village. Tess had spent the day playing with the smiling girl who held Tess's hand.

That respite from fear was brief.

The smiling girl climbed a tree where a venomous snake bit her. And very quickly, she was dead. The Ya family fled into the night, chased away by the villagers who thought the light-skinned child attracted demons. They truly believed that because Tess was there, the girl had died.

Tess buried the responsibility for the girl's death deep in her heart.

But in the night, the story found its way free and haunted her dreams.

Right now, Tess felt fragile and childlike. It frightened her to feel this way. It felt like as much of a threat to her survival as the snake bite because Tess had worked so hard at being strong.

Was her strength all a mirage?

"Namibia isn't like someone driving by you in Annapolis."

Tess realized she'd missed some of Gwen's words and scrambled in her mind to catch up.

"Out here, people help each other, or people die. Okay, here we go. They're at a good angle. I'm flashing SOS in their direction with the signal mirror. Just so you know, in between flashes, I'm watching the vehicle's progress through your binoculars. I'm trying to aim the flash toward their windshield."

"Can we make a deal?"

"What's that?"

"If that car doesn't stop and come up to us, you'll go down and drive away to get help?"

"If we're not home in time to get dressed for dinner, Mom's going to send someone to look for us. In Namibia, she's impatient with me not being where I'm supposed to be."

"Gwen, I could die by then. I could lose my leg. This is a no-joke emergency. Please. If this car doesn't stop to help, you have to go down. Time is the enemy. I'll blow the emergency whistle to keep predators away."

"They've stopped." There was victory in Gwen's voice.

"Far?" Tess asked.

"Yeah. They're getting out."

"Are they searching for the direction? Flash the signal again."

"I'll flash again, but I don't think they stopped for my signal. It looks like they stopped to change their tire. I know Otto was an idiot on the Big Daddy trip, but flats really do happen quite a bit here. Some of the rocks are very sharp."

"Are they far? Could you get down to them?"

"Down and over to them? No, it's farther than the vineyard, and I'm not leaving you at dusk on a hill in Namibia. It's not happening."

"Which is worse, venom or predator?"

"The problem, Tess, is it could be both. You don't get a choice. Nope, they don't seem to see my signal."

"Okay." Tess's mind was switching away from desperation to something much clearer and more rational. "Think. How do we signal them? You could hold up a mylar emergency blanket, and I could use my head lamp's strobe. Look at them in proximity to us. Could they see something like that?"

"I'm standing on the edge of the observation deck and considering," Gwen walked Tess through her actions, probably so Tess would leave her arm draped over her eyes. "Yeah, I think that would be a long shot. They may see it and not feel curious enough to climb the hill to check it out. It would be different if that were search and rescue, and they were hunting our signal."

"As the crow flies, how far are they?"

"Not taking into consideration the trek down just straight out? I'm looking through the binoculars, and I'd say, what? My best guess is that they're not that far, quarter of a mile? Less? Four men and a dog. That's good. If we can get their attention they can carry you off the hillside. You can't exert."

"Try the hurricane whistle," Tess commanded. "Three blasts. Count to thirty. Three blasts. On repeat."

"Hurricane … okay, where is it?"

"Attached to the handle for easy reach. It's orange."

"Got it."

The shrill pitch of the whistle moved through Tess's system.

11

Levi

Between Etosha and Metz Vineyard

Enrico pulled off the narrow, paved road into the dirt. "Flat tire," he said, sliding the gear to park. "The longer you visit, the more you realize how typical that is in Namibia. Like an Irish fisherman sits in front of the fire fixing their nets at night, we sit under the stars repairing the holes in our tires."

The four men piled out.

"What can I do to give you a hand?" Levi asked as Mojo clambered out the door and immediately put his nose in the air, checking his environment.

"Nada," Enrico called from the back, where a spare was tethered to the hatch. "After doing this a hundred or so times, I have my system down to a science." He held up his hand with the fingers splayed wide. "Five minutes tops. You want to time me?"

Levi kept a watchful eye on Mojo to see how he reacted off-leash in the open space.

Yes, Levi's heart knew Mojo was *his* dog.

But when lives were on the line, Levi's heart wasn't enough to make a final decision. The dog Levi picked needed to be mission-ready, on point with his skills, and trainable to hone his behaviors to meet Iniquus's field protocol. While Mojo's tactical work and bite were phenomenal, tomorrow, they would test Mojo's ability to work a scent and effectively communicate with Levi.

Right now, Mojo was facing the mountains. His ears lifted and rotated to capture a sound. His nose wasn't scenting. Whatever caught Mojo's attention was far enough off that his sniffer hadn't found anything interesting to latch on to.

"Yo! Hate to break your flow. Take a look at Mojo."

"Was that an attempt at rap, brother? Because that was weak sauce." Enrico leaned the spare against the side of the car.

"It was unfortunate, I'll give you that." Levi gestured to Mojo. "Tell me about this posture."

Mojo stood statue-like, leaning forward.

"Yup," Reaper said, "he's on to something."

"I don't know." Enrico's gaze swept the flat space between them and the hillside. "It could be a wild animal of some kind." Enrico laughed. "At least we know it's not a rhino. If it were a rhino, Mojo would be going ballistic, trying to herd us to safety and fight the monsters at the same time. It isn't pretty."

Levi had focused on Mojo's coat. This was the second time he flinched three times. It was as if in a precise pattern and not a random muscle twitch. It was curious. Levi had never seen a dog do that before.

Mojo turned to Enrico with a whine and stomp of his foot that was clearly asking Enrico to take some action. "You will pay attention," it said. Then Mojo's focus swept back to the hillside.

Enrico must have thought this was odd behavior, too, because he put his hands on his hips and pulled his brow together, watching Mojo carefully. Looking up to catch Levi's gaze, he said, "Let's see what happens. Mojo, show me."

Mojo looked indecisive—as if loathe to move off his X. Suddenly, he lurched around and raced over to Enrico, lifted up on his hind legs, and bit the air twice right near Enrico's hip. Then Mojo circled around to sit in front of Enrico, waiting for his next command.

Levi read Mojo's look as, "Did you understand?"

Enrico was scrubbing the scruff on Mojo's neck. "Got it, buddy. I'll take a look."

As Enrico grabbed a go bag from the cargo area, Reaper asked. "You usually hang a bringsel on your waist when you're working a search and rescue mission?"

"Exactly." Enrico pulled a pair of military-grade binoculars from his bag. "Mojo prefers to use his mini-Kong instead of those pillow types of indicators. I don't mind as long as he gets the job done. I hang the toy from my belt on my left. After he makes the find, he comes back to me to report in by biting the Kong, then sitting. It's exactly the lost-person skill sequence that you just watched." Enrico lifted the binoculars and scanned the ridge. "I don't see anything right off. If you want to grab your lenses, boys, we can set up a search grid."

Mojo moved back to the exact spot he'd abandoned. His skin twitched three times in succession. And like before, he whined and stomped.

"On it, Mojo," Enrico said. "Give me a second. Sit. Wait."

Mojo reluctantly tucked his back legs under him as he sat, but his focus never wavered.

Binoculars in hand, Levi took a knee so close to Mojo that

Mojo's side pressed into Levi's thigh. "What have you got there, boy?" Mojo's skin twitched in succession. "I'd swear Mojo's hearing something in groups of three," Levi called out.

"Distress call?" Goose had his binoculars trained on the rocky hillside. "Lots of places to get hurt. Lots of boulders that would block our view."

Levi ducked so that he could line up the angle of his lenses with Mojo's focal direction. Slowing his breath, stilling his movements, Levi chose a landmark in about the right spot. Drawing a circle, Levi cleared the center. Each time his binoculars reached the twelve o'clock position, he adjusted the circle to be a bit larger. Working this circular grid was often an efficient search pattern once you locked onto a clue. Levi thought he'd never seen such a relevant signal that someone was in distress than what Mojo had performed.

"Anyone?" Reaper asked.

Mojo's skin rippled.

"According to Mojo's nervous system, there are three indicators of some kind—I'd guess whistle blast. Enrico?"

"That's what I'm seeing."

"They're imprecise but consistently around thirty seconds apart," Levi observed.

"Okay, then," Enrico hung his binoculars from the cord on his neck, "it looks like we're mounting a search party. As we discussed during training today, radio signals in the hills are hit or miss because of boulders and line of sight. Mostly miss. I think we have to assume one or possibly multiple people are injured and incapable of getting down."

"Is that part of the winery?" Goose asked.

"I don't know their boundaries." Enrico scooped his backpack onto his shoulders.

"Enrico, you know the terrain and how to track with Mojo," Reaper said. "Goose, if there's an injury, you're the best man amongst us. Take your vet pack with you. Levi, I want you to observe Mojo. I'll stay back and change the tire, then drive over to you."

It was as if Mojo was holding himself back, waiting for the command. He wanted to leap into action. Once Enrico set him in motion, he rocketed over the open space.

The men picked up a steady cadence as they jogged in the direction that Mojo had streaked.

"I've lost sight of him," Goose said. "He's camouflaged against the colors of the terrain."

"We just keep going in the same general direction. Mojo knows when he's getting too far ahead," Enrico said. "He'll circle back and check on us if we lag behind on our wimpy human legs."

"Ah, yes. Wimpy human legs," Goose laughed, "but we make up for that with our opposable thumbs. How else would they get the lid off their dog food?"

Levi tapped his ear. "There it is. Three whistles." He pulled his whistle from his strap and sent back three blasts. *We hear you. We're coming.*

Enrico lowered his binoculars and pointed. "There's a pickup parked in that shadow."

Mojo had run back to check on them, just like Enrico said he'd do. When the whistle sounded again, the men stopped in their tracks.

No sense in running up in the wrong direction. With the sound riding the wind as it slid down the hillside, finding the source would be tricky.

Mojo's gaze fixed on a spot. And that's where Levi trained his binoculars. "There's a woman on the ridge line waving her arms," he called out, blading his hand in the right direction.

Enrico followed the line with his lenses and said, "That's Gwen Metz, the owners' daughter."

Levi blew three more times. Then he watched as she lowered herself out of sight. Who knew how long she'd been signaling? The effort probably exhausted her energy stores.

The men were in motion, trailing Mojo.

Levi assessed what might have happened to Gwen up there. His first thought was a twisted ankle. "Goose, do you have a portable stretcher in your vet kit?"

"I do, but it's K9 sized. It's not going to help with the length of an adult woman." He tapped his backpack with its K9 first aid patch. "This is just a stabilization pack. If she's severely injured, we're going to need more help. Do you think she's up there on her own?"

"Trailhead," Levi pointed.

"Looks like Gwen went for a hike," Enrico said, "and her day took a turn."

Reaper roared to a stop beside them and climbed out. "Anything?"

"A whistle signal led us to locate Gwen Metz on the ridge-line." Enrico pointed. "Gwen is Iris and Craig's daughter."

"Is she solo?" Reaper asked.

"We visualized one," Levi clarified.

"How are we doing this?" Goose dropped his heavy pack to the ground.

"Radio is line of sight only. Connectivity is sketchy at best in the hills," Enrico explained. "We can try it, but we need a backup plan. Someone needs to hang back to communicate the situation."

"All right," Reaper said. "That'll be me. Let's start with a whistle signal. If there's no time pressure to deal with the situation, we can try the radio or send someone down with the specifics. I'll listen for a whistle blast and repeat back what I heard. We'll go through the process three times to make sure the understanding is clear. One blast means the team can handle the situation on their own. Two blasts escalate the situation, and more help is needed. Three blasts are an all-hands-on-deck emergency, and I'm pulling in a rescue team."

"Copy," the men said in unison.

Goose moved off to look in the pickup truck.

"That's the plan," Reaper turned to Enrico. "Where would I go for help if it's three blasts?"

"Give me your phone." Enrico stretched out his hand. "I'll put in the emergency numbers. It's for the same team that we worked with today in Etosha." He tapped out the information as he spoke. "If it's a three-blast emergency, they know what equipment to bring. They'll come. Meanwhile, one of us can run the trail to give more information."

"Keys in the ignition," Goose called as he headed back. "Do you need a scent source?"

"Nah," Enrico called back. "Not if we can't be sure that the source belongs to Gwen. That can just confuse the situation."

"Good that we have access to a second vehicle," Reaper said as he accepted his phone and glanced at the information. "If someone comes down the mountain and I haven't gotten back yet, take the pickup to the vineyard where we can use cell phones. We can set up a command center there if need be."

Levi tipped his head back, taking in the trailhead, and followed it to the ridge. "A thirty-minute run?"

"That's my estimation," Enrico said. "But we're going to be burning energy doing it. That's not an easy climb."

"Challenge accepted," Levi said, tightening his shoulder straps and pulling the sternal and hip straps into place.

"Since it's thirty minutes up," Reaper set a timer on his watch. "I'll take the vehicle back to the vineyard and grab our team's equipment and something that could be used as a backboard or rescue basket. I'll be back to hear the whistle signal." Reaper headed out.

"Closest hospital is Tsumeb?" Goose bent to retie his laces and get his equipment adjusted for the run. By far, he carried the heaviest day pack.

"It's an hour away." Enrico whistled to recall Mojo. "Everyone's wearing boots, that's good. But just so you know, the oddity of our weather in recent days has been affecting our snake population. Snakes are shy creatures. In a normal year, we don't see any snakes at all. But just in the last few days, over a dozen sightings have been reported by our rangers working in this area."

Mojo ran full tilt toward Enrico, coming to an abrupt seated stop. Tongue long, excited for this new game they were playing today, Mojo waited for his next command.

"Any words of advice?" Goose asked.

"Yeah," Enrico said, "stay directly behind Mojo." Enrico looked down at Mojo and commanded, "Mojo, search for the human, hunt for snakes."

Mojo's nose went up in the air. After a moment, he crouched until his nose was a hovercraft, sucking in and processing scent as he moved swiftly and purposefully up the rocky slope.

"Let's give him a minute to settle into that search. It's a complicated scent puzzle."

"He performs the two tasks at once?" Levi asked.

"It's imperative that our K9s have that skill. The dogs need to focus on their primary task, in this case, finding a human. But they must also be situationally aware. If they're doing a great job following a trail, but they get kicked in the head by a mountain zebra, it's a lose-lose situation." Enrico kept his gaze on Mojo's progress. "When it comes to wildlife scents, they have to process two directives at once. This snake tracking is one that we practice consistently, simply because this is Namibia, home of eighty different snakes, eleven species that are potentially deadly to humans. More than that can kill a dog. Anytime we're out walking an uncleared area, we couple the directives no matter the season because that skillset is imperative to the safety of our ranger teams."

"For example, they'd clear a campsite before the rangers bedded down?" Goose asked.

"Exactly, but unlike when Levi and I were over in the sandbox clearing for insurgents and explosives, the animals of Namibia are dynamic. What was clear at the beginning is not clear a moment later. And we train for snakes not the other crawlies that are here, spiders, scorpions."

"Scorpions, they're a treat," Levi said. "He's stopped. Did Mojo find something?"

"If it were a human, he'd run back. If it were a snake, he'd signal with a sharp bark. Then he stands very still, trying not to agitate the snake. Let's start walking up. We can pick up the pace when Mojo gets moving. He clears pretty fast."

"Anything else up here we need to be worried about?" Goose asked as he fell in line behind the other two.

"Baboons can mind their own business, or not. And there's always the chance we'll come across a black rhino. Some of the rangers have seen them in this area."

Levi was scanning the ground, figuring out what hazards to keep an eye for once they started the run. "Rangers are outside the park, and the police and military guard Etosha?"

"That's right."

"What's their emotional state with the culling that's going on?" Goose asked.

"They're hungry, to be honest. Their food supplies have been cut. Except for the tourists, everyone's food supplies have been cut. I have the good fortune to supplement my wages with my savings. I can afford to go into the city centers and buy imported Western food. That isn't true for the men and women who work for the Namibian government. Most people have pinched bellies, much like the people we worked beside in the sandbox."

"Sorry to hear that," Levi said.

"We're hoping for rain." Enrico picked up his pace to a jog.

"And that's coming soon?" Goose asked.

"Maybe in a few weeks." Enrico gestured up the hillside. "Here we go." And he took off, racing up the barely visible trail.

The men fell silent as they concentrated on where to put their feet. The rocks were loose here, and a fall might start them down a very rough slope.

Hearts pumping, sweat dripping, the men rounded a last boulder. Levi saw a lone boot wedged between two rocks.

One woman stood. "Oh, thank goodness!"

Another woman stretched long with her arm thrown over her eyes, lying perfectly still. Mojo sat on the platform next to her, looking pleased with himself with a "Look what I found!" wagging tail.

"What's going on Gwen?" Enrico slowed his pace.

"A viper bit my friend, Tess. Be careful. There could be more in the area."

As soon as Gwen said *viper*, Enrico and Levi stepped aside to let Goose pelt toward the woman lying prone on the platform.

When Goose kneeled beside her, the woman dragged her arm away from her face.

And Levi's heart stopped.

12

———

Tess

There he was, larger than life.

From the tension around his eyes, he was as surprised as she was that they were suddenly in the same spot at the same time.

Levi, by nature, was stoic. He kept his thoughts and feelings to himself. But in his blue eyes, Tess could see the storm.

Here he was, a natural hero, the kind of guy who would dive off the bridge to save a drowning person. He'd do his best to help her. Of that, she had no doubt. But it would come at a cost. Just her presence would stir up old ghosts.

If Levi hated her, she completely understood.

There was a moment of hesitation. A moment when he pulled back as if the mental shock was a physical one.

He dragged a hand over his face as if painting a mask into place.

But in a split-second, he was by her side, scanning Tess from head to foot, looking for a problem to solve. An enemy to take down. A village to save.

"Shit, Tessy," he hissed between clenched teeth.

Tess could decipher those two words in a handful of ways. And he probably wanted to convey all of them.

Gwen leaned forward. "The bite was to her right calf."

Kneeling beside her, Levi lifted her wrist with a light pressure on her pulse point. He'd find her heart racing. She'd done a good job keeping her cool through this situation right up until she saw his face.

Frowning at his watch, Levi gently laid her hand back on the wooden platform, then pulled a pad and pencil from his thigh pocket. "You've stayed still?" Just a trained medic running down his medical checklist.

She deserved that.

He wouldn't feel the same for her as she did for him. They were a long-ago dream. And this was a brutal reality.

"I haven't moved," She chattered out. Her whole body was awake and buzzing. The flutter of her heart when Levi's fingers touched her skin was nothing new to Tess. She remembered it so well.

It was the same reaction all these years later.

With venom in her veins, Tess's body's response to the sight of Levi was a betrayal of its limbic system.

Tess knew from her early days that survival comes before emotion. You may fear the roaring waters, but you swim them anyway. Then, you sit in front of a fire and tell your pain to the flames that carry your words away with the smoke.

The snake app said this was a life-threatening event.

And until she was told otherwise, the bite was her priority. All the Levi feelings, all of them … she'd deal with that at a later time.

If she had a later time.

The future was a luxurious thought. People walked around, not realizing what a treasure it was to consider the future, to think beyond their present moment.

Lying here, processing the idea that she could have deadly venom flowing through her body and that she might very well not see the sun rise on a new morning, had a familiar sensation.

How was it possible that she was lying on a platform in Namibia, and Levi was the one who climbed to her rescue?

While Tess was scolding herself into the right frame of mind, Goose was off to the side, reviewing the chain of events with Gwen. "And when did this happen?"

"About an hour ago. I have the time stamp on one of the photos. It took a few minutes to get Tess lying down and put an action plan in play. But I spotted you on the road right away and tried to signal with a mirror. Before you had your flat, that is. That's when I switched from the signal mirror to the whistle. I guess you heard that."

"Mojo did." Goose tipped his head toward Mojo, who lay down on the wide platform, sweeping his gaze over the vista as he guarded their activity.

"So, about an hour. You said you had photos of the snake?"

Gwen pulled up the video. "Just the skin markings, not the head."

Goose took the phone and held the video out for Levi to see.

"Do you know what kind of snake it is, Goose?" Levi asked. "My bet is zebra cobra."

"That's what I came up with." Goose lifted his head. "Which leg, the right?"

Gwen's voice rippled with anxiety. "Yes."

"Hey there, Tess. I'm Goose," He knelt beside Levi. "I'm a vet for Iniquus and trained in field medicine. Do I have permission to render first aid?"

"Absolutely. Yes. Thank you."

"Levi, get her shoulders." Goose edged closer and reached over her legs. "Tess, we're going to roll you onto your left side so I can access your wound."

Tess's teeth chattered.

"You're going to keep your legs sealed one to the other. On the count of three, Levi and I will do the rolling. You're not to help."

There was a count, and as the men moved her, Tess tried to be water and let them manipulate how she flowed.

Once Tess was on her side, Levi held her in place with a hand on her shoulder and waist while Goose leaned over to look.

Levi was scared for her. She could feel his concern radiating out of his hands.

Scrambling around to the other side of Tess and sitting where Tess could see her face, Gwen provided moral support.

"I see two puncture marks. So we are dealing with a venomous snake." Goose turned to Gwen. "An hour?" he confirmed.

Gwen nodded vigorously.

"The good news, Tess," Goose continued, "is that as I look at the puncture site, it's not red or swollen or oozing. That's all encouraging. Enrico, thoughts?"

"In my years in Namibia, I've never known anyone, man or dog, with a snake bite. I know the basics—immobilize and race for the hospital."

"Reaper is waiting for a whistle report," Levi said. "Enrico, as far as the race to the hospital, which whistle count will make that happen?"

"One. People coming up aren't going to help. That trail is one-man-wide. We take her down, put her in the vehicle, and hightail it out of here. Rounding up a rescue crew means their climb up with equipment and then down. Broken leg, I'd make a different assessment."

"There are risks to that," Levi said. "And Tess needs to make the final call."

"Levi, just get me down," she whispered. "I trust you."

"Gwen," Levi said. "give one whistle blow and wait for the same in response. Do that three times."

As Gwen moved off the platform onto a boulder to blow long and hard, Levi scrambled to pull his pack off, one arm at a time—so he didn't release Tess's shoulder—and placed his bag under her head. "Are you in pain, Tessy?"

"I can't tell," she whispered. Pain? Yes. Absolutely. The sight of Levi splintered her. And though she fought the distraction, it absolutely took up head space. How could it not?

Tess preferred one crisis at a time.

The noise of the whistle sequence completed, Enrico asked, "Gwen the snake bite happened in this location?"

"There where that boot is." Gwen pointed.

"I'll give the area another sweep. Mojo," Enrico commanded as he went over to retrieve Tess's boot, "hunt snakes."

Mojo jumped from the platform and wedged his body underneath.

"Aren't you putting him in danger?" Gwen asked. "If he's sticking his nose under those rocks, he could be bitten as easily as Tess was."

Enrico's response was lost on Tess. She was watching Goose pull a syringe from his pack.

"Hey, Levi," Goose said, "while I prep this, get her boot and socks off. Rings. Anything that could constrict and cut off circulation if Tess starts to swell."

Levi started with her boot and socks, then moved around to face her.

He'd aged. Levi's face had new crinkles around his eyes. His skin had roughened. There was a determination in his eyes that she didn't remember. But that might be the situation—both being in rescue mode and the fact that this particular damsel in distress was someone he *must* loathe.

As directed, Levi pulled off the rings on her right hand, then lifted her left hand where there were none. "Where's your wedding ring?" Levi's voice was unusually gruff.

"I was widowed about fourteen years ago. Abraham was sick when he moved to America. He fought as long and as hard as he could for his children's sake," she said softly. "But he died."

He died.

And she had made promises to see the children into adulthood. She felt her sense of loyalty and commitment to the boys straighten her spine. After everything, wouldn't this be a horrific way to break her vow?

"Fourteen *years*?" Levi's eyes hardened.

And Tess forced her face to go blank.

"I'm sorry for your loss," he murmured, handing the rings off to Gwen.

"Thank you." A churning tide of conflicting emotions was dragging her to someplace she didn't want to be. As Mama Ya used to say, "The only way to survive was to float and wait until you find the eddy."

Tess made that her mantra—*Float*. She steadied her breath.

But she couldn't quite raise her head over the river of shame.

She'd always felt her cowardice in not finding Levi and telling him in person the whys of her marriage. Writing it would have put Abraham's visa status at risk, even though it shouldn't have. Her vows to Abraham had been true, she would love and care for him for all his days. But, the devotion she felt for Abraham was vastly different than the love that Tess held for Levi.

Had *always* and *unwaveringly* held for Levi.

Tess knew she'd go to her grave loving him.

Each of those thoughts was a crashing wave that pulled her under. She was drowning in the profound grief for what she'd lost.

Pulling at her shirt as if that would give her more space to inhale, Tess gasped for air.

"Tessy. Tess!" Levi's face hovered over hers, his thumb stroked over her cheek. "What's going on right now?"

She had no idea.

Was this cobra venom attacking her system? Or was this Levi?

13

Levi

"Okay, Tessy, listen to me." Levi modulated his voice to the tone he'd used when they were young and together. The tone that had pulled Tess out of her nightmares without waking her. Because if she woke from the nightmare, she'd be awake and terrified. "I know this is scary. I know that. You're not alone. I've got you." Levi stopped himself.

That was from before. And the last thing he wanted to do right now was make her more uncomfortable than she already was.

His focus was squarely on the emergency.

So he amended. "You've got a good team here. We're taking care of you."

Goose sent her a smile. "You're doing great, Tess. And the next step is for me to do a blood draw. I have dog equipment, so we're making do."

"Thank you," Tess closed her eyes. She always hated the sight of blood.

"What's the reason for the blood sample?" Enrico asked.

Goose wrapped a rubber tourniquet around Tess's bicep, then swiped an alcohol swab over the crook of her arm. "I'm capturing a blood sample so the pathologists have a sample from earliest possible. It might be informative to do a comparison over a sequence of time. I'll take another once we're down and a third on the way to the hospital."

Tapping Tess's vein, he inserted the needle. As the rich dark maroon filled the vial, Goose said, "In case it's helpful to you in the future, Enrico, there are different ways the hospital can test for venom. I'm thinking specifically of the D-dimer test for blood coagulation. That's usually taken at the two-hour mark."

"If someone survives that long," Tess murmured.

"We're just over the one-hour time marker." He laid the vial on a cotton square, put a Band-Aid on Tess's arm, and released the tourniquet. "If the snake experts don't have enough information to identify the snake from the skin pattern, they'll do an enzyme test. It's imperative to get the diagnosis right because they need to balance the amount of venom in Tess's system with the amount of anti-venom they'll administer." Goose wrote Tess's name, date, and time on the white label. "If you don't want to open your eyes, Tess, that's fine. You do what you need to keep your system calm. But be aware, I'm about to stomp on this chemical pack to get the ice reaction going. I want to keep the blood sample at the right temperature."

"Thank you."

Enrico took over that process.

Levi kept his hands on Tess, so she didn't need to exert to lay still on her side.

"You'll feel my fingers on your right leg," Goose said. "I'm going to inspect your wound and take a picture." His finger pressed into Tess's flesh.

Levi watched to find any subtle clue that Goose might not be sharing with Tess. "So far, your tissue looks like it's in good shape. In the few minutes I've been treating you, I haven't seen any degradation. Having said that. Levi and Enrico, you two need to come up with an extraction plan. There's a saying," Goose said, "Time is tissue. We need to get her down to the vehicle stat."

Goose produced two telescoping splints to stabilize her right leg, pulling them snuggly in place with hook and loop closures.

"Once we're down. It's an hour to the hospital," Enrico said.

Gwen sat cross-legged at the far corner, staying out of the way. "You all sprinted up the side of the hill. But it took us forty-five minutes to get up here, walking steadily. From past experience, down is slower."

"We'll put in the effort," Goose said. "I want Tess in the hospital by the three-hour mark. It's an hour's drive. We'll aim for thirty minutes carrying her down."

Enrico scanned the path. "That's aggressive." He turned to Levi. "Typically, we'd run a line to keep everyone safe. No rope. And no time. We need to factor that in when we're weighing the risk."

In his mind, Levi formed a workable plan. It was going to be a trick. Not only did he need to jog down the mountain with Tess in his arms. But she needed to feel secure. Any anxiety that caused an increased heartbeat or the tensing of her muscles meant the venom might be speeding to her organs, speeding the degradation of her system.

"Tess," Levi squeezed her shoulder, and she blinked her lids open.

He couldn't believe she was here. That he was touching her. Surreal.

He'd process all this later.

Right now, he needed to see trust looking back at him. He

needed Tess to believe that everything they could possibly do to save her was being done professionally and safely.

"Enrico and I trained to get our dogs down an angle if they sustained an abdominal wound or it's ill-advised to drape them around our necks. We use a three-man team. The man in front is there to watch for anything in the path that might cause an issue and to act as a stop to prevent a fall."

"I'll take point," Enrico said. "That way, I can manage Mojo. And Mojo can manage any animals on the way."

Having finished administering first aid, Goose was throwing his supplies back in his pack, then yanked the straps over his arms. "I'll take anchor."

"And I'll take Tess," Levi confirmed before turning his gaze back to Tess. "If I can't drape my dog over my shoulder to get them to safety, I've trained to run down mountains with that dog in my arms. And that's how I'd carry you, with your permission."

"Tess is much bigger than a dog," Gwen pointed out.

"But she won't be fighting me," Levi explained, "and can curl toward me and hold on."

"Do you think piggybacking might be better?" Gwen asked.

"I don't advise that," Goose said. "It's best if Levi holds Tess in his arms against his chest. It's the most stable way to move her. And will be the least exertion for her."

"Thank you for carrying me, Levi," Tess whispered. "Truly."

Levi forced his gaze away from hers. He had to keep his thoughts and emotions squared away. This was the time for strategic thinking. "Goose, you and I will switch packs. I'll wear the medical ruck."

"It's a lot of added weight," Goose said, pulling the pack off again.

"I think of it as a counterbalance. Goose, your job is to

keep a hand through the top handle of the medical pack. If you feel me falling forward, you brace and keep me upright. I'll try to vocalize any time I feel my footing is off by saying 'kip.'"

With the medical pack on, the straps adjusted and hooked across his sternum and hips, Levi squatted behind Tess's back. "You ready? I'm going to roll you into my arms and stand."

She lifted an arm to wrap around his neck.

How many times had he found her sleeping on the sofa and scooped her up to carry her to bed, hoping she could cling to a calm sleep as long as possible? Tess often woke up more tired than she was when she'd gone to bed.

He scooped an arm under her knees and pulled her to his chest as he pushed from his squat to standing.

"Good?" Enrico asked.

Levi adjusted his hold. It wasn't the same.

She weighed a little more. Her body was stiffer than before. She didn't meld and cuddle into him. There was no little sigh of contentment.

This was a potentially life-or-death situation. Her brain wasn't processing normally. She needed clear instructions to know what to do now rather than his assumptions that she'd remember how it used to be back then.

With her hips squared to the ground, Levi couldn't see over her. It would be fine to carry her stiff like this across a flat field. But it would throw off his balance on the rocky hillside.

"Tessy," his voice caught, "I'm sorry if this is awkward, but we've been in a similar situation before. Remember when you sprained your ankle on the hike?"

She took in a sharp breath and then rolled until her breasts crushed against his chest, her hips rotated. And, with her arms wrapping his neck tight enough to hold herself in place and loose enough that he was able to breathe, her head rested on her own shoulder so her weight was as close to his center of gravity as possible.

"Better, thank you." Levi called out, "Stack up."

"Mojo, lead, find the vehicle," Enrico commanded, then called over his shoulder. "Levi, you set the pace. I'm just going for it. If you need me to push harder, I will. If you need me to slow, just say the word."

And with that, the team raced for their vehicle below.

Every step he took, every single step, meant they were closer to getting Tess to the hospital and the medical attention she needed. He'd just keep putting one foot in front of the other.

14

———

Levi

At the bottom of the hill, Reaper stood with Iris and Craig, waiting for word on what had happened on the trail.

Sweaty and out of breath, Gwen stepped forward to keep her mom from fussing over Tess and slowing the extraction.

Goose gave Reaper a rundown of events.

With no connectivity, Goose pulled up the documentation on Gwen's phone and then his. Goose held them out for Reaper to take pictures of the pictures and video of the video. Then, Reaper took pictures of the field notes delineating their actions.

Back at the winery, Reaper would convey that information to the hospital, giving them a heads-up that an urgent patient was inbound.

Meanwhile, with Tess in his arms crushed against him, Levi leaned back against the sun-heated surface of the vehicle, catching his breath.

Goose performed the second blood draw, and Enrico opened the hatch on his Etosha vehicle, rounding to lowering both passenger benches to make a flat area for Tess to lie in.

The team moved Tess into the back, putting Mojo on one side of her and Levi on the other. "We're going to be going fast," Goose said. "We were longer on the trail than I wanted. If you're getting rocked around too much back there, Tess, tell me. We don't want you clenching your muscles or expending effort to keep yourself from getting slung about."

"I've got her," Levi said.

Seat belts pulled into place, the engine roared to life as Enrico catapulted over the bumpy stretch of dirt and onto the highway.

They were all exhausted and silent for a long stretch until Goose called out, "When we drove past the Etosha guard station, I had Wi-Fi just long enough to pull up the zebra cobra page on Tess's snake app. This looks right." He turned in his seat to flash the picture to Levi. "Tess, we won't be a hundred percent sure what kind of snake bit you until we get the blood tests back. It could be that one snake bit you, and another slithered by. We won't make any assumptions. It's a matter of taking the right diagnostic steps."

"Go ahead and tell me what it's saying about zebra cobras," Tess said. "My imagination is absolutely worse than anything you could read to me from that page."

"The good news is that if it is a zebra cobra, they are cytotoxic. That means that their venom affects cell activity."

"And that's good why?" Levi asked.

"This is not an immediate life or death situation. Tess has an opportunity to get to the hospital for the anti-venom in time."

"In time for what?" she asked.

"I've got bars," Levi called out.

Goose looked down at his screen. "Yup. Me, too. Tess, in time to get you help before the DNA in your cells gets affected. I'm calling the hospital. Even though Reaper has conveyed everything we documented by now, I'd like to know if I missed any first aid steps." He made the call, spoke with their specialist, and gave the hospital an updated ETA.

Enrico understood the assignment. Barring slower-moving traffic ahead, they'd make the hour-long drive in forty minutes.

As the sun went down, the wind picked up, buffeting the sides of their vehicle.

"Levi," Goose called out.

"On it." Levi pushed his boots into the back hatch, sidling closer to Tess. Once she was tightly sandwiched between him and Mojo, Levi reached across to Tess's immobilized leg, catching hold of the brace, then he pressed his elbow into his ribs and his back to the side of the vehicle, cutting down the jostling as much as possible.

Mojo rested his head on her chest, and Tess rested her hand on Mojo's neck. Levi knew that she was gaining calm from the K9's empathy. And Levi was grateful that she was getting emotional support from a source that didn't have baggage attached.

Levi was struggling.

In the long minutes of breakneck driving, he had time to think and for memories that he'd pushed away to resurface.

All of them were wonderful.

The good, the bad, and the ugly, with Tess, it was *all* wonderful up until the letter arrived.

"I'm engaged to marry Abraham. I'm so sorry."

For fourteen years, she'd been a widow. She hadn't looked him up. In Levi's mind, he'd always thought Tess's marrying Abraham was an act of duty. She was living her ethos. He'd imagined that something very bad had happened, and Tess marrying Abraham was the only solution to making it better.

Levi had imagined that, given the choice of free will without moral pressures, Tess would have chosen to marry him as they'd planned from the day they met.

But if that were true, Levi reasoned, wouldn't it follow that once Abraham died, Tess would find him, explain everything to him, and return to his arms?

The story he'd been telling himself for the last sixteen years was merely a fantasy bandaging his heart.

Yeah, he was struggling.

Enrico shouted back, "We're here. Levi, when I pull up, just stay where you are."

"Wilco."

"They have medical staff and a gurney," Goose said.

Enrico glided to a stop, checked the time, and said, "Close to your timeframe, Goose. We're here three hours and five minutes post-bite."

Goose grinned. "Hell of an effort."

"Thank you," Tess called out.

As soon as they pulled up and Enrico put the vehicle in park, the hospital staff swarmed in the practiced choreography for moving emergency patients.

The men stood at their vehicle as the nurses pushed the gurney through the automatic doors, then ran down the corridor and away.

Mojo, standing in the cargo area, moved forward and draped his head over Levi's shoulder. "Thank you, buddy," Levi whispered as he scritched Mojo's ears, then turned so he could give a double-handed reward. "You did an amazing job today. I'm grateful for you."

Mojo gave a whining yawn, releasing stress. He'd been part of the team. And like the team, he'd felt the mission pressures and met the needs in ways both commanded and intuited. As Levi looked into Mojo's eyes, he thought that he read compassion there.

It was really something for Levi to finally find the dog of his heart and, at the same time, realize that the connection he'd always felt with Tess had been a figment of his imagination. It spun his head.

Goose petted a hand down Mojo's side. "Damned impressive training."

"I'm not taking credit for everything today. Yeah, it was part training. But a whole lot of that is heart. Once Mojo understands a mission, he gives it his all. He's a solid partner."

Because of Mojo, the men stayed on the benches outside the hospital. The nurses knew where to find them with any updates.

While Levi passed what information they had to Reaper and Gwen, Enrico took off to find some grub to replenish their depleted systems.

They'd eaten in silence.

After sitting long enough, the adrenaline that had fueled the rescue left their bodies, and they were too tired to speak.

As the sunset and the stars blinked against a crisp black sky, a man in a white lab coat, stethoscope draped around his neck, strode through the automatic doors.

"Levi Elliot?" He lifted his brows.

The men stood.

"Miss Dagomba has asked that I tell you where we are in her care."

"Thank you." Levi's heart was in a vice.

"We have identified the bite as a zebra cobra."

"She's receiving anti-venom?" Goose asked.

"Right now, we are observing and waiting for lab results," the doctor said. "We're balancing the risks and have decided to take a conservative approach."

"Why?" Levi asked,

"Her wound seems stable, and anti-venom has its own risks."

Levi opened his hands. "Like?"

"People who have allergic reactions to the anti-venom can

go into anaphylactic shock, and there's the potential that they would die. This is why anti-venom is only administered in the hospital."

Anaphylaxis. And death.

Hearing that was a gut punch.

"If it was a dry bite—a bite where no venom is released—then we do not wish to stress her system further," he explained. "The good news is, I don't see any redness or swelling. Of concern is that the fang marks are larger than we'd expect. It means that it is an older, larger snake that could put the venom deep within her gastrocnemius."

Levi wrapped a hand behind his neck. "That means?"

"We might miss something by observation alone. The lab results will give us another piece of information."

"But it's *possible* it was a dry bite." Levi pinned his hopes there.

"Studies put the chances of a dry bite at around fifty-fifty. That, of course, depends on the species. We don't have good clinical data about zebra cobras. The nurses are attentive, and I have asked them to inform you once the labs are up. This should be very soon."

"Thank you," Levi said.

With a nod, the doctor went inside.

Alone again, Enrico turned to Goose. "So what do you think? What's our game plan?"

"Why don't you two head home, and I'll hang back?" Levi suggested. "Someone needs to be here to advocate for Tess. A friend's face might be helpful if they need to give her some bad news."

Enrico stood and raised his hand as a car drove in and parked under the light. "That's my staff. I need to get back and file a report. And that needs to be in place before the morning meeting so our personnel at Etosha know about this and can be vigilant."

"Goose and Mojo could go with you if you don't mind leaving the park vehicle with me."

Levi didn't know what to do with the sensations coursing through his body. He had never wanted to see Tess again, but now that he had, Levi felt the internal conflict. Even though his wounds were raw again, Levi also knew he couldn't leave her side. Not while she was endangered.

Before they landed on a plan, a nurse poked her head out the door. "America?"

Levi turned. "Yes."

"Miss Tess would like to see you all if that is all right."

15

———

Tess

The men let themselves into her hospital room.

Her first question was, "Where's Mojo?"

"He stayed with Enrico's colleague in their vehicle," Goose told her.

Levi didn't say anything, not even hi.

Dressed in a hospital gown, there was an IV flowing saline into her veins.

As the team found places to stand, Tess looked from one to the other. My god, what feats of strength and courage they'd displayed today. Following a signal, racing up a mountainside, applying their skills, then getting her down and to the hospital, it was a miracle.

They were a miracle.

"Why are you crying?" Enrico stepped forward. "Are you in pain?"

With her fingers wrapping the edge of her sheet in tight fists, Tess shook her head.

"You're afraid?" Enrico was grasping.

Levi pulled Enrico away and said quietly, "She's crying because we were kind."

"*Kind*?"

"We're helping her. Kindness is the *only* thing that makes Tess cry."

Enrico posted his hand on his hips and tipped his head. "Silently?"

"Yup, silently."

Enrico turned his gaze to the ground and was quiet for a long minute. When he finally looked up to catch Levi's gaze, he said, "That is some heavy shit, brother."

"Yeah. It is."

Tess could hear it in their voices that they had a deep understanding of what that meant. Coming from their backgrounds in the military with brothers and sisters who experienced things that rewired their brains, she felt they wouldn't judge her or press her for more than she could give.

For some people, life would always be a wrestling match with the past.

But Levi was wrong when he leaned into the word "only." Tess remembered vividly the stream of tears she shed that gathered all the feelings in her body when she accepted Abraham's marriage proposal. Those feelings from that day still felt raw.

The appearance of one of the two doctors conferring on her case relieved Tess of the need to deal with the awkwardness of Levi knowing something that intimate and sharing it with a near stranger.

Could they be strangers after what had happened today?

No. Impossible.

"Enrico," this doctor said, a wide smile brightening his face as he held out a hand for a shake, "all is well?"

"For me, yes. Good to see a friend is taking care of a friend." Enrico held out a hand toward Tess.

"How are you feeling?" The doctor moved around to peer at her face. "Would you turn so that I might inspect the wound?"

"Uhm." Tess blinked at Levi.

Levi turned his face to the wall, and the other men followed his lead.

Lowering the head of the bed and pulling the sheet to the side, Tess held the back of her hospital gown together so she wasn't mooning the man while he checked the wound site.

"Yes, good. I see no changes. You can turn over again."

Tess situated herself before calling out, "I'm covered," so the men could turn back around.

"My nurse is arriving with the results of the lab work." He circled her bed and moved to the chair in the corner. Pressing his feet together, he let his legs fall to the sides. A metal chart hung from his hand between his knees.

Tess thought that he looked tired and was probably on his second shift of the day.

He smiled at Tess. "You are not the first American woman I have spoken with this week about snakes. I had an American woman visit me the other day. She brought a picnic with things that I had never tried before. There was a dish called deviled eggs and another that was called Texas caviar. Most interesting."

"Another bite?" Enrico asked, his brows furrowed with concern.

Tess thought there was a lot to his worries. There were life and limb dangers to people and that meant mounting emergency interventions. But too, Namibia had three main industries, and tourism was the most important one. If word of tourists dying from venomous bites spread, an already difficult economic environment would worsen.

"No, this woman, she was doing research. I think perhaps she was a travel blogger."

"Tell me the story," Enrico smiled.

That was a phrase that Tess loved to hear in southern Africa, "Tell me the story." Gathering for stories was an important part of the culture.

"This woman was interested in learning about tourist encounters with our wildlife and what they could expect if something should happen to them as they roamed around the country."

"You told her that the hospitals are few and far between?" Enrico asked.

"I did and also that we can't fly antivenom out to people. They need to have it in the hospital because an allergic reaction can be every bit as deadly as snake venom."

"I was in the south at Sossuvlie climbing Big Daddy," Tess said. "The nearest hospital was four hours and forty-nine minutes away."

"That is quite a precise drive time," Enrico said. "Did someone need the hospital?"

"No. I looked it up as the result of a conversation about wearing flip-flops to the bathhouse." She shrugged. "It doesn't matter. I guess my point was that five hours with a venomous anything bite is dangerous. But, excuse me, I've interrupted your story about the blogger."

"Yes. Yes. She asked me an interesting question. You will enjoy this, Enrico. It is a question that is both far-fetched and yet—" He waggled a finger near his ear as if there was a subject to contemplate. "A question that has planted itself in my mind to be mulled. Here in Namibia, in the winter, during the night, it is typically too cold for reptiles to be out. Some days are warm, and they might wake enough to sun themselves." He opened a hand toward Tess. "As your zebra cobra seems to have done. But, typically, from June to September, the reptiles rest."

Levi pushed his hands into his pockets and pressed a shoulder against the wall, listening.

"This is not true for several of our more venomous snakes. For example, for the black mamba, it is mating season. The male snakes are out seeking a female. The female, she wishes to be found. To this end, the female mamba will secrete a pheromone and leave a trail that the males follow. Sometimes, two males will arrive at the same time, and they will fight. Rising up, they will entwine themselves, each trying to press the other one's head into the sand."

"Until one of them says 'uncle?'" Levi asked with a grin.

"Exactly so. The weaker of the two must slither away and allow the stronger one to mate. Knowing this brief backstory, this is what she asked, 'Is it possible for someone to unwittingly walk along the pheromone trail of a female mamba and get the scent on their boots, go to their lodge room, and look up to find a bunch of male black mambas were chasing her down? And would this person be in trouble?'"

The men's laughter was loud and bawdy.

Enrico clutched his stomach and stammered out between guffaws, "Wow, that's a vivid imagination."

When the hilarity quieted to smiles, Tess canted her head. "So? Is it possible?"

"I do not know." The doctor placed a hand over his heart. "No one has ever posed this to me before. I would like to find out for certain. Would I say possible?" He shrugged with open palms. "Why not? Would I say probable?" He shrugged again. "Since I have never heard of such an event, I think not. Surely, if it had ever taken place, there would be fire stories and songs about it. But when I return to my family's village, I will ask the elders."

A nurse came in with Tess's lab work, and the doctor took a moment to review it.

"This looks to me to be a dry bite." He stood. "Until tomorrow, I will not jinx these results by saying you were very lucky." He tapped the folder on her bedtable. "I think you should go to sleep if you can." He caught Tess's gaze. "This has been a very anxious situation. But so far," he tipped his chin down, "you have no signs that concern me. The nurse will monitor you on the half-hour. We'll draw more blood around five. And we will see what we see."

16

———————

Tess

THE MORNING WAS STILL DARK WHEN TESS WAS HANDED HER paperwork, and she walked out the door to find Levi and Mojo sitting exactly where the nurse had told her. "I can go home," she said.

It was still cold out, and Levi handed her a wool blanket to wrap around herself.

She knew that Enrico and Goose had gone back to the vineyard, and Levi had stayed.

Tess wished he hadn't. And she was immensely grateful that he had.

Dry bite.

All of that effort, all of the exertion was for not.

The long-ago face of her new friend in the new Ghanian village smiling down at Tess as she climbed the tree was vivid in her imagination.

Up the tree with laughter.

Back to the ground in agony.

And then dead.

No one knew whether Tess's circumstances were life-threatening, inconvenient, or somewhere along the length of the spectrum. It was always best, she'd found, to err on the side of caution—to stand in the shade under a tree rather than sunbathe on a dune when water wasn't available.

A crisis? Maybe or maybe not. In the end, it was not. That didn't mean the chances of an emergency weren't there.

Don't tempt fate.

And wasn't that an interesting phrase to run through her head, Tess thought, just as she opened the door to climb in next to Levi and head back to the vineyard?

Her lips quivered as she found her seat. So she rolled them in and greeted him with a nod. Pain oozed from her pores. She knew she reeked of distress and wondered if Levi could smell it, too.

Levi didn't seem to mind her silence. In fact, he seemed relieved by it.

They were almost to the vineyard before he cleared his throat. "Look, I'm in a new job. I brought my boss and colleague halfway around the world to see a dog based on my belief in Enrico's training methods. I have a lot at stake here. Picking the right K9 can mean mission success and lives saved down the line. I need to make sure I pick the right dog for a dedicated and trusting relationship."

He wasn't the kind of guy to hit below the belt. Hadn't been. He seemed to realize what he'd just said.

"I didn't mean that as a jab."

"Right." Her lips dragged into a deep frown, and she hid it by turning to look out the side window.

The vast emptiness of Namibia stretched out under the predawn sky.

Tess felt like, after yesterday's forced proximity, Levi was trying to gain a little space. She could respect that. It was probably best for both of them.

"Look, we're gonna be here together." Levi's voice was gruff. "I'm in a new professional capacity. How about we act like we get along and give everyone a break from the drama? I don't want our past to be a thing here. Also, not a jab."

"Agreed."

"Sunrises at seven."

She had nothing to say to that. She sat in the dark cab, and they drove in silence the rest of the way.

She could play-act in front of the Metz family and Levi's team. It would only be a matter of days. He'd head back to the U.S., and she'd keep moving through her life, taking one day at a time.

"Good?" he asked as he turned off the highway onto the long stretch of the private road leading to the vineyard.

"Yes, thank you."

The trees stood black against the brightening sky. Their leafless limbs tangled the trees together. It had an other-worldly feel to it.

"Eerie," she said, then sucked in a gasp.

An enormous animal was sailing over their hood. With horns slicing backward like curving sabers, it turned its head toward them, peeling its eyelids back until the whole whites of its eyeballs were visible.

Levi came to a screeching halt as, mid-leap, the beast twisted its body all the way around and landed its feet at the side of their vehicle.

Tess's hands pressed into her cheeks, then lowered to her chest.

With another bound, it was back out of sight.

They turned to each other with startled faces, then broke out in peals of laughter, a relief after the stress of sitting side by side for the last hour.

She gulped. "That was terrifying,"

"I know what can happen if you hit a deer, and they put their hoof through your windshield, but I have no idea what could have happened there. Nothing pretty," Levi said, starting them back down the drive at a crawl, his head turning this way and that, probably looking for the next wild adventure. "Was that an oryx?"

"It was." Tess's heart was still thundering in her chest. "I had no idea they were so big. I've only seen pictures. Whew!"

"Paybacks are hell." Levi turned to her and popped his brows. "I ate oryx for dinner last night. I thought it was delicious."

As they finished driving up, that moment, that respite, that oryx-horned pop of a balloon, shifted the dynamic between them.

There was still tension. And Tess still felt deep shame. But this felt tolerable enough that Tess wouldn't try to hide in her room for the rest of her vacation.

When they climbed from the vehicle, Craig and Iris were waiting for them on the front steps.

"There you are, Tess." Iris ran forward and gathered her up in a deep hug and didn't let go for a very long time as she rocked Tess back and forth. "We were so worried for you." She painted a hand over Tess's long curls. "But Levi let us know you were okay." She held Tess out at arm's length. "And here you are, probably starved." Drawing Tess with her, Iris turned. "Perfect timing, we're heading to the veranda for breakfast."

Craig was next in line to grab Tess into a hug. "You're good, Tess?"

"Good. And grateful."

"That's right." As they passed into the reception area, Craig reached out and knocked on the wooden door jam. "In all the years we've been here, nothing that dramatic has happened to a human. The property? Yes. But up until now, our guests had always been safe."

17

—————

Tess

Enrico, Iniquus, and Tess had joined Iris and Craig at the family table when Gwen swished down the walkway, looking uncharacteristically girly. She'd not just washed but curled her long black hair. Makeup accentuated her eyes. And she was wearing contact lenses instead of her normal geek-girl glasses.

Dressed in the sundress that she schlepped around in her backpack in case she was invited on a date, Gwen had even polished her toenails and pulled on a pair of strappy sandals.

Tess reached back into her memory, trying to remember Gwen ever doing any of these things—let alone *all* these things —before.

Tess stood to give her friend a hug. "What an adventure, huh?"

"I'm so glad it turned out the way it did." Gwen held their hug, swaying back and forth just like her mother had. And there was the same sweep of a comforting hand down her hair. "I was so grateful when I talked to Levi this morning. You slept? You're good?"

"I am."

And when they pulled apart, Tess lifted a single brow to tease Gwen for this departure from her norm. Tess knew Gwen would interpret that correctly.

Gwen gave her a hip bump before lifting a bottle of wine in the air. "Here you go, Mom. Tess and I brought you something." She held the bottle out to her mother.

"Gosh, thanks, sweetheart," Iris accepted it and turned it to inspect the label. "You know, as the owner of a winery, I was just sitting here, looking out into the distance, thinking I'd like a nice bottle of wine on hand to sip of an evening. If only I had one on hand."

"Stop, Mom." Gwen turned to Tess. "That's Mom's sarcastic sense of humor. She calls it wry." Gwen looked at her Mom. "It's *sarcastic*. Since you like to taste other regional wines, Tess and I picked this up for you."

"It's very nice of you." Iris kissed Gwen's cheek. "Thank you. We'll enjoy tasting it." She held the bottle out to Craig. "Do you know this vineyard?"

Craig pulled his readers off the neckline of his T-shirt and slipped them on. "I don't think so, no." He looked over the top of the rims toward Gwen. "Did you pick it up in Windhoek?"

Gwen batted a hand through the air. "It's a whole story."

"The one you promised me about sleeping in a vehicle?" Iris asked. "Let's have it."

Craig turned toward the Iniquus men seated at the breakfast table. "I don't know if you gentlemen have spent time in Africa, but I've found Namibia to be the land of storytelling and conversation. I hope you enjoy that about the culture."

With that, Gwen took the seat across from Levi with her

focus turned to her dad as he asked, "How did you girls come across this wine?"

"Tess, why don't you tell it? I think I'd lace the story with profanity, and Mom doesn't like that."

"It's sunrise," Iris said. "Perhaps you can save the saltier language for this evening."

"I think we can share the storytelling." Tess smiled. "But I can start us off." She took a sip of water and then put her hands on her lap. "Gwen and I were heading back to Windhoek at the end of a tour to Big Daddy when we happened upon a side adventure. First, you should know that we were in a vehicle with eight other tourists and the driver."

"Otto." Gwen sneered.

"Behind our vehicle, Otto pulled a trailer with camping gear and our personal items."

Gwen made a "can you believe?" face. "But no freaking water."

Tess stopped and smiled.

"Sorry, more coffee, less cranky." Gwen reached for the carafe. "Keep going."

Tess turned to the head of the table. "As you were saying, Craig, Namibia is a land of storytelling. Unfortunately, some of those stories are tall tales. For hours on end, our guide, Otto, waxed poetic about his months-long forays into the jungles in Botswana, Angola, and South Africa. He had tales of his mighty feats as he overcame situations that required cunning and might. Unfortunately, the times when we depended on him, he proved to be," Tess sighed, "perhaps telling someone else's stories of expedition glory."

"Fertile imagination," Gwen said as she lifted her coffee mug to her lips.

"A bloated ego is hazardous anywhere, but especially in

places like Namibia where so much can go so wrong so quickly without access to resources," Enrico said.

"Exactly." Tess nodded. "And when you couple an ego with a four-wheel drive vehicle that somehow functioned as only a two-wheeled rear-drive vehicle, you run into trouble in certain terrains."

"We got sand-bogged at Big Daddy." Gwen set her mug down.

"That's dangerous," Iris said with a scowl. "He took you out into the dunes in a two-wheeled heavy vehicle? Mercy."

Tess reached for her own mug of coffee. "To be fair, he seemed pretty surprised to discover the situation. Just like we were pretty surprised that he forgot to bring water."

"What?" Iris scowled.

"Not just forgot but made the decision to unload the drinking water at our campsite. Luckily—" Gwen leaned to the side to give the server space to set her plate down. "Thank you." She straightened herself and lifted her fork. "Luckily, we came out of the Big Daddy debacle no worse for wear."

"Not entirely true," Tess said. "We began the trek with four spare tires, and Otto went through all of them. As each tire punctured along the way, we'd keep stopping and changing them over."

"That's part of driving in Namibia." Enrico accepted his breakfast plate from the server. "Thank you, ma'am."

"I understood the problem with the tires. That's not the outfit's fault," Gwen said. "Where they were at fault was that there was something seriously wrong with the vehicle."

"Two-wheel drive with a trailer is difficult," Enrico told the Iniquus men sitting across from him. "The roads are sometimes flat, but there are a lot of elevation changes."

"Yes, that too, but there was a bigger issue," Gwen said,

cutting into her sausage, "On the way to Big Daddy, the car suddenly stopped. Just completely stopped. There was nothing. No click, no turnover, it absolutely flatlined."

Tess said, "Otto looked at things, trying to figure it out. And finally, he announced it had something to do with the fuel."

"He had an extra fuel tank in the trailer?" Enrico asked.

"Exactly," Tess said. "He started the pump to move the gas from one tank to the other. It took a while, but at this point, we were all in good spirits, on our way to desert camping and dune climbing. The vehicle started after he did that."

"Was the fuel the thing that made it start again?" Levi asked. "Or did resting for a few minutes do the trick?"

"That's astute." Gwen sent Levi a warm smile. Her gaze held his just a second too long.

Tess whipped her head around to see how Levi responded.

He was reaching for the salt and pepper.

Averting her eyes, Tess looked down at her plate of eggs, toast, salad, and slices of meat.

Craig followed her gaze. "It's wild meats from our range lands. We culled the ones causing issues. So if the meats a bit tough, well, so were their personalities."

"Dad!" Gwen wrinkled her nose. "That's so not funny."

"We're having zebra and wildebeest," Iris said with her knife in her hand. "The one on the right is wildebeest. Try that one first."

Gwen laughed at how long Tess was chewing that bite. "What do you think, Tess?"

She held a hand over her mouth to answer. "It tastes exactly how one would think wildebeest would taste."

"Gamey? Tough?" Gwen asked.

"Yes, that."

"The zebra?" Iris pointed to the left side of her plate.

Tess cut a piece to try. "Hmm. I think I did myself a disservice by assuming zebra would taste like horse. It doesn't."

"Where did you eat horse?" Reaper asked.

"Iceland. They raise horses as a meat source like we raise cattle for the same. These aren't pet horses that they name. It's all very similar to cows in the United States. But I found the meat more tender. Zebra is still a bit tough and maybe a bit—I know this is the traditional Namibian way of serving meat—a bit of sauce or spice might help."

"To mask the taste?" Gwen asked.

"It's not my favorite to be honest." Tess wiped her mouth. "Back to the wine. With the vehicle back story in place, this is the tale of how Gwen and I came to be in possession of your gift."

Craig rubbed his hands together. "Yup, I'd like to hear."

"I was sitting up front next to our guy, Otto. And Gwen was in the middle of the bench behind us, forming a conversation triangle," Tess explained. "Otto told us that he'd decided not to take the normal route home. The route would take us up into the mountains. He told us how beautiful it was up there and that there were these amazing vistas and these wonderful photographic opportunities." Tess smiled. "He went on and on about what a fantastic opportunity it was."

"He got you jazzed for a thing that wasn't going to happen?" Enrico asked.

"Rude. Right?" Gwen asked. "He told us that up on the mountain, they often see some of the wildlife that we hadn't come across along the road thus far or that we would even see in Etosha."

Tess nodded. "Wild cats at dusk."

Iris scowled. "But he wasn't going to go? Did you pay for him to take you up there? That was part of the package price?"

"Yes, it was. But since he wasn't feeding us either, we

didn't think he was following all the bullet points in the brochure," Tess said. "I asked. He was worried about not having a four-wheel drive with the weight of the trailer. That and we didn't have any more spare tires."

Iris nodded. "It was a sound decision not to risk it."

"I have to say, for all my time working in areas that are off-grid," Tess reached up to press her thick curls out of her eyes. "I find comfort in having a satellite phone. And while I am forever grateful for the effort and care that you all provided me yesterday. Another piece to this story is that no one had a means of communication. No radio, no sat phone, no cell connectivity, and a cantankerous vehicle." Tess grimaced. "After that conversation about rerouting, I started to pay attention to how far we were from anything. And how few and far between were the fellow travelers along our path."

"Just ostriches." Gwen ran two fingers across the table. "It put me in mind of Disney's Fantasia. But Tess is right. We were out in the middle of nowhere. We had been traveling—I don't know, Tess, what would you say forty-five minutes without seeing as much as a house on the side of the road?"

"That's about right. Up until that point of our story, houses dotted along the way. A tiny desert house would be off in the distance like a plastic piece on a Monopoly board. But as Gwen said, we had been traveling quite a while with pink sand, the ostriches running along, and nothing else." Tess looked at Gwen. "Does this remind you of my lone cow in Texas story?"

"No water then, no water this time either."

Tess sent a glance around the table. "Sorry. That's a story for a different time. So there we were in this bleak, sandy place."

Gwen sent the flat of her hand to show the movement of their vehicle. "We were coming up over the hill, and as soon as we evened out the vehicle, 'it stopped.'"

Craig scowled. "What does it mean you stopped?"

Gwen turned to her dad. "I mean that the engine cut off. We rolled to a stop. Otto tried to turn the engine over. It didn't even click. Nothing was happening. It was just dead. *Dead.* There was nothing to work with there."

"He did go back and try that fuel thing that worked beforehand," Tess said. "He moved the fuel, and we waited for a while, and we got nothing. Now," Tess sent a bright smile around the table. "Here's the miracle of this whole episode, just before the vehicle stopped completely. Otto pointed at a small cluster of houses a few kilometers back toward the hills. And he said, 'That's the last there is for the next hundred kilometers.'"

"To anything?" Iris put her hand over her heart. "You girls are going to be the death of me."

"We're here, Mom. We're fine."

Iris leaned toward her daughter. Her voice turned stern. "Out in the middle of nowhere with no communications, and you said you had no water?"

"Tess and I learned our lesson at Big Daddy. We had water and food with us. Not enough for everyone, and you know how that becomes a dilemma. What happens when you come prepared for you while the others didn't."

"Reaper brought up that same dilemma yesterday," Craig said.

"For me, I wouldn't have shared." She held a finger up, stopping anyone from jumping in. "Before we left, Tess and I both told the group about our concerns. We showed them how much water we were bringing and why. We showed them which snacks we picked—salt over sugar—and why. But did they listen? No. They bought chocolate doughnuts and lunchbox-sized water bottles."

"It's a choice." Craig nodded. "And in this case, Gwen, I think I agree with you. They were on their own to FAFO."

"FAFO, Dad?" Gwen tucked her chin. "Where in the world did you hear that term?"

"Fool around and find out? Isn't that a thing you kids say now?"

Gwen grinned. "Yup. That's exactly right, fool around."

"So the miracle was the proximity of the houses and the distance in either direction to something else?" Goose asked.

"Yes, that and Otto happened to roll to a stop in front of a long drive to a winery," Tess said. "The sign said seven kilometers."

"But it was the heat of the day, Gwen, right?" Iris scolded. "Seven kilometers without knowing if the winery was open or still existed?"

"I didn't go anywhere, Mom."

"Otto decided that he'd hike to the vineyard. Half the group joined him."

"With a little water bottle?" Enrico asked with a shake of his head.

"They didn't know what they didn't know. Until you've faced dehydration, it's hard to fathom. Water seems ubiquitous." When she said that, Tess could feel Levi's gaze hard on her. She could feel that protective force that he'd radiate out like a magic shield.

But this time, something was different, like he was trying to tamp down a reaction that was borne of habit.

And it hurt to remember. It hurt to know that wasn't for her anymore.

Tess focused on her fingers, laced tightly in her lap. It was unfortunate that they should cross paths. There was little she could do about it. She needed to get through a few days; then he'd be gone. And she could throw herself into her work.

Licking her lips, Tess screwed her courage in place.

When Tess lifted her gaze again, Gwen was fluffing a hand

through her hair, sliding the strands behind her ear to expose her neck as she looked at Levi. "We stayed back and sat in the shade of the trailer. We figured there were more efficient ways to get some help."

"And the other half of the group?" Levi asked.

"Sunbathed," Tess said. "Gwen and I were comfortable enough in the shade with a gentle breeze except for a Kamikaze fly that continuously dive-bombed us with the most aggressive buzz I've ever heard."

"Tess and I had been successful when we got sand bogged at Big Daddy, flagging down cars. And that was our go-to plan."

Levi pushed his fruit bowl toward Tess with one last plump, gloriously red strawberry.

Gwen's eye dropped to the bowl, then up to Levi.

Tess held her breath. It was another act of muscle memory on his part.

Levi blinked at the bowl, then pulled it back, leaving it untouched beside his water glass.

He was right to retract the strawberry.

That had been a call back to the way they used to be together.

Levi always saved the best bite for last, and he always offered that bite to Tess. Be it a piece of fruit or something sweet—even if they had ordered the exact same dessert—the last piece, the one that was a symbolic show of sacrifice, Levi offered it to her.

This might be too hard to do, Tess thought. Maybe she should take the car and head back to Windhoek until Iniquus left.

Being this close to Levi left her bereft for the death of their future together.

Her heart was broken. Shattered. The sensations over-whelmed her.

But she'd been through this so many times over the years that she knew if she sat very still and held her breath, it would pass. Mojo crawled under the table until he was over to her, digging his nose under her clasped hands and shoving his head forward until it rested on her lap. "Hey there, Mojo. Thank you for coming to say hi." She bent to kiss his brow.

Tess was grateful that with that move she could both hide the trauma that surely painted her face and break the straw-berry-connection spell.

"The vineyard was open?" Iris asked.

Craig leaned forward. "Well, it would have to be, Iris. They brought us a bottle of wine from there."

"We could have broken in and stolen it, Dad."

For her part, Tess felt lucky to have Mojo, and she was lucky that this was not her story alone.

Gwen was taking up the slack.

"A car came up, and Tess stood in the middle of the road. They had to stop. She asked them if they'd mind driving up to the vineyard and telling them our predicament. We also asked that if they saw a group of people walking up the road in sandals—"

"Sandals? It was a fourteen-kilometer round trip." Enrico's brows pinched together.

"Yeah. We thought the same thing," Gwen said. "So we asked that if the driver saw the group would he let them know that the distress message was being delivered."

"When the couple drove off, Gwen and I felt sure the vine-yard would do something. I've found the Namibian people to be generous."

"Did your group turn around?" Enrico asked.

"They did," Tess said, stroking Mojo's ears. "The fortunate thing is that even though Otto has an ego that could have led to poor choices, in the end, he didn't take us up that mountain. It wasn't a road that people regularly traveled. No food, little water, no communication, wild cats, and a walk back to the highway that might have taken days, depending on where we rolled to a stop."

Gwen raised her juice glass. "So kudos to Otto for not being a dumb ass."

"Gwen!" her mother's brows flew to her hairline.

"To be honest," Tess said, "This was one of the most amazing side quests that I've ever been on in my life. What happened next went like this: after about another half hour or so, the vineyard sent a tram vehicle that picked up all of us and took us to the vineyard. They said we could camp there. This was not a tragedy because we had camping equipment. The other people on the tour, though, were adamant that we not stay the night. They were all these digital nomads. They all had work meetings in the morning, and the Wi-Fi reception was too weak for them to do their jobs.

Dad nodded. "They'd have to send a new vehicle from Windhoek to pick you all up, turn around, and drive it back. You couldn't depend on a patch repair on your vehicle."

"Exactly," Gwen said. "And that was the plan."

"How far were you from Windhoek at this point?" Levi asked.

"We were still about three hours away, then we'd have another three-hour drive back." Tess looked under the table as Mojo turned and curled onto her feet. "So our magical side venture—the vineyard picked us up, and we arrived to have a lovely bottle of wine. The same as we brought to you." Tess let her mind take her back to that time, seeping back into the care-free moment when everything seemed to go right. "It was very relaxing on the veranda. The temperature was comfortable. The sun painted beautiful colors across the sky as it was setting. Gwen and I were perfectly content."

"And, as it turns out, about a decade ago, someone brought the owners some cheetah kittens without a mother to teach them survival skills, making it impossible to return them to the wild. Much like our Betty, the cheetahs came to call that vineyard home."

"Not walking around like Betty, though, surely," Iris said.

"They were penned. Not a sturdy pen, mind you, but I guess it was enough of a pen if the cheetahs never learned to climb. As we finished our first glass of wine and were feeling very mellow and happy, they said it was time to feed the cheetahs. To go out and watch cost sixty dollars."

"To offset the cost of feeding, I'd imagine," Goose said.

"Yes, that's what we thought," Tess agreed. "They did have a big bucket filled with meat. They took us out in an open-sided safari vehicle. The views were spectacular. The angle of the sun made the hillside look like something that would inspire an artist's brush. We got to the enclosure, and the cheetahs were waiting for the guy. It was a little bizarre to see un-mothered adult cheetahs. They seemed to have been stuck in kitten mode, mewling and tumbling with each other. And so our adventure went. We had our little cheetah experience, then went back to the vineyard, where we enjoyed a lovely meal. And eventually, two vehicles showed up. They drove us back to Windhoek and let us out at the hotel. The end." Tess smiled.

"We got in at four in the morning, Mom. That's why we told you we were sleeping in vehicles. We had a bit more sleep in our rooms, then rented a car and came here, a bottle of wine in hand."

"Well, girls, I'm glad you have those memories. What a great story," Craig said, shoveling up a forkful of eggs.

Iris turned to Tess. "It seems that there's some magic in the air. In the last few days, you've been in situations that very easily could have turned dire." Iris squeezed Tess's hand. "We feel so fortunate that things have turned out the way they did."

"You gals need to stay safe," Craig added. "We need you around telling the world what catastrophes are heading our way."

18

———

Tess

WITH BREAKFAST COMPLETE, EVERYONE MOVED ALONG WITH their day, leaving Tess and Gwen at the table.

Gwen shifted over to her dad's seat so the friends were kitty-corner and better able to see each other and speak in tones that wouldn't carry.

"Who the hell are you?" Gwen thought friendship was no-holds-barred. Once a certain threshold of intimacy was surmounted, she took down any mask and said what she wanted.

Take it or leave it; that was who she was. And Tess, for the most part, found it refreshing because it meant she too could relax her social vigilance.

"Why are you acting that way around him?" Gwen pressed.

"Around whom? What way?" Tess knew; she was buying herself some time. She absolutely did not want to divulge her story to anyone.

"Levi, of course," Gwen turned toward his voice out in the courtyard where a group of children had gathered around him.

As she turned back, Tess raised a sardonic brow in response.

"When you're around Levi, you're stiff as a board, and you avoid eye contact."

Tess shrugged. "Maybe I'm just embarrassed that I was such a damsel in distress. That I needed to be scooped into this man's arms and carried feels ridiculous, even more so when there was absolutely nothing wrong with me. Yeah, grateful and embarrassed are weird bedfellows."

When Tess was coming down the mountain, she was ultra-aware that she was in Levi's arms only for pragmatic hero reasons. He would carry anyone. A guy, a grandma—it was nothing sexy or romantic.

God, he smelled so good.

Lying in her hospital room, unable to sleep with the constant nurse checks, Tess remembered all the times Levi had swept her into his arms and carried her to bed. When he was in *that* kind of mood, what followed was always amazing.

When he was standing on the platform at the top of the hill before the breakneck descent that had her clinging to him with eyes squeezed shut, his voice caught as he said, "Tessy, I'm sorry if this is awkward, but we did this before. Remember when you sprained your ankle on the hike?"

Did she remember?

Of course, she did. They were new to dating, out hiking for the first time when her foot went in a hole. He carried her down the mountain, took her to the orthopedic emergency center, made sure nothing was broken, ordered her favorite food, and took her back to his place at their shared apartment building. He wanted her to stay at his place on the ground floor so she wouldn't be stuck in a 3rd floor walk-up apartment while on crutches. He'd offered his bed and slept on the couch. He even called Shanti that night, asking her to bring down clothes because Tess's things were muddy, and she'd need her tooth-brush and pajamas.

Shanti arrived, giggled, and left.

And Levi couldn't have been more amazing.

Shanti said that when Levi opened the door to her, he had been such a super alpha hero protector that even she'd gotten a rush.

And Shanti was a card-carrying Gold Star Lesbian.

From Gwen's behavior this morning, she, like Shanti, had gotten the same kind of tingle when they saw Levi in full go mode.

It was completely understandable that Gwen found Levi appealing.

Who wouldn't?

"Oh my god, the whole scene was movie-worthy," Gwen gushed. "The way he lifted you, the way he held you—I mean, he treated you as if you were precious." Gwen paused and stared over to where he was laughing with the children. "To be honest," she said softly, "I'd like to be treated as precious at some point by a man who could scoop me up and carry me down the rocky trail, racing to save my life." She turned back to Tess and forced a smile. "Sometimes, it's hard to get my date to share his umbrella with me."

"Wait a minute," Tess scowled for oh so many reasons but voiced only one, "You wish you were the one that went through that yesterday?"

"Absolutely not. I would like that scene only if Levi wasn't actually racing to try to save my life. But you have to admit, that whole thing was rom-com worthy." Tipping her head, she added. "You seem embarrassed. That's not at all like you."

Embarrassment? She was just trying to make it through Gwen's Levi-gushing.

It hurt. All of it. And yet, Tess had no right to feel that way.

"Obviously, you hadn't planned for your foot to slip off a rock," Gwen pressed on. "There's nothing embarrassing about your actions. So that's *not* it."

Still nothing from Tess.

"He knew your name. He calls you Tessy. At least he did on the hill. That seems intimate."

"I knew Levi a long time ago, back in college."

Gwen leaned forward. "And he did something heinous? Some frat brother douchery?"

"Levi?" Tess pulled her chin back. "Never."

Gwen canted her head, assessing Tess for a long moment, gears obviously whirring as she tried to make sense of her clues. "You knew him when you were married to Abraham?"

"Before my marriage. Abraham and I were married during Levi's first deployment.

"But Abraham knew him?" Gwen was starting to see the picture.

"Yes, they liked each other a lot and got on very well."

Gwen tipped her head back and forth. "So, is there something going on between you two now?"

"Levi and me?" Tess looked away. "No, why?"

She pushed harder. "He's fair game then?"

Tess forced her focus to land on Gwen, forced her voice to sound unaffected. "He's his own person. Why would you ask me about that? I don't know anything about his life. I haven't seen him in almost two decades. You should ask Levi if he's relationship-free."

Everything in Tess's body clenched. And it shouldn't. Tess wasn't a jealous person by nature. But she hadn't asked, and he hadn't said—there very well could be a Mrs. Elliot and their children at home waiting for Levi's return.

It was probable that was the case.

There was no reason for her to be jealous about any part of

his life, and equally, there was no reason to be jealous of Gwen's interest.

All that was left of Levi and her were memories. Their separation was something she had imposed on him. And now she was a thorn in his side, a moment in time he needed to get through until they could both go on their merry ways, tossing this chance encounter into their memory boxes and shutting the lids.

Gwen had turned her full attention to the yard.

Mojo was outside with Reaper, Levi, Goose, and Enrico. The kids were nearby playing with their jump ropes.

"What are the men doing?" Tess asked.

"See that pole near them?" Gwen pointed. "Enrico uses it to train the puppies to bite the rope and play tug of war. It builds their jaw strength and the endurance of their hind legs as they pull. The working dogs still have fun with that when they're here making their etiquette rounds."

"Etiquette rounds," Tess laughed, relieved that the conversation had turned to something else.

"The K9s need to keep up their people skills. So they come here to hang out with visitors in a domestic setting instead of the kennels."

"But why is the rope coming out of a pipe?"

"Enrico explained that pipe is chest-high on a man. They want to make sure that they don't allow the dogs to train too high up for fear the dog wouldn't just take someone down but catch the neck where they could puncture an artery."

Tess gave a full-bodied shake.

Levi pointed at one of the kids, and the boy handed over his rope. He pulled out his phone and tapped until a song blared out.

A moment later, there was Levi doing his rope thing. He'd told Tess back in the day that he'd learned to do a hip-hop dance with a rodeo accent with a jump rope because he wanted to impress the head cheerleader at his school. And he had. She was very impressed with his skills. But that didn't make her any less a lesbian, so he'd put in the work and had this fun skill but never got the kiss. He did gain a friend, though. They were still close when Tess was in the picture.

That song over, the kids were jumping up and down, begging for another dance.

The music changed, and once again, Levi was twirling the rope seamlessly and effortlessly through his dance routine.

Gwen grabbed Tess's hand, shooting a quick look in Tess's direction. "Look at him! How is it you're not drooling?"

You can't drool when your heart stops beating.

Gwen turned her attention back to Levi without needing an answer.

Now Tess was looking at the back of Gwen's head as Gwen said, "So there's nothing there anymore. You're sure? It's okay with you if I see if he's interested in getting to know me?"

"I don't understand why you would ask me such a question."

"You obviously used to be a thing back in college."

"When I was in college, I married Abraham. I was a loyal married woman. That's all you need to know about my past relationships."

Knowing Gwen couldn't see her line of focus, Tess watched Levi showing the children how to do one of his moves and said, "I have loved deeply, and I have lost profoundly. I don't think my heart will ever be whole enough to love anyone else."

"Yeah, I'm not so sure about that." Gwen turned to her. "If there isn't something there, why do you act that way around him?"

Tess forced herself to turn away and drop a curtain on her emotions. "What way?"

"I don't know." Gwen peered at Tess. "Cowed? Ashamed? Vulnerable? Maybe the right word is fragile."

"You're misreading my emotions."

Gwen reached out to lay a hand on Tess's arm. "Then help me understand. Can I help?"

"I'm grieving. You're seeing me feeling grief for my loss. It bubbles up to overwhelm me at times. All I can do is move through it."

"I sometimes forget that you were widowed. That's," she shook her head, "not fathomable to me. That seems like something for much older people. But your husband died like ten years ago." She squeezed Tess's arm. "Not to diminish the pain of your loss, but still, there's hope for the future to feel brighter."

Was it okay for her to let Gwen believe that these feelings were for Abraham?

Did it matter?

Grief was grief.

What Tess decided to say was, "Back in college, Levi was on a gymnastics scholarship. Go ask him to do a dance on that dog rope and see what he can do. It's amazing." She stood. "I'm going to go grab a hat for Etosha. You should go enjoy the talented Levi Elliot."

19

Levi

They were leaving the vineyard just after lunch for a day testing Mojo's field skills.

Enrico had invited the others.

Levi wasn't sure he was glad that the Metz family and Tess had accepted.

But here they were. All of them.

"The plan is to watch Mojo do a search and rescue mission, then at dusk go see the animals in the park." Enrico stood by the open park vehicle as the group piled in.

Levi loaded Mojo into the cargo area then rounded to the vehicle to find everyone already seated and Gwen patting the seat beside her.

Doors shut, buckled, and engine running, Enrico glanced over his shoulder, "Gwen, your mom told me you're working with the effects of weather on feeding human populations. We're in a bad stretch here. Starvation for man and beast is a real possibility. If you're still on for a drive through Etosha at sunset, would you and Tess mind if one of my commanders came with us? You can see the animals, and we can pick your brains?"

"Talk about the weather?" Craig put on his ball cap and adjusted the bill. "Nothing makes Gwen happier."

"Sure, that's fine with me. What is the subject of the brain picking?" Gwen asked.

"As you may know, our emergency food stores are being depleted at an unprecedented rate. Everyone is hoping that with the rain, we'll recover and start rebuilding the reserves back to where they were. In the meantime, we need to cull our wild herds."

"That bad?" Goose asked.

"Worse," Enrico said. "The international news found out that a cull is planned."

"What are we talking here?" Reaper asked.

"Around seven hundred animals in all." Enrico put the vehicle in drive and started toward the highway. "These are round numbers: eighty elephants, thirty hippos, then impalas, about three hundred zebra, and another hundred of elands. The culled animals will come from five different parks for butchering, then be turned into biltong, a kind of dried meat from this region that's a bit like jerky and distributed to the people."

"We knew about that," Gwen said. "The reserves emptying so quickly and the upcoming cull is what spurred WorldCares to send us in and see what we think might happen with the drought. Our headquarters is worried that culling the animals will put significant pressure on your tourist economy. When jobs go away, hunger follows."

"It's a different world here," Enrico said. "When Westerners hear about the cull, some things will be easier for them to accept; the buffalos will be okay. "

"Impalas," Goose said. "They'll think of the car, not the animal."

"I couldn't tell you what an eland is," Gwen said, reaching for the shoulder seams on her shirt and shifting them back and forth until it fell smoothly over her chest.

"Why would increasing the food supply create economic pressures?" Iris asked.

"One of the problems is that people often don't read anything beyond a headline," Enrico said. "And the explanation will be the buried lede. In the United States, we're taught that wildlife in Africa is endangered and should be preserved. That took hold in a big way in the eighties and nineties when researchers shared their findings on elephant psychology, proving they're sentient beings with complex emotional lives."

"I remember doing fundraising to protect the wild elephants. There was the fear that they were dying out," Goose said. "Being from a tiny island in the Caribbean, the idea of animals as large as an elephant really caught hold of my imagination as a boy."

"Exactly, sentiments changed, and that has profound ramifications. Take Zimbabwe as an example," Enrico said. "Depending on tourist money to help protect their animals and help their economy, they benefited from the concern over animal extinction. People wanted to see elephants before they went the way of the dodo. Around forty years ago, Zimbabwe stopped culling their elephants. Right now, they have over a *hundred thousand* elephants, and their ecosystem can only sustain half that."

"What do you do with a surplus of fifty *thousand* elephants?" Iris asked. "Seems there wouldn't be enough food for them to forage or water to drink."

"They're encroaching into human spaces, which pits the farmers against the elephants, each trying to survive. It's a big problem with no easy answer."

"We have that situation on the East Coast in the United

States," Craig said. "Not elephants, deer. There's not enough food or water or space to roam. The deer end up too close to humans, causing accidents on the roads. The government arranges for rifle hunters in the country and bow hunters in the suburbs to come in and cull the herds. My hunt club participated in that regularly. We got to join in the sport of hunting. The butchers distributed the deer meat to needy families. It feeds the people, and the deer can survive because there's enough food, water, and space."

"Yes," Enrico agreed. "The numbers are figured out in an office as data points. Go here. Kill this number. Distribute them there, right? But people become very emotional about the idea of culling African wild animals."

"Strong feelings without the benefit of a lived experience," Goose said. "It's a balancing act."

"And this is the dilemma," Enrico turned onto the highway headed east of Etosha Park. "We have three main industries: mining, fishing, and tourism. Tourism is king. Now, the animals are dying. The people have little food. The supplies are depleted, and the government has decided that, like the deer that Craig was talking about, we need to cull the herds in order for everyone to survive. You're exactly right, Goose. It's a balancing act. If the tourists believe we're exploiting the animals rather than caring for them, Namibia could develop a reputation for bad stewardship when, in fact, this is not the case. The risk is that the tourists would find another country to visit."

"Sometimes treating them well," Craig said, "means culling them in a systematic and careful manner. It's hard to get that across when you're talking about elephants and hippos."

"It's a difficult set of circumstances," Levi acknowledged.

"Rain is the answer," Enrico slowed to a stop as a wildebeest moseyed across the road.

"At the vineyard, too, we're hoping for rain," Craig said. "That might turn things around."

"Over Africa right now, there's a new weather system. It might be promising," Tess offered. "It's nothing we've seen before."

"Ever?" Levi asked.

"Never," Tess pulled in a deep breath. "We're going to have to get used to the idea that what used to be predictable, like the start of the Namibian monsoon, isn't going to be as straightforward anymore."

Craig looked over his shoulder at Gwen. "That new system could mean rain here in Namibia soon?"

Gwen shrugged. "Hard to tell. The spaghetti lines look like they trace farther north."

"North like Angola, then?" Iris asked.

"Mom, I honestly haven't looked at the modeling since we started our vacation. I can get you the specifics once we're back at the vineyard if you want."

"Yes, please. I'd like to know that." Iris shifted around in her seat until her back was pressed to the sidebar. "I just thought the monsoon timing might have been something that came up at the conference you girls just came from."

"I'd say that conference was just a source of frustration and incredulity."

Levi heard an uncharacteristic note of defeat in Tess's tone.

"Why?" Craig asked. "What did you learn?"

Gwen laughed. "I learned that Tess has a theory that because of social media, we're all going to die. And very soon."

"What?" Reaper's smile became a chuckle.

"Gwen thinks it's my conspiracy theory. I don't think I'm that far off, honestly," Tess said.

Enrico tipped his chin up. "Okay, let's hear this."

"Fact, not a conspiracy theory," she started, "research tells us that the human brain gets a dopamine reward when it perceives patterns and connections."

"Basically, what you do for work with the prediction of how weather affects populations," Iris said. "So that accounts for why you girls like your jobs so much."

"I hadn't really put that together. But you're right. However, Gwen and I base our predictions on quantitative data. In a conspiracy theory, the connections aren't real. And interestingly, it seems to me that there's a significant social reward that comes with being a conspiracy theorist. People who are following the same conspiracy theories seem to feel like they're privy to secret information, and they form a kind of clique. For people who have trouble connecting, it's a social club."

"There's the monetary side of developing conspiracy theories, too," Gwen added. "Disinformation equals clicks, and clicks equals money. Because quacks on social media are treated as though their opinions have the same weight as facts, the words of people who make the subject matter expertise their life's work are relegated to the same level of importance as Jane the Human Weather Vane."

"People say, 'Do your own research.'" Tess pressed the flat of her hand to the side ledge, "They have no idea what they're talking about. I mean, to do this personal research, are they heading out in the field or into a lab? Or are they watching shiny influencer videos that are chasing those clicks? There are sources that debunk the bunk that are reputable. But a video link sent by a bestie far outweighs the academic, mainly because the academic is often inaccessible because of the vocabulary and advanced subject matter. We are living through an extinction period, the death of expertise."

"But this is weather, girls," Iris said. "What could they possibly be making up?"

"I have an example, Mom. Did you hear that for nine days

last year, a strange rumbling was detected?" Gwen looked around, and there were only shaking heads. "A seismic signal appeared in scientific stations all around the globe. They looked like the squiggles of an earthquake. A couple of theories were postulated about the cause."

Tess grinned. "The most popular was that aliens had landed, and their spaceships were being detected."

"Another prevalent conspiracy theory was that the government was doing experiments on controlling the weather."

"These are the scientists or the conspiracy theorists who are saying this?" Enrico asked, flipping on his signal and passing the slow-moving truck in front of them.

"The conspiracy theorists—who read the scientific data and made up what they wanted to—presented at our conference advancing the idea that something nefarious was going on that the government was trying to keep from the citizenry." Gwen bent to dig her water bottle from her pack.

"That had to spring from something," Craig said.

"Around the third day of the rumble, we saw the speculation start popping up on social media," Gwen said, unscrewing the top. "Of course, scientists came on to the threads, explaining that they thought that the signal machines were broken or that something had caused them to fail. But after more days of rumbling, the machines were all checked and deemed operable. The conspiracists grew louder and more alarmed. After nine days, the vibrations disappeared. The event was over."

"We have people who monitor those chats because we use citizen scientists," Tess explained. "They might, for example, track temperatures in their backyards or identify and count birds during migration. We include the volunteers who are willing to gather data for us in our forums. We could hear the alarm in their word choices. And we couldn't comfort them because we didn't know anything. In a vacuum of information, conspiracy theorists emerge. And once someone believes something, it's tough to change their minds."

"So it *was* aliens then?" Levi asked with a smile.

"This is the current scientific theory," Gwen paused to take a long drink, then screwed her cap back in place, "The concentration of greenhouse gases has increased the volatility of weather patterns. In our traditionally frozen areas, ice is melting at an unprecedented rate. The conclusion, as of now, is that there was a mega-tsunami. It was created by a wave when an ice break splashed into a fjord. What the apparatus was measuring was the sound of the ensuing wave."

Craig shrugged. "So the nine-day rumble is no more. That conspiracy theory will fade."

"It wasn't just that," Tess said, "we're facing a significant problem with the tech-bros and their philosophy: move fast, break things."

"My," Iris put a hand to her chest, "that sounds downright ominous."

"I was out in California a lot last year, volunteering for a science experiment," Reaper said. "And I heard something about that. Are you talking about the guys who are developing a way to offset carbon emissions with space pollution?"

"That's them. They were at our conference. Scary as shit." Gwen turned. "Oops, sorry, Mom."

"What now?" Goose asked.

"I don't remember the specifics, but in general," Reaper said, "they're releasing some kind of pollutants into the sky to try to cool the planet."

"It's a startup company," Tess explained, "that got a million dollars in venture capital to run their experiments. The future money would come in when industries offset their carbon footprint by purchasing sulfur dioxide balloons and shooting them into the sky."

"Is that a real thing?" Levi asked.

"It's called solar geoengineering, and it's a research subject in all the major universities right now," Tess said. "They think it might be an option to put a reflective substance into the sky, sort of like ozone sunscreen. Until I went to the conference, I thought that was only happening in the laboratories."

"People are actually out there sending sulfur dioxide into the atmosphere?" Iris asked.

"Into the stratosphere," Gwen said, "But yeah, that's what's happening."

"Who's funding that?" Craig followed Enrico's finger as he pointed out the front window.

"That's the training grounds over there," Enrico said. "Looks like they're ready for us."

"I think it's crowdsourced, Dad."

"There ought to be a law!" Craig railed.

"You don't know to make a law until someone does something like this that can impact the population," Goose said. "Mexico is leading on that."

Gwen pulled her pack up from the floor and set it on her lap, getting ready to get out. "And when they make those laws, the conspiracy theorists believe that the government wants to keep control of the weather all to themselves as a power move."

"You know what? I actually saw that playing out on a real-world mission." Levi said. "My clients believed our government targeted their colleagues for retaliation, and the U.S. showed their hand through the precision use of weaponized weather."

"Are you serious?" Gwen looked at him with flirtatious eyes, which startled him. Levi sent a glance toward Tess; yup, she was paying attention, and she'd seen it, too.

"Was this with Tidal Force?" Reaper's voice had a cautionary tone.

"A private contract I took on before I interviewed with Iniquus. The group that was affected was not my client. Client adjacent. They knew each other through business."

Reaper nodded.

"I was coming off my military contracts and started going through the process of interviewing with Iniquus. I took a week-long private contract with some buddies of mine to do close protection on the island of Capri."

Iris smiled. "There are worst places you could've been."

"Yeah, it was a hardship," Levi laughed. "Absolutely gorgeous island, beautiful water, just an amazing experience. The only thing that marred it was when we learned that there was—" Levi stopped and looked at Gwen, saw the same look in her eyes, and turned to Tess instead, "There's a stretch of water that Phoenicians used for thousands of years. There's a specific wind."

Gwen tapped her shoulder against Levi's. "The Mistral is a strong wind that comes down from the north and makes the Mediterranean choppy."

Levi felt a blush rise from his collar. "Yes, thank you. The coast guard assured us the Mistral wasn't blowing, and the area would have calm sailing. But then we got word from them that big storms were coming up, and so we insisted that our people stay in their hotel until the danger passed. That wind was intense. It was almost like a hurricane. It shook the buildings like an earthquake. My client's buddy was out on his sailboat. It was supposed to be unsinkable."

"Let me guess," Craig said, "it was named the Titanic?"

"It did go under quickly like the Titanic. Something wild and, as Gwen and Tess have been saying, unprecedented happened. There was a—I'm uncomfortable throwing out weather terms in front of you two—a downward pressure wind that I think they called a downburst."

Though he was looking at Tess, it was Gwen who answered. "Yes, that's pretty fierce.thought"

"The authorities believe it was a downburst or a waterspout, and it so happened to strike the exact spot where this billionaire's yacht was anchored. It was a tragedy. People died."

"And the government tie-in?" Gwen asked.

"The billionaire, who died in the event, had been under investigation for fraud, but, apparently, the grand jury said the prosecutors didn't have enough evidence to take it to trial, and the charges were dismissed. The conspiracy is that where the Russians might have accidents like falling off a balcony or down a flight of stairs, the United States could use precision weather to remove people from the equation. Making it worse, the billionaire's partner, who had been part of the same scheme, had died the day before. He'd been riding his bike along a bluff in Oregon when a gust of wind blew him over the cliff."

Iris's eyes were wide. "My goodness, I might see how a person could latch on to that conspiracy theory. What are the chances? Two acts of weather. Two different countries. Two people tied to the same crime?"

"In two days' time," Levi added as Enrico pulled to a stop next to a building, and the group all piled out.

But rather than walking toward the waiting rangers, they formed a circle.

"Gwen, this conversation started with you saying that conspiracy theories were creating problems for you at your conference?" Iris said. "If it affected your work, does that mean it had to do with Africa? Or even Namibia in particular?"

"In a way. Are you ready for this?"

"Doubtful," Craig said, leaning back against the vehicle.

"We'll explain more this evening when Enrico's colleague is along. But in general, there is an unprecedented shift in the winds. The conspiracy theorists think that the American insurance companies have developed a way to manipulate the winds in such a way as to make themselves more profitable. And that this year, they're testing it out."

"Wait." Reaper closed his eyes with a quick shake of his head, then popped his lids back open. "What now?"

"More tonight about the weather issues happening in Africa and Europe, but in America, the theory goes that the insurance companies were able to hold the winds on the east side of the Atlantic near Africa and Europe, saving East Coast USA from hurricanes. Then they tested to see if they could bring a hurricane inland and thrust it northward."

"Following that thought," Iris wrapped a hand around her neck. "Why would the insurance companies do that? They lost billions."

"They did it to test their equipment," Tess was definitely looking defeated, and Levi wanted more than anything to take her into his arms and comfort her. He shoved his hands in his pockets instead.

"Mom, the conspiracy theorists are saying that the insurance companies can manipulate the winds. The goal this year is to make the market hot by destroying homes. Everyone desperately wants to protect their house investment and will pay whatever it takes to keep their insurance in place. Next, the insurance companies turn off the wind and rake in the premium money caused by this year's panic. But the insurance companies have no fear they'll need to pay any future claims since they can direct the wind. The insurance industry gets mega-wealthy, and the executives go on to live plush lives."

"Wait," Levi stabbed his hands onto his hips, leaning forward. "They're saying what now?"

20

———

Levi

WHEN LEVI OPENED THE HATCH TO GET MOJO DOWN FROM THE transport, he jumped to the ground, his tail wagging happily. He obviously knew where he was and what was coming. "Mojo, we could light a house with the amount of energy pouring off of you, dude." Grinning down at Mojo, where he sat patiently impatiently at his side, Levi was grateful that Reaper and Goose had been on the same page with him so far.

They were all impressed with Mojo's actions yesterday when he moved with ease from a staged training session with copters and take-downs to a real-world mission with possible life-or-death consequences.

Enrico gestured toward the man approaching. "My colleague, Kimba, is a military K9 handler here at the park."

Kimba held a hand high, and everyone called their greetings.

"Okay, here's the scenario," Enrico said. "In a minute, I'm going to take control of Mojo. My colleague there is going to drive you farther out to a starting point. From there, you will walk to the find site. As of now, I don't know which site he's chosen. He'll send me the GPS for the rallying point after you're in place. Reaper, just so you know, this is a fresh location where Mojo hasn't trained before. We keep a map for each of our K9s and pin the area where they made a find so that there are no repeats."

"Interesting," Reaper said.

"It's important that these are real skillsets that will save real human beings. The vanity of a quick find has no place in the work we do. Every minute lost in the park with the predators is a dangerous one." Enrico turned to Levi. "You can calm your fragile nerves, brother. You're not in the park right now. And we have a soldier on overwatch with a high-powered rifle, lest a lion be out looking for a snack."

"Comforting."

Enrico turned back to Reaper. "At this location, we have a dedicated build-out to hide our search subject." He turned his head to catch his colleague's movement when he held up two fingers. "Two subjects?"

Kimba grinned and rocked back on his heels.

"Great. Well, Reaper and Goose, we've already decided that you'll be following along with a drone. Is there anyone else who wants to hide in the rubble for a bit?"

Gwen shook her head. "Nope, after yesterday, I'm good with the excitement."

"Craig? Iris?"

"Thank you, but neither one of us is good with walking too far these days. Our knees."

"All right," Enrico scanned the group, "well, we can leave it just Levi, Tess, I wasn't going to ask. It might be too much after your event yesterday. I could get one of the off-duty rangers to go along. What's the call?"

"What does this build-out look like?" Tess asked. "I feel like I'd like to help."

"No pressure, Tess," Levi said. "You don't owe anyone anything."

"I know," she smiled at him. "I want to. But I'd like to know more about the structure, before I commit myself, to see if I can handle it."

"Kimba?"

"Yes, this structure is for two lost persons. The main subject, Levi, will be in the front of the structure. You would enter into the back side of the structure. There is a box that has spaces for air and is very safe. Before you go, one of our K9 will search the entire area for anything that might bother you. Either of you can signal at any time and for any reason that you want to be removed from the training. But we ask that you lay still and not make any noise. We are testing Mojo's ability to track a single individual's scent from a scent source."

"That sounds okay." Tess nodded. "I can do that."

"The idea," Kimba continued, "is that Levi's scent will be offered to Mojo. He is asked to find the one scent. Once Levi is found and rewarded. We want to see if Mojo is aware of another lost person that he was not asked to find and how he handles the situation. And we have added a twist." He clapped his hands together and rubbed them back and forth in anticipation.

Levi leaned in. "Are you going to tell me, Kimba, or is it a surprise?"

"There is a camping site set up near where you will hide. Mojo will pass that before he gets to you. We have placed three of the scent sources you gave Enrico yesterday in the tent. These were positioned near objects that Mojo might see."

"Listening." A slow smile spread across Reaper's face.

"When Mojo finds Levi, I will lie down on the ground and

tell Mojo that I'm hurt and that he needs to find a solution to help you."

"A puzzle," Reaper said with a full-on grin. "I like it."

"We shall see what we see," Kimba concluded. "This is a complex rescue for him."

"But he's trained for it, right?" Levi asked.

"Here in the park, anything can happen at any time," Kimba said. "Our dogs are trained from the time they are puppies to identify items by their names and retrieve them. They are also trained to assess a situation and figure out the best item to bring when there is no command other than 'Help.' When they do this well, they get what Enrico likes to call a 'high-dollar reward.' That makes it one of their favorite games."

Enrico clapped a hand on Levi's shoulder. "All right. Luckily, today, it's not as hot as yesterday. For those lying in the structure, there are blankets for padding and water for your comfort. Remember that at any time you wish, you may leave the scenario." His head swung toward Tess, and Levi was relieved that his gaze continued on without making eye contact. Tess absolutely despised the idea that someone would think she was weak.

No one should *ever* think that of her.

There were few people that Levi had met in his life who had such a strong moral character and who faced their demons with such determination.

From what Levi had learned about the job that she and Gwen did, it looked like Tess was right there witnessing the human condition at its most vulnerable, facing her triggers.

Her desire to help was what made Tess Tess.

Leaving Mojo with Enrico, Levi followed behind Tess and Kimba to a quad.

As Kimba drove over the bumpy ground, the wind caught

up Tess's curls, and she pulled her hair around, holding it in her fist.

The drive was farther than Levi had thought it would be, but he understood the location once they'd arrived. Out in the distance, there was a thick grove of half-dead trees. Short and scrappy, the trunks weren't much taller than his six-foot-four frame.

"I will not walk with you," Kimba explained. "I don't want to add my scent to the trail. And Tess, if you coul maintain a path about ten feet or more to Levi's left, it would be helpful. When you get to the structure, Tess should circle clockwise and Levi counterclockwise to the openings, get comfortable, and then close the door. Mojo will be trailing only Levi's scent." Kimba handed Levi a GPS unit with a flag marking a spot. "Follow this out. If you want to circle trees and wend yourself around, that will complicate the trail. A K9 swept the area ten minutes ago, and we have a man with a radio on overwatch to warn you. Inside the structure, it is safe from most things."

"Most?" Tess pursed her lips.

"Rhino and elephants would be a problem. Now, as you get out toward the far side, there is a tent. We prefer that you not go into the tent but do walk up to the door and walk to the waypoint that I've handed you. The zipper is at a height that will force Mojo to crawl inside if he wants to search there."

"Excellent," Levi said.

Kimba pulled out two walkie-talkies, handing one first to Tess and then to Levi. "You know how these work?" He looked directly at Tess.

"Yes, I use them in the field."

"Good then. The station has been set specifically for this rescue mission. You will hear our radio chatter. We wish you to have them as low as possible so as to not alert Mojo. But you must be able to hear, lest we need to warn or instruct you." He smiled broadly. "Are you ready for some fun?"

"Absolutely." Levi grinned and stretched out a hand to shake with Kimba. "See you in a few."

As Tess set out walking by his side, Levi tucked his thumbs into his straps so that old habits weren't muscle memory. Her hands weren't his to hold.

"You look very happy about everything that was said. I'm sure it all means something to you as far as Mojo's training goes." Tess stepped to the prescribed ten-foot distance.

"This is a terrific setup. Enrico is a master of his craft. I really want Mojo to succeed here. If this goes as well as yesterday went, I am pretty sure that Reaper and Goose will sign off on Mojo, and he'll come home with me."

"He'll be your dog?"

"My dog."

"Mojo reminds me of you," she said in a voice that was reflective rather than conversational.

No one had ever known him better than Tess. "I'd like to hear more about that."

"From the beginning, he's been lovely. Hasn't he? Protective by nature, but not in a look-at-me kind of way. He's done what's necessary without hovering and being overwhelming. Steady, skilled, dependable. He's obviously a thinking dog. And when he offered emotional support, it was subtle. Soft. He didn't call attention to the fact that I was struggling. There when I needed it, and then went on about his doggy day when my system calmed. Mmm, that's vaguely right." Her gaze was on the ground ahead of her.

She walked in silence for a while.

"I'm still thinking about this," she said without looking his way. Then, she lifted her hand to gather the air and rub it through her fingers.

That gesture was something she'd done since he'd known her. It had a magical, graceful quality.

It seemed to Levi she was doing it more than usual.

"Qualifying the sameness in your characters isn't easy. I don't like what I said earlier. It's too surface, like a veneer thought." She painted a hand down her chest from neck to belly. "I've seen you two communicate. You're on the same wavelength. Enrico needs to call Mojo's attention to him and make a command. You and Mojo work together like old partners, each doing the thing that needs doing. I think, for now, that's the best I can come up with."

"Thank you. I value your opinion."

She stopped and turned to him. Ten feet away was much too far. Levi wanted to walk closer as he asked this, but he wouldn't chance messing up this evolution. Too much was riding on Mojo's performance.

"Tess, I hope this isn't uncomfortable for you. I'm mean ..." He flipped his hand over and drew his arm to the side in an arc. "I take it that you wanted to keep your private life private. Gwen ... " He let that trail off. "Seeing you has meant a lot to me. When I was at the hospital with you and on the drive back to the vineyard, it took me some time to process you being back in my sphere."

She gave a short nod, obviously braced for what came next, and Levi didn't want that. Deciding to ease into things and see where it took them, ready for any decision she might make, Levi tried, "I would like to stay part of your life going forward. I hope that we can be friends."

"Friends." She said it like she was trying to pronounce a foreign word for the first time. "I ... I ... I ... Yes, I think I'd like that too."

"Good then?"

"Good." She started walking again, but her head was turned away from him.

When she angled back she asked, "Do you think your wife will be okay with the idea of being friends with someone from your past?"

"No wife. No girlfriend. Just a guy in a new job and a new city. You're pretty close, right? Gwen said Annapolis?"

"When we're not in the field, yes." She bent and picked up a stick and whipped it back and forth through the air, making swooshing noises, and he let her process. Was she checking on his status, or was she simply trying to avoid future drama by accepting his offer of friendship?

Tess tossed a glance his way. "You had a dog in the military, right? You were about to go train in Texas last we spoke those many years ago." She turned her head completely away from him.

Levi liked that they were talking, trying to talk. Awkward—that he could acknowledge. And there was that tender spot that hurt when any kind of weight was put on it. But dogs were neutral ground.

"I did. I loved it. It's been a great career choice."

"When you left the Navy, what happened to your dog?"

"This will be the first time I have a dog that I train with consistently. In the military, I chose a dog for an assignment. That could last a day or several weeks if I were moving off grid for a mission. Having a dedicated dog was for specific roles. Otherwise, we had to share. They're just too expensive and long to train to tie a single fur-force to a single handler when they can be shared around."

"That sounds hard on everyone." Tess reached up and adjusted the strap on her bag, patting her water bottle. "And you had to carry your stuff and the stuff for your assigned dog?"

"Right."

"Water and everything, I'm assuming. That sounds heavy."

"Could be. That depended on the amount of time and if we were dropping in or hoofing it."

She sent him a grin. "*Paw*ing it, you mean, cowboy?"

"Yeah," he chuckled. "I guess that might be the better way to put it." Still awkward.

"Why does Mojo need to leave Enrico?"

"He's rhino sour. He can't work near them in the park, and the black rhinos are coming back because of a local initiative to protect them in their natural habitats around Namibia. So working with the rangers won't work either."

"What happened that made him act out around rhinos?"

Should he tell her? He should tell her. He should always be as forthright and straightforward as he could be with her. "A poacher killed his handler."

"Oh."

They reached the tent, and Tess waited as Levi stood at the entrance, circled it, wove in and out of the trees, and then started forward again.

"You're taking him, aren't you?" she whispered. "You're going to give Mojo a good home and an interesting job? You're going to keep his brain busy so he can redeem himself in his own mind?"

Levi knew that question came from a bruised place. But he couldn't promise Tess that was what would happen. "That's why today is so important. I think this is the last test before Reaper and Goose sign-off. Barring some crazy twist today, I'm all in."

"You, not your company?" She pointed. "I think I can make out the structure on the horizon. We're almost there."

"Iniquus is the company, Cerberus Tactical K9 is my division. Our operators handle their own dogs. In Command's view, it makes for a better team. They purchase the dog to do the work, but he's given to me, so the bond is tighter."

"How much would it cost to buy Mojo?"

"Seventy thousand."

"Seventy?" She sucked in a gasp. "Wow. To me, that's, whew! But then I work for a non-profit. They treat me fine, mind you."

"You have a PhD. They should treat you fine."

"Our resources go to doing as much good as we can. Fifty thousand sounds like a fine car that gets paid for over a six-year loan. Seventy?"

"It's a bargain. Well-trained dogs with good genes like Mojo can go for double that."

"Training time, yes. But how will you get—sorry, none of my business."

And Tess was doing that thing again, reaching out as if capturing a handful of air, then rubbing it over her fingers. She looked up at the sky and scowled. When she turned to him, her face had lost its color.

"Everything okay?" he asked.

"Something's coming."

A shiver slid across his scalp.

She'd never used that tone around him before.

Tess had never said *anything* like that to him before.

"I've felt the vibrations change from the time Gwen and I landed in Namibia until now."

The structure was easily visible now at twenty yards. Levi shoved the GPS in the side pocket of his pack. "Any idea what you're sensing? You were at Big Daddy, then Windhoek, then here. The ecosystems are different. Would that change the air quality for you?"

"Not this," she scanned from her left to her right, then startled and swung her head to look over her shoulder.

The ice that dumped through his system was the closest thing to terror Levi experienced outside of a combat zone.

21

———

Levi

THE STRUCTURE THAT THE SOLDIERS SET UP WAS PRETTY SLICK. Under a dome of branches, there were two long boxes at different levels. His was on the ground, and Tess's was high enough up that he lifted her into place.

They lay silently on the folded blankets, which were meant to cushion their bodies from the hard floor. Tucked into the corner, extra water bottles were within easy reach.

While the ceiling and floor of their crawl spaces were solid wood, the sides were constructed of randomly placed sticks that had been nailed into place. This camouflaged the person inside and removed any sense of claustrophobia. The sticks weren't solid sides like the plank boards he'd imagined; if need be, one could kick themselves free.

Not quite cage-like, this design gave Levi a fairly clear view of the search team moving toward the tent.

Mojo was working off-lead, nose to the ground, legs splayed wide, chuffing loudly as he moved along. This tested

Mojo's ability to track a subject-specific scent, ignoring all others.

While Levi's trail was fresh, there was a significant wind rustling the trees around them. When a dog air-scented, they usually searched for a generalized human scent rather than a specific person's scent. Whether that human scent lingered around for detection was weather and time dependent.

Colder was better; it held the scent toward the ground.

Heat, like yesterday, meant the sent would rise faster.

If it rained, things got difficult fast.

Today, neither the temperature nor precipitation should cause Mojo issues.

But there were two confounding elements. First, the wind had really picked up. The scent would spread in a cone shape. The wider the cone, the harder it was to track back to the source. And second, no one was going to signal Mojo that he should be searching for a second subject.

Now that Levi thought about it, when Tess made her gathering motion, it seemed like the movement came from the same place as a K9's scenting the wind. She would draw something through her sense of touch that other humans couldn't, just as K9s sniffed the air, finding the essence of something discernable to them, while Levi had no sense of the situation at all.

Right now, Mojo had tracked Levi all the way to the tent and, squatting low, had thrust his nose under the zippered tent door. Without a command, he wiggled his body inside.

Levi was excited to look at the video when the team got back to the vineyard that evening. Reaper and Goose were monitoring both drone footage and footage from Mojo's collar camera.

From Mojo's collar cam, the team would know exactly what Mojo was up to in that tent.

Levi was particularly interested in that information because when he squatted outside the tent to leave his scent by the door, Levi saw a Kong, some tennis balls, and a tug toy. All were poised as temptations to distract Mojo from his task.

The first test tracked Levi's scent from his last known location to the tent.

The second test was coming back out of the tent and back on the trail without further commands.

Levi was holding his breath.

Out Mojo came, nose to the ground, he circled the tent, then came right over to Levi and peered through the twigs.

Levi said nothing.

Mojo's nose twitched, and he rounded to where Tess lay still and quiet. He lifted on to his hind legs, put his paws on the structure, and looked in. He sent off two sharp barks.

Tess said nothing.

Mojo traced back to Levi, caught his gaze, and barked with a stomp of his foot before turning of his head toward Tess.

Levi said nothing.

Two barks, two stomps, and an extra-long glance toward Tess, Mojo was clearly angry that Levi wasn't helping her. When he didn't get what he wanted, Mojo ran back to Kimba, who was now lying on the ground. "Mojo, help."

Mojo came back to yell at Levi. And at this point, Levi felt it was okay to say, "Help." So Mojo understood he was also in trouble.

Mojo backed up and swept the area. He ran this way and that, back over to Kimba, licking his face. "Mojo, help."

Mojo's body held stiff with concentration. His ears twisted as he searched for the sound that could assist. He sat and sent three sharp "help me!" barks up and listened again.

Now, he was chuffing the air, looking from Kimba to the tent to Levi. He shot off, rounded the structure, and lifted up to check Tess, who stayed silent as requested.

Levi thought this whole process of Mojo's fact-gathering was fascinating.

Mojo pushed his nose as far into the twigs as he could force it, sniffing Levi, and then went into the tent.

Disappointment washed over Levi when Mojo reemerged with a tug toy in his mouth and brought it over to Levi, dropped it, and then barked.

Levi was at a loss for what to do here. He knew not to tell Mojo, "No, not that." The only word he was told to command was "help."

Biting the ball at the end of the tug toy, Mojo lifted it toward Levi, caught his eye then whined. Obviously, this wasn't about play. Mojo was too intense for that. He brought "help."

Mojo stood there waiting while Levi tried to imagine what Mojo had in mind. His gaze traveled from the ball up the rope to the loop at the end. "Good job, Mojo. Good help."

Levi reached through the space and accepted the toy. It wasn't easy, but Levi was able to get the rope around the door of his enclosure, slide the ball through the loop, and pull his hands clear.

Immediately, Mojo grabbed the ball and tugged at the door. He settled back into his haunches and pulled harder.

The structure shifted.

Mojo dropped the ball and ran over to check on Tess. He ran back to check on Kimba, licking his face and trying to rouse him. Then, he went back to his task of tugging his ball. And sure enough—sure enough!—the door popped open, and Levi was freed.

"Good job, Mojo. Good help."

Levi crawled free as Mojo ran around to check Tess, barking his very distinctive "Come here!" bark then peeked around to see what was holding Levi up.

Once Levi helped Tess down, Mojo led them back to Kimba so that he, too, could receive help.

Tess eyes were as bright as her smile. "That was absolutely the best. What a gift to take part in that."

Levi freely admitted that it was an absolutely magnificent sequence.

Mojo deserved all the pets and scritches that followed.

"The construction is supposed to simulate someone caught in a structure collapse?" Tess asked Kimba while Levi wrestled Mojo as a reward.

"Possibly. During past rainy seasons, there have been flash floods that have swept people along as the rainwater fills the dry riverbeds. When that happens, they're often tangled in the debris that is cleared by the water flow."

"Drowned?" Tess whispered.

"Often not. Sometimes, they're just tired from the swim and tangled in something like this." Kimba spread his arms to show the hide. "And they could use assistance getting freed up."

"If the pull toy wasn't one of them?" Levi asked. "What were the helpful objects in the tent?"

"There was a radio, an ax, and a hammer. We thought the best choice would be the ax to get yourself out, second, the radio, so you'd be in there longer and need someone to assist."

"Any would work."

"Any would work, but he'd bypass a first aid kit, the water bottle, and the staged distractions."

"A pile of steak might have done it."

"A pile of steak would have called in a lot more interest than Mojo. You might have been in trouble. The guy on over-watch only brought three bullets." Kimba elbowed Levi.

Enrico's quad pulled up.

Goose and Reaper climbed out of their open vehicle, all smiles.

"Consider my mind blown," Levi told Reaper as he shook Enrico's hand. When Enrico moved off to talk to Kimba, Levi said softly. "That's it, Reaper. Mojo's my dog."

Reaper nodded slowly. "I am right there with you. Mojo is extraordinary. Let's sit on that decision for one more day, though. I want to chat with Enrico about his program tomorrow."

22

———

Levi

Enrico rounded the back of the safari vehicle. He'd taken Mojo back to his house since the group would be out in Etosha Park, and sunset was prime rhino time as the animals made their way to the watering holes to drink.

Upfront in a covered cab, the driver climbed under the wheel and opened the little window cut into the back glass so he could speak to his passengers.

Behind him, there was an open space with a roof and bench seating.

The air was turning chilly, and everyone was grateful when Enrico produced the winter coats, hats, and mittens they'd all brought with them from the vineyard and left in his vehicle.

Enrico's commander, Josef, sauntered from one of the cabins with a stack of wool blankets. "Here we are. The temperatures will continue to drop as the sun goes down, and of course, we will have the wind blowing us." He handed a blanket to each of them. "Do not worry. I've told our driver we must be back here before the sun slips behind the horizon. The predators won't be prowling quite yet."

"Thank you," Gwen said, then slid onto the bench next to Levi, where he'd hoped Tess would sit.

Gwen slid all the way over to him until they were thigh to thigh, patting the seat next to her as she looked at her mother.

Josef settled in the front seat and Enrico climbed in next to him. "I had the opportunity to speak to Gwen while Mojo was hunting for you," Josef told Tess as she slid in behind Levi, sitting next to Craig. "She has shared some of her story. If you do not mind, I will pose the same question I asked Gwen. What motivated you to work with WorldCares?"

Tess pulled the wool blanket open and tucked it around her before she spoke. "When I was a child, I was a refugee of sorts. The weather had a significant impact on my family's daily efforts to remain safe. I want to protect people as much as possible. That was my aim when I worked on my doctorate, and I was very fortunate to find like-minded people," she held out an open palm to indicate Gwen, "with the same kinds of global interests. While it's wonderful to partner with other scientists at the university, I wondered where the information would go and how it would be acted on. Any research I conduct needs to support people and not be sold to an organization that might exploit a situation when those people are at their most vulnerable. WorldCares saves lives. While suffering will remain—it's the human condition—it can be mitigated to some extent."

Tess looked to her left as she spoke. And Levi wished he could see her face and read her emotions as she explained her story. She had, on occasion, told him pieces about her years-long effort to stay safe.

A familiar theme was that Tess and the Ya family weren't just trying to survive the civil war but were doing so through extreme weather events.

Until he went to war, Levi had to admit that he hadn't understood.

He knew Tess was telling him things about a life that she'd lived. But it was so far from his own experience—growing up a typical Oklahoma ranch kid—that in his mind, he'd filed those stories in the same place he might put a fictional novel he'd read or a movie he'd seen.

It wasn't that he disbelieved her. He *absolutely* believed her.

But without the lived experience, he simply couldn't fathom what life had been like for her as an eight-year-old child.

Night after night, she seemed to relive the horrors to the point that Tess tried to avoid going to sleep.

One thing Levi had learned through his experience with Tess was that when she felt endangered, his remaining a calm and steady force was imperative. Her cries sent his adrenaline through the roof, and everything in his body told him to fight for her. But there was nothing to fight. All he could offer was that calm and steady harbor.

Later, when Levi was in his own battles overseas, he'd used those skills he'd honed over the years with Tess to maintain his focus and calm. He felt sure that those skills helped him to stay alive and protect his brothers.

Of course, when he had those thoughts, Levi had to push them away because they tore at the hole in his heart.

Levi reached for his water bottle and tried to swallow down those memories.

Everyone seated, the safari vehicle drove down the pale grey dirt road.

"If you don't mind, I would like to start right away with knowing what the weather is doing here in Namibia."

"I apologize, Josef," Gwen said. "Because when we left this morning, I didn't know that we would be speaking with you, and since Tess and I are on vacation, neither of us has looked at the weather modeling in over a week. The best I can tell you is that when we left the conference in Spain, there was some agitation about the wobble near the equator and how it would impact both Europe and Africa."

Tess leaned forward to stick her head up where she could better speak to Gwen.

"Oh, here, this won't do," Iris said. "You girls need to sit together. Driver, could you stop for a minute?"

"What do you want us to do, Mom?"

"Well, switch places."

"We're not allowed out of the vehicle." Gwen protested.

"Can you pull over for one moment, please?" Iris called.

And, with laughter in her eyes, Tess switched places with Iris.

After retucking her blanket, Tess faced Gwen. "That one model of the wobble impacted Angola all the way down to the Namibian border."

"What did you think?" Gwen asked.

"It would be unprecedented. But these are the times we live in, right?" Tess tipped her head. "Never say never. Since it wasn't my model, I didn't follow through to see if Angola was warned to put it on their radar—so to speak. But if that outlier proved to be accurate, the wobble would have a significant impact."

"When would this happen?" Craig asked. "Wobbling? I didn't know that was a weather term."

"Dad, it's like this. When there's a powerful storm, it's not on a highway heading in a straight line. The movements that modify the storm elements around are called 'wobbles.' When you're looking at them on satellite, the shifts can seem pretty insignificant. But just the smallest movement can create an enormous impact."

"The air current is wobbling now," Tess said. "It's been impacting the weather in Europe all summer,"

Gwen turned to Levi. "Look there." She pointed to an animal nibbling on a tuft of dried vegetation. "That's a kudu."

"We think that wobble accounts for the torrential rains and floods in Europe," Tess explained.

"And that's why it's been a relatively calm hurricane season from the Caribbean up into the United States, except, of course," Gwen added, "for the system that affected my aunt."

"What would that spaghetti look like?" Enrico asked. "I'm sorry, I'm jumping back to Angola. What would happen if that one outlier wobble line was accurate, and it impacted Angola?"

"A deluge," Tess said. "For example, Morocco had six years of drought. Suddenly, there was a lot of rain in a short time span."

"Caused by the wobble," Gwen said. "Sounds innocuous, it absolutely isn't."

Tess gathered her hair and held it in a tight fist as the wind picked up. "One of their lakes, Lake Iriqui, had been dry for over fifty years, and it filled back up."

"Wow. How much rain came down?" Iris asked.

Gwen shrugged. "Like four inches in twenty-four hours."

"I mean," Iris fussed with her blanket, pulling it up under her chin, "that's a lot of rain in twenty-four hours, but enough to fill a lake?"

"Because there are sand dunes." Gwen shuffled around a bit, and now it was her hip that pressed against Levi.

There was nowhere for him to go to give her more room. He didn't want Tess to think that he was inviting this behavior, so he put his hands on the seat back in front of him.

"There's no vegetation to absorb the excess water. What's going to happen to all that rain? It's going to run directly to low-lying areas and pool."

"And the people?" Enrico asked.

"On the positive side of the human equation," Tess said, "the reservoirs are full. Those who suffered from the drought will now have a source of water."

"And the negative?" Levi asked, looking over Gwen's head.

"Because of the length of the drought and the arid conditions that persisted for decades, the people might well have built their homes in that area," Tess said. "Or houses were built of materials like clay that worked well under the baking sun but would disintegrate in water. Also, looking forward, the weather in the area may change for years to come because of the increased moisture in the air as the water evaporates again. What will that look like? We have no idea. This isn't something we account for in our computer models. More rain, at this point, will degrade their infrastructure and might make getting supplies over the Atlas mountains as difficult as it was when they had their earthquake." Tess pulled her hat lower over her ears. "The fast-changing weather patterns have become a challenge for WorldCares. We work hard to stabilize populations so people don't feel pressured to migrate away from the land and culture they know. But the weather is shifting faster than the people can adapt."

"WorldCares has a team of biotechnologists like my Mom and Dad, trying to forecast what strains of crops will survive weather extremes."

"Ah, the advancement of science. Did you know they've figured out that feeding cows red algae reduced cow farts?" Craig grinned.

"Thanks, Dad, that's good to know." Gwen laughed. "Or, like I was talking to a colleague and found out WorldCares is investing in a research initiative that sprays modified bacteria DNA on corn seeds so they don't need as much fertilizer."

"Okay, well, good," Craig said. "The sooner, the better. A

healthy planet is something everyone would aspire to." He leaned toward Gwen. "I'm stuck on wobbles, Angola, and its impact here in Namibia. Our vines are desperate for a long drink."

"No one has any idea. It's a stranger wobble than normal. But in a normal El Nino year, this sometimes happens," Gwen said. "Our colleagues are saying with the combination of El Nino plus the temperatures in the northern Atlantic, we might as well use a Magic Eight Ball."

"To Gwen's point," Tess said, "when you hear the term "breaking records" it means we've never seen the event before. If we've never researched it, it's hard to model. We don't know how to interpret the data. The predictions that Gwen and I generate are becoming more an art than science. Basically, we're taking an educated guess."

"And now?" Enrico asked. "What's the guess?"

"Personally, I've had my eye on a spaghetti model that dipped into Angola. I'd lay my money on the outlier."

"The outlier," Enrico repeated. "Then Namibia would come into play. If there are heavy rains in Angola, the flood basins in northern Namibia will fill."

"Which could help with our drought situation," Craig smiled.

"Maybe, Dad, but if it's too much, it's too much."

"El Nino, that will pass," Craig said. "Things should be right as rain next year." He turned toward a baby elephant, curving its trunk around the dry leaves.

"I'm not completely convinced it's all El Nino," Tess said. "The winds aren't getting that spin they need to get into the Atlantic. If they sit here, Europe gets slammed. If they move over to the United States, then the storm gets energized by the heat in the Gulf waters and becomes the mega storms that tried to skate your Aunt Pat down the mountain, Gwen."

"We saw that this summer's European flooding was probable and warned the Mediterranean countries' governments. Well, our org warned them nobody would have answered the phone if I said, 'Hey, it's Gwen Metz. Y'all are going to flood in August.' But WorldCares staged to go in and help in several areas where resources might be stretched thin." Gwen caught Tess's gaze. "I think we did a pretty good job calling it."

"Did you catch the flash flood in Spain?" Enrico asked.

"No." Tess turned, looking over her shoulder at him. "A flash flood is hard to predict and hard to prepare for. In general, we leave that level of granularity to the governments. Our goal is to project out between three and six months. We're looking at trends that will affect mobility—will people need to flee an area? That's something that is best to avoid. We have other specialists that consider the present government to predict how long recovery might take. From there, WorldCares positions resources in places where the weather will have the biggest effect on population survival."

"And you're here in Namibia." Enrico let out a long, low whistle.

"To be clear," Gwen said as she lifted her binoculars, leaning past Levi to scan, "things happen that we have no ability to predict—some aspects of war, some natural disasters mostly around geological issues like volcanos and earthquakes, and the resulting tsunamis. Morocco, last year, we were unprepared. It took us weeks to get help to the people stuck on the eastern side of the Atlas mountains."

"Houses made of mud in that area," Craig said. 'You know, if we had a torrent like that in Namibia, the suffering would be immense. You may not know this, Tess, I don't know if you went on a tour or not, but in cities like Windhoek, after the Nazis left the region, the South Africans took over governance. And South Africa Apartheid laws impacted the native people."

Iris added, "Namibia just got its independence recently. It's only a few decades old."

"Ancient and yet brand-new," Craig said. "The good people of this land have followed the laws regarding what kinds of shelter they can build and where. In the cities, they're compressed into a small area of packed earth. Their homes are neatly built, but they were allowed little more than wooden pallets and plastic tarps. They remind me of pictures of back in the Great Depression and the Hoovervilles."

With Gwen leaning across his lap, resting her elbows on the side of the vehicle as she scanned with the binoculars, Levi could see Tess. And he saw that look in her eyes she got when she was fighting down some memory from her past that had inadvertently sparked.

It might be that she recognized the structures from her past. It might just as easily be something he had no clue about. But there was a certain veil that closed over her, a dimming of the light that he looked for in her eyes, the muting of her normally gentle countenance. It was as if she could do something that made her disappear from sight, like an animal that sank into the environment to camouflage itself.

Levi knew that when she got like that, she needed a moment to remind herself that she was safe. He'd wait it out, keeping his hands visible, sitting still, and protecting her space.

He'd guess she was thinking of the children in harm's way. The kids who didn't have an Abraham who, as a teenager, swept a child into his arms and ran pell-mell for safety instead of dropping her to save himself.

Or a Mama Ya who took Tess under her wing in the years of unrest and kept her alive even though it put their family in lethal danger.

In Levi's experience, people like that were uncommon.

Right now, in his heart, Levi was right back to loving Tess

with the same fierce devotion he had when he'd left for that fateful deployment.

It was as if these last years were parenthetical for him. A sentence began (information was added) and now he could continue with his thought.

He was also right back in the raw pain of knowing how much he loved her when she didn't feel the same. If she had, she would have sought him out at some point over the last fourteen years since she'd been widowed.

That had been the double-edged sword that stabbed him all the way down the steep hillside when he didn't know if Tess would live.

To find her and lose her again wasn't something Levi thought he'd survive.

It had to mean something, her being here with him, right?

Hailey knew Gwen and suggested the vineyard; Gwen brought her friend, Tess, home with her on vacation; his connection with Enrico—all of that was like the weather systems that Tess and Gwen were talking about.

The convergence of elements could shift everything.

Maybe, just maybe, Fate was moving the game pieces around the board, and she had a plan.

Maybe he could hope just a little.

23

Levi

That night after the safari, Levi was too riled to sleep. He tossed and turned, and Mojo kept lifting his head to check on him. Mojo seemed to be on edge, too.

Levi thought maybe taking Mojo for a run would help them both unwind.

Tennis shoes tied, Levi was dressed in fleece for the chilly night.

It was well after midnight when he rounded the corner of the vineyard, and he found Tess reaching for the handle on the pickup.

Where could she be going this late and alone? He wondered if she was retreating to Windhoek until Iniquus left.

He made sure that she could hear his shoes crunching through the gravel so that he didn't startle her when he asked, "Where are you going?"

"Hey there. I thought I'd drive a bit to get away from the light pollution and take a look at the sky."

"Alone?"

"Out here? Yes, who would get me out here?" She climbed in and rolled down her window before she shut the door.

"Who? I don't know. Maybe you're thinking of the normal dangers. I know for sure you're the kind of a woman who would rather be alone in the woods with a bear than a man. Right?

"Statistically, that's a no-brainer. But you're the only man. And not a single bear to be found."

"Other critters?"

"Maybe." She pulled her hat lower over her ears. In the glare of the outdoor light, her nose was already pink from the cold. "I brought some pillows and blankets and thought I'd just go out, lay, and look."

He peeked into the bed of the pickup—pillows, sleeping bag, hiking bag—it looked like she'd planned to camp.

"I was in bed, flailing around, unable to sleep," she added.

"I'm sure you didn't sleep much at the hospital either, not with all the nurses' checks." He kept his voice low so as not to wake anyone. And he kept his tone light so as to not impose his emotional upheaval on her.

"And the night before that, I slept in the car—"

"Your cheetah side adventure." He smiled.

"Exactly. And the night before that, I was on a jackal-dotted search and rescue in the middle of the night to help a fellow traveler who was lost coming back from the loo."

"Which is what one does for a fellow traveler." He put his hands on her window sill. "You're exhausted, Tess. Why can't you sleep?"

"Too riled."

"Me, too. I get that. And so you thought

..."

"The Metz have their exterior lights on so people can move about safely at night. I thought I'd drive out a bit, so it was just me and the stars." She hitched her thumb toward the bed of the truck. "I sleep best when the air is cold, but I'm warm and snug."

Levi held back his, "I remember." He wondered if that was the easy part of the story and if there was something difficult that she'd left unsaid.

Nights for Tess had always been tricky times.

When she'd been on the run in Ghana, Tess had explained, she learned not to make any noise. Mama Ya told her that emotions rode the wind. Sobbing could be heard at long distances. Crying out at night could get someone killed. Tess knew that during the war, she hadn't made a noise, or Mama Ya might have had to abandon her to save herself and her own children. As an adult, Tess could understand the peril that this woman took on for a stranger.

In Ghana, sleep was silent.

Once Tess arrived in America to live with her aunt and uncle, they'd turned to medication for both Tess's sake and for theirs. But Tess hadn't liked the way it left her foggy for most of the day. As soon as she went to university with her own apartment, she stopped taking it.

Her roommate, Shanti, slept with a face mask and noise-canceling headphones anyway, so that hadn't been a problem.

Back when Levi and Tess were dating, and Tess had her ankle twist on the mountain, and they started living together more-or-less, she'd been embarrassed to wake him and offered to take the medications for his sake.

Levi refused.

He was afraid that Tess would still be having nightmares but would be so deep under the influence of the medication that he wouldn't know. She might experience the terror and not be able to wake from it.

After Levi got to Afghanistan, that kind of night terror activity wasn't unusual for his fellow service members, especially if they'd been on more than one deployment. It was just better hidden because bases ran twenty-four-seven, and there was always the noise of activity.

Levi considered that it was possible that the events of the last few days made Tess feel vulnerable to nightmares, and she didn't want the noise to call attention to her.

Maybe it was him. Maybe he triggered her.

Or maybe he was overstepping and jumping to conclusions. After all, Tess had always loved the night sky and the stars.

He didn't have to make this hard.

In fact, it was doing her a disservice.

She reached through the window and grabbed a handful of the sky, felt it with her fingers, and scanned the bowl of the Milky Way. When she focused back on him, she said, "That's a bemused look on your face."

"When you do that, I think you're an air whisperer." He grinned.

At first, she returned his smile. "Sounds magical." Then the smile fell off, her brows furrowing in the middle. She said quietly, "Yeah, there's something down low in my gut."

"Parasites?" Levi raised his eyebrows toward his hairline. "You've been eating the game meat."

"Yes, but it's cooked." She started to roll up her window. "Nice seeing you."

He left his hand on the top of the glass. "Tess, I was teasing. Come on now. I want to hear. And I want you safe. This isn't a country either of us is used to visiting. You don't know what you don't know until it's damned dangerous that you didn't know. And you're thinking of sleeping out here all alone?"

"Okay." She lowered the window again. "I think I followed that. You look like you're going for a run. It's—what do you call it?—zero dark thirty? But if you and Mojo want to ride out with me away from the vineyard lights, I see no reason you shouldn't."

He ran around to the left-side passenger seat and climbed in.

Mojo insisted on sitting between them.

"Hello, Mojo, sweetest of all the sweet boys." Tess crooned. "Are you getting along with Levi?

After Levi pulled the door shut. She lifted her foot off the brake, and they rolled forward.

Mojo laid down and put his head in her lap.

Watching her profile as she drove out, Levi's pain started to lose its barbs. He had high hopes that he could get some of his questions answered.

He'd always understood that there was more to the story than he was being told. He had always believed that she truly, deeply, cellularly loved him. He just couldn't understand, under those circumstances, the betrayal of her marrying another man.

But this wasn't just any guy. This was Abraham.

And Abraham had sacrificed everything for her. The food from his plate, the last drops of his water. When she was weak and tired, he carried her on his back as the family made their way from space to space, trying to find a safe place to rest their heads.

If Abraham had needed her, Tess could do nothing other than to help him.

If she could turn away, she wouldn't be the Tess that he loved so ardently to this day, the pain still fresh and throbbing.

As a SEAL, he knew the debt he felt to his brothers who saved his life not once but time and again over the years. What would he do for them?

Anything in his power. Absolutely anything that they asked of him.

He understood. He'd understood for a long time. And there was the boulder, sitting on his chest.

Keep it light, man, Levi counseled himself. "How's your family? The children?"

"Adam and Mordecai! You wouldn't recognize them. When you saw them, they were toddlers, and now they're men. It's astonishing. Adam is working on a master's in urban planning, and he plays bass in a jazz band. Mordecai is my athlete. He's finishing his bachelor's degree in physics. He's applying to graduate programs."

"Smart kids."

"Humble, generous, kind children. They are a balm when life chafes. I'm so very lucky to have them in my life."

"And you?" he asked, resting his hands on his knees.

"Me what?"

"Did you have children?"

"That's not the kind of relationship that Abraham and I had. When he reached America, he was very ill. I think he waited too long to call me. Sometimes I think, perhaps, if … But had he called me sooner, I would have missed out on us. And that would have been a great loss." She didn't look at him when she said that. After a moment of silence, she added, "I don't think that's what you want to know. I think, for closure's sake, you want to understand why my letter was so short with no explana-tion." She threw a glance his way, then turned to stare out the windshield. "When I got the phone call from Abraham. Shanti said that you would never forgive me. And I believed that to be true." She sucked in a breath and held it for a long moment before she said, "I knew the pain I was feeling, and I imagined the impact of my decisions on you. I was selfishly guarding myself. If you … I don't know that I have the right words for this. I'm going to try. I knew where my heart and where my duty stood. Adam and Mordecai needed me. To abandon them would be impossible. *And* I owed you an explanation. But if I saw you, I was afraid that I wouldn't be able to follow through with my vows to Abraham. I was afraid of myself and what I might do."

"He died."

She looked out over his shoulder with a million-mile stare. "Yes."

"Fourteen years ago."

Her lips barely moved. "Yes."

"And you didn't look me up, Tess." Levi couldn't keep the wound—or the recrimination—out of his words.

"How could you have forgiven me for our past? And how would you forgive me if I showed up out of the blue? What if I stepped into your life only to remind you of pain and anger? And since I knew nothing about your life, I wondered if I would step in and possibly cause conflict in a new relationship. But there was more. When we were together, you were my priority in every decision I made. But fourteen years ago, I was a twenty-something-year-old single mother of two little boys who had lost their whole world—their mother, then their country, then their father. I made vows to Abraham and vows to myself. To keep those vows, I would have had to shuffle you into my family life, and that wasn't a place that you would recognize. Would I ask that of you?"

"You stayed away to protect me."

"Of course."

She stopped the truck in the middle of nothing, put it in park, and climbed out.

And Levi was glad.

He wanted this conversation. But the pickup cab was too small for his big feelings.

Tess held her arms wide and began to spin around and around until she was stumbling sideways, and Levi caught her.

She used to call that being "drunk on starlight."

Levi brushed the curls from her eyes and let his hands fall to her hips. He was looking for a reaction to an intimate move. Was that all right? He decided it wasn't.

Instead, he rounded to the back of the truck, lowered the tailgate, and climbed in, sitting on the nest of blankets and calling Mojo up beside him. "Come sit, Tess. Let's have this out. Okay?"

Without answering, she clambered up to sit across from him. Folding her legs into a crisscross.

And there they were.

Time passed in silence.

Someone needed to start talking so he took this approach, "I remember this, the meditation of sitting in silence, looking into your eyes. On particularly hard nights in Afghanistan, I'd recall those times, and it settled me. It's how I fell asleep."

She pressed her lips together and looked down to rub the edge of a blanket between her fingertips.

"Knowing your heart like I did, I can't imagine the weight you've borne. It occurred to me from time to time that it was a kind of compliment that you thought I was strong enough and resilient enough to take on the burden of your decision."

"Did you doubt my feelings for you?" she whispered.

"That no, never. Which might have made it harder in some ways. I knew there was a damn good reason." Did he want to go there with this conversation? Yeah, he did. "When we went to Momma Ya's funeral, and I met the Ya family, the ties were palpable. But you know, at that time, Abraham was married with a third child on the way. I liked him, I respected him, I felt nothing but deep gratitude to him."

"Yes," she murmured.

"So when you told me you were marrying him, let's just say I was deeply conflicted. And I'm not proud of my thoughts or my emotions. Fast forward to when I found you on the hilltop. I was so damn pissed at you. Not about the past and not about what happened to our relationship. I was just so angry. My thoughts? The moment I saw you again, you were trying to leave me. It was irrational, I get that. But there it was. I didn't want to lose you and mourn you again."

Mojo crawled into Tess's lap, and she looked down at him, stroking his fur.

Look at her. She is so beautiful.

Levi couldn't pull his gaze from Tess. He drank her in. Drank in all the changes from the last time he'd seen her.

Her intelligence shined through as always.

Tess's mind had always been an aphrodisiac to him.

"I trusted that you were making decisions about something bigger than you and that you were acting selflessly. And I put that here on my shoulder with the good angel that whispers in my ear. You always lived on that shoulder." When she looked up, he tapped his right shoulder.

"On the Angel side."

"Yes, exactly."

Her hands kneaded Mojo's ears, and he let out long, low rumbles of pleasure. "Tell me about the other shoulder, the devil one."

He caught her gaze and let it hold. "I'd rather not."

Tess sat quietly, waiting.

"I've been angry, honestly."

"Fair."

"No, Tess. The rage I felt wasn't fair, which made me angry with myself, with life, and my future."

"I'm sorry, Levi. In my mind, you mourned the end of our relationship and moved on."

Levi monitored his tone to make sure he didn't sound bitter when he asked, "What did that look like to you? Wife, kids, mortgage, and gutter cleaning? Beer and football?"

"A wife who was athletic and beautiful. I imagined you had three kids, and they were all adventurous like you. You'd pack the babies into backpacks and climb mountains. Black Diamond ski vacations with hot cocoa around a roaring fire. I pictured beautiful things for you because I wanted beautiful things for you. I wanted you happy. I wanted your wife to have come through a normal childhood without my baggage. I wanted you to forgive me and forgive the situation."

"I'd told you you're my life," Levi said quietly.

"I thought that was youth talking."

"Well, as it turns out, it wasn't. And honestly? I tried for what you described. But whenever I was in a relationship, I'd look into the woman's eyes and realize I was trying to make it work, but it felt plastic and unnatural. And ultimately, it was unfair to let someone I cared about feel that, on some level, she wasn't up to being—"

"Me?"

"Yep."

"You told women about me?"

"As a parting explanation. I'd explain that I felt unfaithful to you by being with them, and that was obviously my crap and had nothing to do with them."

"You wanted them to move on to better relationships."

"I did. But I didn't have to do that frequently. I mostly kept people at arm's length. Like I said, anything else felt like cheating."

Tess nodded. "Same."

"Since you were married, that must have sucked."

"Abraham had stage three testicular cancer. It sucked for sure, just not for the reasons you're imagining." She sighed.

"I'm sorry for all that. For everyone involved. I'm sorry that there has been so much pain and heartache and that it seems to spread like ripples in water. Touching so many people."

"You're not responsible for my emotions, Tess. I'm a big boy. I'm just calling it like it was for me. Seeing you, I'm suddenly standing alone in a storm with no shelter."

"Same." That word sat between them. Then she asked, "What happened after you got my letter?"

When he learned that Tess would marry Abraham, her choices hollowed him.

His heart was a rock dropping in a well, pinging against his insides with its descent.

Levi could guess the bigger picture was dire for whatever reason and that Tess was acting on the strength of her personal courage and sense of integrity.

Yeah, Levi understood what it meant to have an ethos. It was one of the things that had always made him feel a hundred percent comfortable when Tess said she loved him. A thousand percent comfortable that if *he* went to war, he would never get a Dear John letter.

For a long time after that letter arrived, Levi didn't give a crap if he lived or died.

He got all the ribbons and metals to pin on his uniform because he was the first to raise his hand and run into the fray. Frankly, he'd hoped a bullet found him and put him out of his misery.

But while he put himself out there, willing to die, it didn't make him a loose cannon. Levi understood that poor judgment on his part would put not only his Team brothers but also the pilots and the PJs at risk while they tried

to make the rescue.

If he were hit, his brothers would be responsible for his body, either saving it or transporting it.

Levi wasn't going to allow his misery to endanger others.

He credited the dogs he worked with for keeping him going. His work with the K9s was the only thing that tempered his grief.

"After the letter?" Levi asked. "I haven't gotten my feet under me since. I just roll from mission to mission, focusing on the three feet around me. Head down because there was no horizon line to focus on, I tried not to trip myself up. Yeah, untethered." He rubbed his thumb along his jawline. "Seeing you was a gut punch, Tessy. More so because your life and limb were at risk, and I was right back in my gorilla emotions.

"Gorilla emotions." Tess chuckled.

"You've heard of turning into a Mama Bear."

"Been there. Done that."

"So, for me, it's more like a silverback four-hundred-pound gorilla. I wanted to protect you with my life, for you to know that you were safe, for the nightmares, and the screams to stop. And my ego wanted it to be me that did it."

She touched her left shoulder, "And your devil side thought that the reason I chose to marry Abraham was because Abraham had always kept me safe?"

Levi leaned forward to look deeply into her eyes. "Exactly. Abraham kept you safe, and I wasn't up to it." He tipped his head back to see the heavens and to remember that in the grand scope of things, he was like a tiny speck of dust. When he lowered his head again, he added, "I believed for a time that that was why you married him. And then it occurred to me that there was more to the story, and I didn't know what it was. I got to the point where I thought you hadn't married him for your safety and your mental health stability because he would be a daily reminder and a daily trigger. But then I wondered," he tapped his left shoulder, "the devil side wondered, why you wouldn't tell me the story? Tess, I didn't know you were bringing up the children by yourself. I didn't." He shook his head. "I didn't know."

"And had you known, you would have stepped in and been your guerrilla self." She sighed. "During that time, I had the boys, and they gave me purpose. I had to get out of bed every day to make sure they ate. Did you have something? The dogs?"

"I have leaned into dogs, yes. But because the dogs kept getting rotated, I put up a wall. I'd just pretended that every dog that came through was one of those people you meet on vacation. You have a great time, you promise you'll keep up, and you all move on with your lives. I would talk to the dogs as we went out for our runs. And it helped, bark therapy. Tess, here's the brutal reality—for a long time, I couldn't stand being in my skin. I'm telling you all of this because I think you need to hear my experience. I didn't look you up during those years, either. Those gorilla feelings that would protect you from anything included protecting you from me."

She looked at him with surprise. "Why would I need protection from you?"

"Ha! I'm trying to get up the courage to say this. I won't turn away from any fight, and I, by nature, run into any danger. But this feels … I don't really have a word for it, but here I go. One of the reasons why I was angry—and have been angry—is because your decisions deprived us both of love."

Those words hung between them, and Levi held his breath. Was that too much? Had he crossed a line?

Tess's words were barely audible. "Mama Ya always talked about how Fortune's Wheel turns, and it feels like the wheel is right back to the top again. Like the time that needed to pass has passed, that the things that needed to be done on our own were done, and that we're back to each other. I want to ask you if you think that—now that our lives have shifted, now that the kids are in college, and you are out of the military—do you think it's possible that we can find our way back to each other?"

Levi leaned forward, capturing Tess's face between his palms, painting his thumbs over her cheeks, then angled his head to kiss her.

Her lips, soft and chilly, radiated warmth through his whole system, and his blood pulsed with joy.

24

———

Tess

As Tess reached the corner of the veranda, she heard the murmur of Gwen speaking to Levi.

Approaching, Tess was able to make out Gwen's words.

"—that she was raised in Ghana. From her early childhood, I think something's there. I would never ask. I'll tell you this, though, Levi. Tess is one of the bravest women I've ever met. I mean, we have been in some very dangerous situations, and she seems to know somehow how to escape the bad guy, or the weather, or out-maneuver the destruction of force. I'm always glad when I'm assigned to work with Tess because, as fragile as she looks, it's only one of her adjectives. She can think in the moment. And no insult, but I'd honestly feel safer with her than I would with like someone like you. You might have skills and brawn, but she has tenacity and creativity."

"She's a remarkable woman," Levi agreed.

Tess looked behind her. Should she retreat? Make some noise so they knew she was there?

Iris waved good morning as she and Craig approached. Now, Tess was stuck there, waiting for them.

"Tess said she knew you back in school," Gwen's voice floated around the corner. Her voice was no longer flirty like it had been yesterday on the safari. There was a cautionary tone. Tess could imagine that Gwen had realized there was something between Tess and Levi and had adjusted to the circumstances.

"We knew each other in undergrad," Levi said, "after I joined the Navy, we fell out of contact. Life gets in the way sometimes."

"I feel big-sisterly toward Tess. Levi, listen to me. I am asking you not to hurt her."

Before Tess could hear Levi's response, Iris scooped an arm through Tess's as she kept walking. "Looks like you're heading out for an adventure."

The sky was a brilliant blue, shining through patches of clouds.

As they rounded the corner to approach Levi and Gwen, a change of conversation was in order. Tess pointed up. "They look like the spots on a giraffe's hide." Then she reached out and gathered the air.

Something was *wrong*. More wrong today than yesterday.

Tess scowled at the sky. Whatever this sensation was, it was new to her, and she couldn't predict what would come next. That made Tess feel as vulnerable as Gwen had described her.

As the group approached, Levi and Gwen swiveled outward to include them in their conversation. "What are you seeing, Tess?" Gwen asked. "Those are just cirrocumulus clouds."

Tess rolled her lips in as anxiety clutched her chest. What *was* she seeing?

Mojo left Levi and came to sit beside her.

"What's this?" Craig tipped his head back.

"Those are high-altitude tropospheric clouds," Gwen pointed.

Tess dropped her hand to Mojo's head. "It shows that there's convection and small amounts of liquid water droplets."

"As opposed to ice crystals," Gwen explained.

"Water?" Craig held his fists up as if he might be ready to thrust them high overhead in a victory dance. "Rain?"

"Yes and no," Tess muttered under her breath. "If it does precipitate, you're looking at a virga—a dry storm."

"Like Tess's dry bite," Gwen explained. "You think it's going to be something, but it's not. The precipitate evaporates before it reaches the ground. Namibia won't get any relief from those clouds."

Tess looked at Gwen, unblinking for a moment. Her brain was racing so fast that she didn't even have a clue what she was processing.

"Right, Tess?"

A growing storm were the words that filled Tess's head. But nothing was there that looked concerning. It was all as expected in Namibia at the very end of the dry season.

Tess exhaled, pulling her lips into the figment of a smile.

She felt the crush of too many people and too much unwanted focus when all she wanted was to look at the sky and understand.

Levi's instructions today were to hang out with Mojo and see how they got along when they weren't mission-focused.

When Tess said she was interested in going to visit the Himba village, she'd invited him along.

And now that they were here, walking toward the chief

sitting under a single tree, carving a giraffe for tourists to buy, she was glad she hadn't come alone.

This experience was very awkward for her.

After receiving permission to be there and walk past the *okuruwo*—their sacred flame, Tess, Levi, and Mojo moved forward with their guide.

There were groupings of women in their traditional garb—belts and decorations but little else. The women glowed from rubbing a paste of crushed ochre and fat into their skin. And their hair was protected by encasing their braids in red clay.

Around them, their babies, naked except for cowrie shell belts around their waists, played peacefully outside the huts.

Tess and Levi had an English-speaking guide from the tribe who was there to educate and translate.

And it was all so very uncomfortable. *Very* uncomfortable.

The best metaphor that Tess could land on was a day when she went to the amusement park with her aunt. There, they had a bird show. A handler would come out with a bird on his finger and start describing the bird, pointing to the body part being discussed.

In this case, a teenage boy from the Himba tribe had a stick in his hand. As he moved through his explanation, he would tap that area of the woman with the end of the stick.

For Tess, the point when she was so uncomfortable that she turned away happened when the teenager talked about how the tribe removed a bottom tooth. He tapped the woman's mouth, and dutifully, she dropped her jaw to show her teeth.

The Himba people seemed fine. It was Tess who reacted.

Levi leaned in, "What are you thinking Tess?

Then she stopped to consider his question.

Yes, the situation felt wrong to Tess.

But was that the whole problem?

Or was there something more?

"Men and animals have use of the water," the guide said, "women do not. Instead of bathing in water, they bathe in smoke. A woman will hold her armpit over the smoke of a small fire, trapping the smoke with her cape. She will sit there for some minutes. And then she will move on to a different body part."

"Smoke bathing," Tess said, her mind flooding with questions. No water to clean themselves *ever*? And what about the monthly cycle? Surely, the women would need water to wash up from that. Those questions were on the tip of Tess's tongue, but she was not sure she wanted to know.

On the way to the village, Levi shared what Enrico had said the other day, that the tribespeople lived in regular houses. This was their day job. It was like going to see a historical reenactment in the States; the people worked in the eighteenth century during the day with hoop skirts and powdered wigs, and at night, they were just like everyone else, pushing a cart down the grocery aisle and eating ice cream from the carton in front of the television.

Still, the guide was poking the woman with a stick again.

The guide turned to Tess, "What questions do you have?"

Tess turned to an elder. "Are you anticipating rain today?"

After an exchange, their guide said, "No rain any day. Those clouds are normal for this time of year, but rain would be improbable."

Tess scratched the back of her head and reached out to feel the air again tipping back. "Do you ever get thunder and lightning?" she asked.

The guide looked up at the sky and then at the women. "I've never seen it, no."

"Huh." Tess held her arms out wide, palms up. And then let her gaze sweep the sky from horizon to horizon. She weighed the air in her hands as if she were a scale and then lifted one hand up over her head as if she were scooping air into her palm. And then she rubbed her thumb against her fingers.

Mojo had his nose in the wind, nostrils quivering as he sniffed the air, then he gurgled a whine from deep down in his throat.

"Talk to me, Tess."

Tess focused on the guide. "I don't want to be an alarmist, but I have a question. Are there precautions in place for flooding?"

"Here?" The guide turned and conferred with the elder, listening intently, then told Tess, "When the rains fall in Angola, the floods happen in the villages farther north." He lifted his chin to show the direction. "Aunty said that when the rains come down, they naturally fill the flood basins. It doesn't happen often. This is a problem for the people who are not used to flooding because they built their huts where it will flood. This is a poor choice."

"But here in Etosha?" Tess insisted.

"We're too far from Angola to be bothered by it. Besides, September is the end of winter here, the end of the dry season. We might get some rain next month."

Tess leaned back and looked at the sky.

Levi stood perfectly still, and she was grateful that he kept his energy away from her. She needed to concentrate. She was remembering. It was something from her deep past. But when she tried to grab at it, it disappeared like smoke in a breeze.

"It rarely floods here, and we like it when it does. It seeps into the ground, and after, we have a good harvest," the guide seemed as though he was trying to reassure Tess. "Though, once I was in Windhoek, and we got three weeks of rain in twenty-four hours." He moved his hands to his heart. "Two children were swept away, and later, their bodies were found by the dam."

The event had an obvious effect on him. Tess put her hands to her heart in response. "I'm so sorry. Two precious children is a terrible loss."

The guide looked up at the sky as if trying to see what had upset his visitor.

"This isn't good," Tess said and blew out. "It's really not good, Levi. I need to call Gwen. I need information." She rounded one of the huts where the small children sat in the dirt, tracing their fingers through the powdery soil.

When Tess and Levi arrived, she'd spotted their guide on his cell phone over here near the pen with the lone goat. Tess had surmised there was a hidden WiFi connection nearby.

And standing where he had been, Tess was able to get Gwen on the phone. "Gwen, I need you on the computer. Start with history. Has this region ever flooded?"

"Looking."

The minutes stretched out, and Tess's anxiety mounted.

Finally, Gwen said, "Yes, about twenty years ago. I'm scanning the article that I pulled up on our system. There was a flood that killed forty-two people, mostly children and elders who were swept away in a flash flood."

"Where did the water originate?"

"From Angola. Okay, here's more. WorldCares sent in helicopters to evacuate people stranded on high ground without food, drinking water, or shelter. They dropped MREs and water bottles while they performed the prioritized evacuation sequence—nursing mothers with their infants, then young children, then twelve and up. That was a big mission. But it was in February, which would be the wet season. Wetter than usual." Gwen paused, then asked, "What does your intuition tell you?"

Tess whispered. "It feels like a disaster."

"Mom and Dad are here. They need to know what's going on."

"Tess, sweetheart, are you in trouble?" Iris's worried voice came through Tess's phone.

"Hang on, Mom. Just listen for a minute, okay? Hey, Tess, when we were on safari in Etosha, you mentioned that spaghetti model that trailed down to Angola, the outlier."

"Yes." Mojo had rounded in front of Tess and sat on her feet. He scanned the vista just like he had when he climbed the hill to save her that first day.

"If that was the correct model," Gwen asked, "could the effects of the wobble reach all the way down to Namibia? Do you remember?"

"At the time, I thought southern Angola. But it's been days," Tess said.

"The wobble?" That was Craig's voice. "What kind of weather would that cause?"

"A torrent, Dad."

"As much as Morocco?" Iris asked.

"No, Mom, if that model dipped lower, that would cause catastrophic flooding across the whole of northern Namibia. Looking, Tess."

"If that's what's happening, we need to warn people—Enrico at Etosha, the rest of Iniquus—and you all need to get out."

"Get out?" Iris asked. "But we're near high ground."

"This isn't a time when you could go up there and wait to see what happens. A storm the size Tess is talking about causes mudslides. Up isn't safe."

"Yes. South. Gather up what you need to save and start driving. Don't wait."

"Gwen, dear, this seems excessive."

"Oh, wow, Tess. Yup, you were right. That darned red line is extending straight south into Namibia. I'll start making calls."

"Gwen, now stop." Iris's voice warbled.

"Mom, I've heard Tess sound like this too many times to take it lightly. This is how Tess sounds right before a disaster. It's in her voice."

"You've been in a disaster with Tess before?" Iris sounded bewildered.

"You have no idea how many times. Mom, seriously, if she's talking about floods, you need to prepare for floods. Do you know what Tess does with her hand in the air? It's like she's sipping information. Tess, I'm back. Where should we go?"

"My first knee-jerk thought is the American Embassy in Windhoek. We drove by it, remember? It looks like a fortress, and while it's on an elevation … Gwen, here's the important thing, Enrico knows who you are and what you do. If you just call anyone saying the sky is falling, they won't listen. Call Enrico. I don't know how they evacuate, but the infrastructure in the area won't protect anyone."

Another group of tourists were entering the Himba village, asking the chief for permission to pass by the sacred fire.

Though the sun was out, and the sky hadn't changed from its giraffe-spot-clouded blue, a strobe of lightning flashed.

The Himba tribal members stood and looked toward the sky. Then they turned to look at Tess with distress.

A moment later, thunder rumbled from the north.

"Go home!" Tess called as she ran. "Go home! Get as high up as you can! Don't wait. Go now!" She was sprinting for their Jeep, Levi and Mojo glued to her side.

25

———————

Levi

Following Tess, Levi sprinted for the vehicle.

He knew he was wearing his battle face, yet he had no idea what was going on.

Tess had gone to stand by the hut, a finger in her ear, looking down at the ground with concentration. As she slid her phone back into her pocket, she scooped her hand toward Levi to get him moving as she hauled ass toward the entrance, screaming for people to save themselves.

Had he seen the flash of lightning? Yes.

Beyond the fact that the tour was obviously over for them, he was running blind.

Levi grabbed the handle, jerking the Jeep door wide and loaded Mojo. "The sun's shining, Tess." He shoved the key into the ignition.

"Go. Go. Go." She pushed Mojo's butt back toward Levi so she had space to climb in.

Her face pinched, and her muscles stiff; after pulling her

seatbelt into place, Tess held her limbs tight, making herself small.

Was this a flashback? Some kind of trigger? Levi had been out of her life for a long time; maybe this was new. "Tell me."

"I haven't felt like this since forever ago."

"In Ghana?' He reached over Mojo to wrap his arms around her, but as he kissed the top of her head, Levi knew that was the wrong thing, and he pulled away. "Tell me what to do here, Tess. I'm lost."

"Flee or die is what I'm feeling. Please, Levi, drive!"

Levi glanced out past the windshield, looking north.

The speed at which the clouds raced in, with their purple and green otherworldly colors, reminded Levi of a tornado that would sweep away a beautiful Oklahoma day and leave destruction in its wake.

The sensation at the pit of his stomach was something he remembered from when he was a kid. The sirens whirred, and everyone dropped whatever they were doing to race for their safe place.

Levi sensed the same thing Tess did: *flee or die*.

He wasn't on the road even ten minutes, racing away from the village, when the clouds covered the sun, turning day to night.

Even he could feel the energy stirring.

Lifting his arm, all the hairs stood on end. He turned to show Tess the electricity in the air. She held her hair in a pony-tail to keep her curls from tangling in the open Jeep. But the hair that had escaped her fist was full of static. From his train-ing, Levi knew that the atmosphere was gathering energy for a lightning strike, and they were at the point of impact.

He needed Tess safe.

Stomping on the gas, he rocketed them forward.

Lightning flashed, momentarily blinding Levi. When he

could see clearly again, fire raced along the ground beside them.

Sparks flew. Glowing particles in the wind landed on the trees and bushes, which had dried over long months without water, just kindling, ready to blaze.

The fire spread at an alarming rate.

Tess reached over and scratched sharp nails into the skin on his arm. Her mouth formed soundless words. He imagined this was how she'd learned to communicate silently as a child.

"I've got this, Tess. I'll get you safe."

She reached over and grabbed the steering wheel, forcing it to the right, and suddenly, they were careening off the road toward the fire line.

As Tess locked her arms so Levi couldn't correct the steering, Mojo's gaze was fixed on what was ahead of them. Levi hadn't known Mojo long enough to understand his barks. But it sounded like it might be the same kind of frustrated "Help her" bark as yesterday on the mock search and rescue mission when Mojo wanted Levi to get to Tess.

Then Levi saw it. Just ahead of them, two children raced away from the fire line.

But you can't outrun a fire.

A quick assessment and Levi realized that they couldn't stop to get the children. The vehicle would catch.

The heat was too intense.

"Tess, get over here. I need you to take the wheel. Put your foot on the pedal, don't lift it. I'll slide out from under you."

Holding the roll bar, Levi dragged himself out from under Tess and into the back seat. "Keep it steady, Tess. When the bumper is almost even with the children, take your foot off the gas, but do not brake." Cupping his hands around his mouth, Levi tried to get the children's attention past the roar of engine and flame.

They didn't turn.

He called out, "Tess, lay on the horn."

Tess pressed the palm of her hand into the middle of the steering column. The noise startled the children, and they turned their heads. Levi was standing in the back, his foot shoved under the seat, his toes curled up to brace himself. He opened his hands and leaned out.

The children instinctively reached for survival.

When Tess lifted her foot from the gas, because of the upward slope, the forward momentum was ever so slightly decreased. It was enough that he could lock his fists around two tiny wrists and heave upward, flinging the children onto the back seat.

Levi remembered how Tess described her mother lifting her by the wrist and flinging her at Abraham. What came next was destruction.

He quickly scanned the children, their chests heaving from the exertion, tear streaks where bright trails through the soot and smoke that coated their faces.

Levi climbed back over to the front seat. "Switch again, Tess. Get in the back with the kids. Make sure their clothes aren't smoldering, then get them on the floorboard."

He stood on the gas pedal as Tess clung to the roll bar and scrambled over the seat.

"Come here, Mojo," she commanded, and Mojo didn't hesitate to follow her over the seat.

"Good, Tess, get everyone down as low as possible and pull the wool blankets over you. They'll smolder, but they won't burn."

The first blanket she pulled out, she tucked around Levi, pulling it into a loose knot behind his head so it draped over his arms as he drove. Then she pulled her baseball cap from her pack and put it on his head before working on getting everyone situated behind him.

Catapulting forward, Levi tried to find a break in the flames. But the wind had whipped up the blaze. There wasn't much vegetation, he reasoned, and it was dry tinder, so it should burn and stop. His hope was to get to the rocky hill, climb up into the smoke, and back down the other side, where perhaps they could find fresh air to breathe. That was his plan.

In the back, Tess was asking the children if there were any of their friends who might be out in the brush that they hadn't seen and might need rescue.

"What did they say, Tess?"

"The school day is over. The other children are from rural homes that are too far away, so they live at the school. These children lived close enough to go home."

"All right, let's get them home so their parents won't be frightened."

"The big blaze over there," she pointed past him, "that was their house. When they saw the lightning strike it, they turned to run away but the fire was chasing them,"

"Was their family home?"

A moment later, she said, "No. No one was there."

Levi ducked his head to avert the embers flying around them in a gust of wind.

When he lifted his gaze again, Tess yelled, "Levi! The fire has us surrounded!"

26

Tess

HIS INIQUUS SAT-PHONE IN HAND, LEVI FAILED TO GET A call out.

The engulfing cloud cover made connection impossible.

Tess and Levi stood hand in hand on a boulder, watching their vehicle burn. There would be nothing to salvage by way of transportation or cover.

Levi had driven them right through the flame wall. And while their woolen blankets didn't catch fire, their tires did.

Fleeing into the rocky hills kept them from the path of the blaze, but the soil was dry and dusty here. In the deluge, they could see moving toward them from the north. Tess knew all of this would wash away and them with it.

A mudslide was just another way they could die that day.

Nowhere was safe.

When Tess turned to Levi, he had a GPS topo map open.

"We have to get down and away." Tess pointed toward the line of rain. "When that hits here, we need to be inside some kind of shelter, or we'll become hypothermic fast."

"Agreed," Levi said. "We've got to aim for the school."

"They might have a bus or some other way to get the kids—and maybe us—south to safety."

The children clung to each other as Levi pulled out his binoculars and scanned the area, comparing what he could see and the pictures on his GPS. "Okay, Tess, I have a plan. Can you weigh in?" He moved to stand shoulder to shoulder with her so she could see the map. "We have to go back down there. But it's already burned. It might still be hot. We'll have to carry the children. Their sandals won't protect the bottoms of their feet."

"What about Mojo?"

"I'll put him on my shoulders and hold the bigger girl to my chest. Can you piggyback the smaller boy?"

Tess looked down the side of the hill to where the fire had consumed the fuel, then slid down the buffet table of dead vegetation, gluttonously eating everything in its path.

"One foot on black," she said. "I remember that now. When they were burning the villages in northern Ghana, the only safe place was the area that had already burned."

As Tess and Levi bowed their heads over the map, praying to the gods of direction and wise choices, they calculated that it would be a three-mile hike, and the children were already exhausted.

Levi pointed in the direction, getting his bearings, then slid his equipment into his pockets. "As Goose said the other day, 'Time is flesh.' We need to go now and push hard."

"I'll do my best to keep up." With her hiking bag on her back and the boy's hand trapped in hers, Tess stepped cautiously after Levi.

This trek was a lot slower than her rescue the other day when Levi held her in his arms, and they pelted down the side of the mountain. But that had been a three-man team helping with stability. Today, they didn't have that luxury.

About halfway down, Levi shot a glance toward Tess. "You know what could make this worse?"

"Don't give the air any ideas."

"Black mountain rhinos," he said with a grin despite her warning.

"That's worse than anything else that might rear its terrified head?" She focused on Mojo. "Rhino-sour." That word had such a strange feel in her mouth. "What would Mojo do?"

"Protect us."

"Is that so bad?" Tess asked.

"Enrico warned me that Mojo turns berserker when he sees a rhinoceros."

"You're right. If we added a charging rhino and a berserker-mode Mojo into the mix, the situation would be—what did you used to call that? FUBAR? Yes, FUBAR."

Mojo jumped onto a boulder, coat oscillating in the wind. He reached out and bit at the air. Then turned and barked at Levi.

Levi turned. "Tess," Levi called, "your hair is floating."

Tess knew exactly what that meant. The air was charged with electricity.

"Lightning protocol," Levi yelled. "Get down here, Mojo."

Levi dragged his pack off his back, shoving it under the lip of a boulder. "Tess, put your bag here. It has metal." Mojo was by his side, and Levi unclasped his tactical K9 vest and slung it under as Tess shifted her gaze to sweep over the kids, making sure they weren't wearing metal.

"Okay, here's the deal," Levi said. "We need to have the least connection to the ground as possible. Spread out twenty feet apart. I know it's hard on you kids. Fast. Fast. Balls of your feet, Tess. Crouch down, feet together, lower your head, cover your—" and before he could get the word "ears" out of his mouth, lightning zapped the air. Thunder roared immediately after. It was long and low, tracking slowly over the sky.

Tess felt the vibrations in the marrow of her bones and the fillings in her teeth.

"Stay still," Levi yelled.

The boy stood, arms outstretched, stumbling toward his sister.

"No, get down!" Tess swung an arm through the air to catch his attention.

A second flash of lightning filled the air with the sharp, pungent odor of ozone. She waited for the thunder to shake the hillside before she turned to where Levi was checking on Mojo.

"Well, at least there aren't rhinos," Tess said as she stood and pointed toward a pickup truck bouncing off-road in their direction.

"Yup. I'm on it. Tess, you get the kids." Levi buckled Mojo into his vest then grabbed his pack. "I'm going to get him to stop." He handed Tess's cap back, and she pulled it over her curls.

Slinging her pack into place, Tess grabbed the boy's hand.

The girl—who was older—sprang out ahead, following Levi as he sprinted down the hillside.

Tess moved as fast as she could. The boy's short legs were a hindrance. Finally, Tess dragged her hand up until he was dangling near her hip, and he intuitively wrapped his legs around her and clung to her neck.

The rain began with a few drips and drizzles, followed by a normal rain shower.

Her baseball cap offered Tess a bit of protection, but the rain was coming in sideways. By the time she reached the bottom of the hill and was tracing after Levi and Mojo, it was pelting her so hard that she was having trouble seeing.

Levi stood in the path of the pickup.

The guy came right up to Levi, making Tess shriek as he barely stopped in time.

The man's eyelids were peeled back, showing the whites of his eyes, panicking.

Tess thought that the driver hadn't seen Levi signaling through the curtain of rain.

After slamming his hands onto the guy's hood, Levi rounded to the driver's side. "I need you to take us to the school."

"I cannot. No." He pointed across the blackened stretch. "I've got to get to my mother."

"Look, man. I've got two small children here. We need to get them back to the school."

As the rain beat against the sooty earth, baked to a clay-like hardness, Tess called, "We're not going to make it without a vehicle."

Levi was obviously not playing around.

And the driver, too, was single-minded in his focus.

Their back and forth was taking up precious time.

"Move over, guy," Levi commanded.

"No." He moved his hand to the gear to shift into drive.

Levi unlocked the door, popped it open, and dragged the guy out of the cab. "Look, man, I'm gonna give you your truck back. I just need to get these kids to safety."

As Levi tossed the driver into the back of his pickup, Levi yelled, "Get in. Let's go!"

While Tess loaded Mojo into the front, Levi grabbed the children with their wool blanket shields and popped them in next to the driver in the back. Tess climbed in the back as well.

Following his GPS, Levi raced for the school, squealing to a halt at the front door.

A middle-aged woman was standing in the doorframe, wringing her hands.

As they unloaded, the man got back under his steering wheel.

Tess yelled at him. "Don't go north. Do *not* go north.

He stared at her for a moment, considering her words. A decision made, he slammed the gear into drive and jetted off, heading north.

All Tess could think was that he had family there, and he was trying to save them.

Tess and the children scrambled inside the school. It was a relief to be inside of a structure, away from the stinging rain.

The first thing that Levi and she did was check their phones. Tess had a bar and Levi had none.

Tess dialed Gwen. Her priority was to get an expert opinion on what might happen next.

From the topo map, Tess knew that they were too low-lying for this to be a safe location.

As Gwen came on the line, Levi was asking the teacher about a vehicle, there was none.

"It's raining that hard there?" Tess yelled into the phone so that she could be heard above the deluge.

"Who is that?" Levi asked.

"Gwen."

He reached for Tess's phone. "Gwen, is anyone there from Iniquus? Reaper or Goose?"

Levi turned to Tess and repeated, "They left with Enrico earlier. They were up at the Etosha kennels. Gwen warned them."

It would have been nice if they could come with a vehicle, but Tess knew it wasn't practical, nor was it wise.

"Gwen, write this down," Levi said. "I need you to call this number." He reeled out an eight-hundred number then added,

"You need to say this word for word: Code Red. Code Red Code Red. Yes, you say the code three times. Next, 'incoming message from Levi Elliot, Cerberus Team Charlie.' Yes, Charlie. Elliot E-l-l-i-o-t." He looked aggravated but kept his voice even. "Give them these coordinates." Levi lifted the GPS unit and again reeled off a string of numbers. "Read the number back to me … That's correct. Keep writing. This is our situation: Thirteen children, three adults, including a teacher, Tess, and me, and we have Mojo."

Thirteen children? How had he gotten hold of that information so fast?

"Tell Iniquus about the storm you're seeing. We'll stay inside as long as we can. When the school floods … Yes, it will flood. We're in a low-lying area. Listen, Gwen, I need you to write this down for me. 'When the school floods, we'll take the children to the roof.'" He paused. "I understand that. That's why I'm giving you this information. I need the people at that phone number to send help … I don't know, Gwen. I have no idea what help they can send. But that's their job, so we'll just let them figure it out. Call them now. Do it now."

The teacher had come over and put her hands on Tess's arms. "It's not safe here?"

Tess split her attention between Levi's phone call and the teacher as she explained why this area, along with the school, was so dangerous.

"Then how?" the teacher asked, "how do we keep the children safe?"

27

Levi

There was no easy way to the roof.

And both Tess and Levi knew that's where they'd end up.

Already, there was a slick expanse of water that ran flush to the school's threshold.

Levi fixed a rope with climbing knots to the stove pipe extending above the roof line.

With Mojo wrapping his neck, Levi climbed just behind Tess to keep Mojo as safe as possible.

Tess reached through the hole for the supplies they'd gathered. They moved water, food, ropes, wool blankets, and tarps to the roof.

Tess had insisted that Levi find every jug with a top and a handle that he could and send them up to her.

There wasn't time for explanations or debate. So he did as he was asked. The teacher and the older children went off to search then brought the jugs to Levi to hand up.

Suddenly, a wave crashed the door open.

The children screamed and scrambled onto their desks.

As they were working, the flood waters had risen.

Without a barrier, muddy water raced into the school.

While the teacher worked to keep the children calm, one by one, Levi pulled a child off the desk and waded to the rope.

Hand over hand, they climbed.

Though it slowed progress, Levi didn't let go of the child until Tess had their wrists and hoisted them from his hands. If a child were to fall, it would be difficult to find them in the churning, debris-filled current and save them.

Heck, it was difficult just moving from desk to rope with them in his arms.

Another wave rolled through the school, and now Levi was up to his thighs. Casting his headlamp around the room, Levi made his way back to the rope and called up. "How many do you have?"

"Thirteen children, two adults," she called back, water gushing through the hole.

"The two adults are you and me?" he yelled. "Where's the teacher?"

Tess took a moment to scan the scene, then looked back to Levi. "She's not here."

Levi was back down in the water, surprised to find it was now at his thighs.

Tess leaned over the hatch and shined her headlamp around the dark interior. "Oh!" Tess yelled.

He saw it. The floating white shirt.

Tess started down the rope. But Levi grabbed her ankle and told her to get back on the roof to protect the children.

For now, the kids were probably safe; Levi just didn't want Tess to see what came next.

When Tess hesitated, he added. "Get to the top! I'll get her and hand her up to you."

How long had the teacher been floating?

It was most likely that she was dead, and Levi braced himself.

Grabbing the teacher, he pulled her to him. Dragging her from the water, Levi used his hip to press two student tables together and laid her out.

Struggling against the lifting tide, he rounded to her side to perform CPR.

As he pinched her nose and tilted her head back to blow the first potentially life-saving breaths into her lungs, the only thing that happened was a rivulet of brown water streamed from the corner of her mouth.

Levi continued the compressions, watching the teacher's face for any sign of rousing. He saw that there was a blow to her head and thought that she had been struck before she was floating in the water. Perhaps she had tripped as she was hustling the children toward this classroom.

He wondered what her name was.

He wondered what he should do with her body if this didn't work. The family would surely want to bury her.

If she were dead, he'd have to leave her here. He wouldn't bring her up to the roof. Maybe it was a Western mindset, but out of sight, out of mind might have power here.

There was no reason to heap trauma on top of trauma for the children when this crisis was ongoing.

Levi continued with the compressions, making sure that his thrusts were two inches deep and on the right cadence; for Levi, it was Johnny Cash's "I Walk the Line." But in his lifetime, Levi had only practiced this on CPR dummies during his periodic medic training classes. He'd never tried to save someone's life this way, and most of the words evaded him.

He knew that Tess would be up playing mother hen to the students with Mojo as backup. But she'd be wondering, wringing her hands.

Focused on the battery-operated clock on the wall. He gave this another five minutes. Then he'd have to get up top and see what he could do to keep them secure. The rain was still a curtain of gray. And the brown flood waters slapped against the windows.

The thigh-deep water held small animals, rats, mice, and some things he didn't recognize. Some swimming for their lives, some floating, already dead.

Levi didn't want to be in the water with them; they might see him as a means of escaping the flood.

With a glance up at the clock, he realized the time frame he'd set for himself was up. He didn't want to give up. But the water around the desks had reached the height that the teacher was all but floating.

For no reason other than a last-ditch effort, Levi climbed onto the desktop, straddling the woman. Raising his hands overhead, he interlaced his fingers, And with all his might, he slammed his hands down on her chest like Thor's hammer blow.

The teacher suddenly sat. She puked water from her lungs out into the swirling current that filled the room.

The woman was in full fight or flight. Vomiting and swaying, she gripped at her chest and throat as she heaved air in and out like a locomotive.

Another wave of water came through the open door.

It was time to get to the roof. Now or never.

28

———————

Levi

Between the two of them, Levi and Tess were able to get the teacher up to the roof. Then Levi clambered up after her, shutting the hatch door.

So far, they'd met every challenge.

Everyone was cold, wet, and tired, but everyone was alive.

Levi did a quick head count to make sure that was true.

Pulling the cans of white spray paint from one of the boxes he'd sent up. On one side of the black roof, he painted V/16, and on the other side of the roof, X/1. It was an international code that, when seen from the air, would be read as, "Sixteen people need help, and for one, it was a medical emergency." With that, rescuers would know how to proceed.

Hopefully, this information would stay current.

The water pounded down like it was Armageddon.

The children had climbed under the tarp, sitting in a circle around the teacher, who lay in a fetal position. The lightweight plastic could keep the rain off them and not fatigue their arms as they held it over their heads.

They may need that energy later.

Even with that many little hands holding the tarp in place, the wind could easily snatch it from them. A rope threaded through a corner grommet was attached to the stove pipe. That had to be Tess's foresight at work.

Levi pulled a dry bag from his kit and handed it off to Tess. Then he pulled another for himself. They opened them and put their day packs inside. He assumed everything inside was already damp, but that wasn't the only point of these dry bags. Tugging the mouth wide, Levi swung the bag through the air to fill it before rolling the top. This way, their survival gear should stay watertight and could possibly float. The neon orange might signal someone as they moved about the roof.

As soon as the bag was in place across her chest, Tess grabbed his arm. Her eyes were wide and rigid. "Levi, we're floating."

He stopped his chores and held his hands wide. Sure enough, the building bobbled.

"Velocity and debris," her words barely whispered past the wind. "This is a cement building." She stared out at the water as it rushed around them. Then, seeking out his gaze, she leaned in so her words weren't whipped away by the wind or drowned in the deluge. "Parts of the school were sealed with paint, but this building is cement blocks. It will absorb the water. We're going to sink."

Levi reached for his binoculars to see if there was a possibility for escape up ahead. But nothing sprang into view.

How was it that he and Tess had been apart for so long, and as soon as they found each other, they were put into one life-or-death scenario after another?

As the school bobbled in the water, the children screamed and clung to the edge of the tarp. The teacher, still stunned by the blow to her head and near-drowning, could do nothing to calm her students.

Tess grabbed two of the jugs and squat-walked to the edge of the roof. She opened the top and poured the contents into the flood waters. After recapping the empty jug, she moved to the next.

"Get away from the edge," Levi called. "The rapids can tip you in. "

"I have to do this here. The contents are caustic."

But with a nod to safety, she lifted the rope, still attached to the stove pipe, and knotted it around her waist.

Levi made his way to her, bringing three jugs in each hand.

"I counted," Tess said. "You all did a great job finding this many. I think we have two for each child, three each for us adults, and one for Mojo."

"You're making floatation devices?" Levi wrapped his legs around the stove pipe and crossed his ankles, and then he joined Tess, emptying bottles. "Is this a theory, or have you seen this work before?"

"We did this once when it was rainy season. For months, at that point, we had been playing hide and seek in our survival game. Well, for us, it was hide. The tribesmen did the seeking. We were living in a flood zone, hidden in the grasses. We had been doing all right finding food there. The bark and the fruit from the trees and bushes. But this huge rainstorm came up. It was very similar to this. Abraham took the gallon jugs we used to store fresh water and emptied them. Mama Ya was screaming at him that was all the water we'd been collecting. He ignored her. Then, using ropes, he tied the jugs together for each of us. I didn't know how to swim. Because of the wild animals in Ghana, it wasn't safe to get into natural waters. And there were no swimming pools where I was." As she spoke, she took the spool of thick cotton roping, cut off a length with her knife, then configured a life preserver,

"So the construction that you're tying, that's how Abraham did it?

"To the best of my memory, yes."

"And you survived the flood, obviously. Was the water as roiling and difficult as this flood?"

"I was nine years old. I remember being in the water. I remember having jugs on my chest and the rope running under my armpits and between my legs, keeping everything snug. I remember clinging to the handles to save my life, lifting my chin over the swells of the flash flood. I remember that Abraham had jugs on his chest, too, and that we made a line, Abraham, then me, then Mama Ya, then Moses, all floating along, all locking arms. Abraham yelled for us to kick. I didn't know how to kick, but I tried my best. As I kicked, there were things in the water—animals, tree limbs. Eventually, I remember that Abrahan shoved me onto a branch of a tree. He tied me in place so I could rest for a while. And after that, I don't remember how we got out of the flood. I don't know how long I was in the tree. But Abraham's creative thinking gave me a shot at survival. And I don't know how else to protect these children."

"It's a good idea, Tess. It's a very good idea. But this mess is like white water rapids."

"If they can keep air in their lungs, they can survive. I want to give them at least a chance. Look, their teacher is sitting up again. That'll give them hope."

"She really needs to see a doctor and get to the hospital so they can take a look at her lungs. The amount of muddy water that poured out of her was crazy."

"She was drowning?"

Yeah, Levi hadn't had time to catch Tess up, and he could

see the incredulity in her eyes. "A few rounds of CPR, and she woke up. Right now, she seems fine. But a near-drowning always needs a doctor."

"I didn't know that. Why?" she asked as her hands busily worked.

"Secondary drownings happen when there's water in the lungs, and there isn't the proper exchange of oxygen."

"How soon can that happen?" Tess hadn't stopped her pouring and capping, knotting and tying. Every two jugs, she signaled a child to her. "How fast do you have to get them to a hospital?"

The wind whipped away her question, but Levi was good at reading lips. "Fast, a couple hours is the most I'd give it."

"As if we have any control."

"Surviving the fight means you can stay in the battle. We need to keep racking up the wins." He lifted an empty jug. "This is the last of them."

As Tess stood up to tie her flotation device into place, the corner of the school dropped to the side.

The children released the tarp and grabbed at each other as they slid.

Levi, pressing his foot against the stove pipe, got his hand around one of their legs. As long as the children could keep a good grip on each other, they might be able to stay on the roof.

Tess screamed, "Hold on. Hold on to each other."

But one of the little ones slipped by.

Tess scrambled after her, yelling, "Mojo!"

Mojo leaped toward the child as Tess doubled over with both hands and feet on the roof, bear-crawling her way as fast as she could.

Levi couldn't release the children until the school righted itself—if the school ever did right itself.

The child slid over the side.

Mojo too.

And all Levi could see of Tess was her bottom and legs as she bent over the roof's edge.

Another wave righted the floating school, and Levi released the child's leg as he followed Tess's lead and bear-crawled to her side. Draping his bulk over her thighs to give her added weight, he peered over the edge.

Tess had shoved her hand through the handle on the back of Mojo's tactical vest.

Mojo was dangling off the side of the school. The child was in the water, clutching the handles of the floatation jugs.

Mojo held the rope from the child's make-do life vest in his teeth.

Bracing one hand on the lip that formed the roof's tray top, Levi prayed the decorative embellishment would hold.

Calling, "Good boy, Mojo. Hold," Levi saw the determination of the locked jaw and bulging muscles of Mojo's jowl.

Levi had no idea how they were going to get out of this. Tess couldn't release Mojo because there wasn't enough space on the handle for their hands to grip side by side.

With a single hand, Tess held about a hundred and twenty pounds between the child and Mojo's weight.

While Levi could wrap his hand around hers, moving a good amount of that weight to his own shoulders, bunching up like that meant that if the building tipped again, the child, Mojo, Tess, and he would end up in the flash flood waters.

As the school bobbled and shimmied, the water crept up the sides. All Levi could do at that moment was hold on. This felt very much like the rodeos when he had been a teen riding a bucking bronco.

Tess was taking the brunt of this. The roof apron was grinding into her hips.

"Tess, here we go. I'm going to lift my body. You need to

slither backward. Every inch is a win. You can do it." He bent his arm to give her limbs the slack it needed for her to move.

If the school popped and slammed the way it had been, and she was between joints, she could easily break her arm.

Losing her limb capacity could be the difference between surviving or not. It was up to him to keep the weight off her so she was safe. "Keep going, Tess. Get the edge at the crook of your elbow."

"Oh, yes, that's right." Once she was there, Levi wished he could reach for the child and fling him up onto the roof. But his grip and body position wouldn't allow it.

"Okay, Tess, on the count of three, you're going to move to get your hand on this side of the apron. One. Two. Three." He lifted his weight onto his toes into a plank. One hand on the apron, the other lifting the rescue.

"I can't. I … my body won't move that way. You're still too heavy." But then she yelled her surprise. Levi felt her sliding toward the center of the roof.

Glancing over his shoulder to make sure the new angle of the school wasn't making Tess slide over the other side, he saw that the children had Tess by the legs and were heaving her backward, their bare heels pressing into the gravel as they scrambled.

The child in the water hugged the empty bottles to himself. It was his one possible lifeline should the grips of strangers fail him.

As Tess slid to the center, Levi dragged Mojo over the edge, the rope still tight in his teeth. "Hold Mojo, good boy! Good boy! Hold!" Levi released Mojo's handle, reached for the child's elbow, and flung the boy back onto the roof.

Still clinging to the jug handles, the child scrambled into the circle, where the other students surrounded him protectively, petting and patting him to calm his nerves, his eyes wide and unblinking.

Levi looked over to see blood flowing from the grazes on Tess's legs. There was no point in first aid. Everything was wet.

For the moment, though, the rain had stopped.

Would it hold?

There was nothing else to prepare. There was no action to take other than to keep an eye out for some possible point of safety up ahead.

So far, miraculously, they'd stayed afloat.

Levi had been on boats that hadn't traveled as fast as this schoolhouse had.

Tess's assessment at the very beginning was accurate. The cement that was sealed with paint might be what allowed this structure to be so buoyant. But in short order, the unpainted cement would absorb too much water, and it would sink.

With nothing else to do to secure the roof, this was the part of the fight that Levi always hated—hunkering down.

That was when his life didn't exactly flash before his eyes, but it was certainly a time for introspection. Possibly even some self-condemnation. If this was the end of his life, had he spent his time wisely? Was he doing what he could to add something good to the world?

On the battlefield, those questions centered around Tess.

Levi beat himself bloody, trying to figure out what he might have done that would drive Tess into Abraham's arms.

And now, after last night, he had closure. They were able to love each other again.

It had felt like a miracle to have her in his life again.

But then *this* happened.

And though this moment was a reprieve of sorts, they hadn't survived the day yet.

29

———

Levi

Tess licked her lips as she scanned the children. When she focused on him, she asked, "Levi, how long have we been on the roof?"

Since Levi had watched the clock in the schoolroom to time the teacher's CPR, he was fairly precise when he said, "Twenty minutes."

She shook her head. "It feels like hours."

"It has been, counting everything that happened since we left the Himba village. Getting to the roof is just the next thing." He focused on her face, assessing. "Tess, you haven't slept in days, and now you're running on pure adrenaline. Can you do me a favor? It's going to be hard because, well, we're on top of a schoolhouse bobbing down the river. But can you sit quietly for a minute and center yourself? I want you to feel the air and tell me if it will rain again." He looked up at the steel-gray sky. "This respite from the rain is making a big difference in our survivability. But if you think those torrents are going to hit us again, we'll need to be much more aggressive. That means tough decisions and more hazards."

"Give me a for instance."

He didn't really have a "for instance." He didn't see a way out of this mess. "I might need to try to swim to shore with the rope." What he really needed to do here was plant the seed that everyone surviving wasn't probable. She'd been in enough circumstances that she knew that. But her brain needed to understand the situation and the ramifications. And he could see that Tess had that "no man left behind" conviction in her eyes.

"And pull the school over?" she asked with incredulity. "That would take a bulldozer."

"Those who are able could monkey crawl their way to land." He swallowed. Here it was, point blank. "There's a possibility that we can save some but not all."

Tess's face blanched white.

"It could be that if I strung the rope and got you and Mojo with me to help pull, that we could tie the children to the rope and rely on their jugs to keep their heads above water as we pull them to shore. The school will be underwater at any time now. I think we need a last-ditch plan formed. But if it's going to rain, we need to be proactive right now."

Tess turned toward the children.

"Take everything here out of the picture, and just focus and do that thing you do when you sip the air, please. I need all of the information I can get."

Starting on one side of the flood waters, she swept her gaze upward. Her hand came out. Palm open, gathering the energy in the wind, she rubbed the air through her fingers.

"The sky looks ferocious." Her finger came up, and she pointed at the clouds in the distance. "That's an odd structure for clouds."

Then, dropping her hand, Tess stared at it for a long time. "Are those columns?"

A wave splashed over the school's apron, making the children shriek and shrink against each other. They gasped and gripped even tighter in their circle, scooting back until they were compressed into a tight knot.

Tess reached out and gripped Levi's arm. "Do you still have your binoculars?"

Levi reached for his dry bag.

"I have my phone." She pulled her phone from her bag and took a picture of what she saw. Then she turned the screen toward herself, expanding the image to see the details.

With his binoculars up, Levi and Tess said, "It's a bridge," at the same time.

Dropping the binoculars to his chest, Levi asked, "Are you getting any bars on your phone?"

Before she could answer, another wave of water came up over the apron. Now, water had formed a pool, trapped on top of the roof by the apron that saved the child moments ago.

Levi shifted until he could speak into Tess's ear. "If the water swirls around the bottom of that bridge, it's possible that the school will crash into the pylons. When the school crashes into it, the children are going to fly forward, and then they're going to fly back. We need to position them in the best way we can so they stay on this roof."

She nodded.

"If we can catch hold of something on the bridge, I'm going to try to get a rope from the pipe to the pillar. And when it happens, Tess, listen, it's going to be violent, and it's going to be fast. That water is going to ram the structure against the barrier."

"I wish we knew how deep the water is. Maybe the floor of

the school is very near the bottom of this flood. Maybe that's why we've only sunk this far."

"My hope is that we have enough time to get at least some of the kids to safety."

When Levi was with the SEALs, they were given impossible tasks without a clear means of accomplishing them. It was a challenge he really enjoyed.

The Team would brainstorm possibilities, and even the craziest ideas were put on the table. Right now, without equipment, Levi wasn't coming up with any ideas, workable or not.

The children hunkered together, moaning their distress.

Levi held the binoculars up to assess. "Sweetheart, from what I can see, there is metal undergirding. It's possible that I could put you on my shoulders, and you could tie the rope."

"Then what?"

"You crawl up and straddle the beam, and I start moving kids to you." He pulled off the binoculars and handed them to Tess.

She stared at the bridge for a long moment. "Yeah, I think I see what you're suggesting. And under any other circumstances, I'd say you're crazy."

"A touch of crazy usually helps in tight places like this one."

A wave pressed behind the school, and suddenly, there they were, hitting the pylon.

Without further discussion, Tess reached out, climbing onto Levi's shoulders as she clung to his hands.

With the school sinking even deeper into the water, Tess couldn't reach the beam. "Levi, I need to stand on your shoulders."

The school shimmied and shook; getting her up that high would be a trick. But Levi knew that tone in her voice. She'd committed to the idea and wouldn't be easily swayed.

It was nothing Levi had tried before, but they fumbled through. With Tess's sneakers on his shoulders and his hands wrapping her ankles to hold her steady, he could feel her straining upward.

"Still not high enough, Levi. Grab my ankles tighter, and I'll lock my knees. You can shove me up there the length of your arms, right?"

Levi wasn't so sure about that.

His legs wide and his knees bent for stability, Levi knew just how precarious this all was. But what choices did they have?

When he was a SEAL based out of California, he'd learned to surf. Was this that much different?

Probably.

But Levi was projecting only good outcomes.

"Just another little thrust, and I can hook my arm. Push me a little farther, Levi."

He didn't want to do that. It meant gaining inches by shifting his feet closer together and unbending his legs. Less stability, more danger.

But he did it. Because sometimes there were no choices.

And this time, it paid off.

Tess was able to get her hands on the beam and rest her hips there, allowing her to

throw a leg over and push herself to a seated position. Tying the rope into place, she called down, "Okay, ready."

Thirteen times, Levi pressed a child onto the rope. Thirteen times, Tess grabbed them at the top and positioned them on the beam.

Levi was down to the teacher and Mojo.

The school was breaking apart with every wave.

The water was up to Levi's mid-shins.

"Send Mojo up next," Tess called. "There's a place for him near the bridge pylon, and no one else will fit in there."

Levi squatted to gather Mojo into his arms and moved him to wrap his neck, leaving his hands free. "I'm going to take Mojo up," he told the teacher. "I'm coming back for you. I'm not abandoning you. I'm coming back."

The teacher nodded vigorously, her teeth chattering.

The school banged and lurched, and now the teacher was in the fast-moving waters up to her thighs, with nothing to hold on to for balance.

Levi grabbed the rope and, hand over hand, hoisted himself up as fast as he could.

Tess, straddling the beam, reached for the handle on Mojo's tactical vest.

Ducking his head, Levi pushed Mojo toward Tess, not letting go until Mojo scrambled toward the spot Tess had picked for him.

"No, Mojo, no. Go there." She pointed.

Mojo seemed to get the idea. It wasn't an easy space to get into and fit. Mojo waggled and strained, grunted and growled to get himself up underneath. As soon as he was positioned, Levi went back down to find the teacher clinging with both hands to the rope.

The three empty jugs held her chest high enough in the water that her face wasn't in the current.

There was no schoolhouse to be seen.

"Give me your hand," Levi yelled, reaching for her.

She was obviously terrified.

"Grab my hand!" he ordered.

She was in a state of freeze. Levi had experienced it himself. It's a terrible feeling to think that you might die because—while your brain is processing and begging the body to cooperate with the right action—in freeze, no action is possible.

He moved farther down the rope, closer to the swelling waters.

Catching hold of her wrist, she continued to grip the end of the rope, looking wild-eyed.

With the teacher dangling from his left hand, Levi was grateful for the knots in the rope. He placed his boot on the knot and then shoved his weight into his feet. He slid his right hand up above the next knot. Again and again, he crawled higher.

The teacher was still in shock, clinging to the end of the rope, when Tess reached out and grabbed her. Tess helped maneuver the woman to a spot on the beam.

With the roar of water beneath them, his normal voice sounded like a whisper. "Tess, you never told me—will it rain?"

"Yes, it's coming."

"And this bridge is made of concrete. It's not going to hold up. I can already see side fissures forming from the pressure of the water. We've got to get people on top of the bridge and see if we can't get help. I don't know what's up there. So I need to go see for myself and make a plan."

Levi pried the teacher's fingers from the rope, tied it to his waist on one end, and tied the other end to the undergirding.

Tess reached out to stop him. "No, what are you doing?"

"Tess, up is our only hope."

"Up then." She tipped her head back. "How do we do that?"

He looked around. "I have no idea."

30

Tess

ONE OF THE SKILLS THAT TESS HAD LEARNED IN HER YOUTH was that the first knee-jerk body reaction was the lizard brain, or, as Abraham called it, the ancestral brain. It was the part of the brain that wanted to survive. It was often reliable. But sometimes, modern circumstances didn't mimic those of the ancients.

In ancient times, when predators were attracted to movement, freeze was the perfect stay-alive tool. In this case, it absolutely was not. But the teacher was paralyzed.

The rain was so heavy that Tess couldn't see beyond the bridge apron in either direction.

Here they were: two functioning adults, thirteen children, and a woman deeply in need of medical help. With the others lining the beam, Levi wrapped Tess in his arms.

Despite all evidence to the contrary, Tess found hope in the sound of his heartbeats. "We don't have much time, Tessy, but we have some. Let's think this through."

"We have to take into consideration the volume of rain. It's heavy and slippery."

"Looking at the water levels. We can't stay here."

"And yet … " She turned her head and kissed his chest. She left it unsaid that there seemed to be no way out.

A tree floated under the bridge, scraping the sides with its leafless branches.

"Pull up your feet. Pull your arms in," Levi called.

As it moved through, it caught on the edge of the apron. The trunk pushed left and right, trying to flow with the water.

"We could jump for it," Levi said as he assessed. "Half on one side, half on the other, we link arms, stay buoyed with our jugs."

"Mojo and the teacher."

He drew a line with his finger. "We lay them on top."

"And when the log rolls, what then?"

"We're imperiled no matter what choices we make. There is no safe way out of this circumstance. What we have is hope and effort. If I go first, I can straddle the trunk, and you can lower the kids to me. Mojo, the teacher, then you dangle down, and I reach for you. If we hurry, we might make it before this breaks free."

"I'd have to drop them from my hand to yours. Why don't I untether myself from the beam, and you tie the rope to the trunk so they can climb down as you guide them?

"Because Tess, if you fall, then who will help the children? It's game over."

"What if the tree doesn't break free? What if the water swells, and we're trapped?"

"You know this very well—sometimes, it all just comes down to dumb luck. Children," Levi called. "I'm going to give you instructions. You will repeat them back. I want you to know what to do if you end up in the river. Hold onto the handles of your jugs and hold your heads up where you can breathe. Feet point downriver. Pull your knees to your chest to make yourselves more buoyant. Try to see where the water is calmer and angle yourself in that direction if it's toward the shore. Tell me what you will do. I will—"

As a group, the children repeated his words.

Tess absolutely did not want this to happen. Right now, she was on a solid structure. For the moment, they were all safe. Safe-ish.

The children shivered with cold, and soon, hypothermia would affect their capacity to function and help with their own rescue.

Soon, this area would fill with roiling water, and they'd be trapped. All it would take was one large wave from the north, and just like the schoolhouse, this space could fill in an instant.

She whispered into his ear. "That's the best we've got?"

"Given our limited understanding of the situation, that's the best we've got at this moment. And under the bridge, at least we're not fighting the rain.

"Okay. Okay. I'm just going to amend that you go first, and Mojo goes second. Put Mojo further up the tree. Since he caught the boy earlier, I think that if one of the children slips, he might catch hold of them before the water makes the decisions."

There was no more discussion. It was as if those words flipped a switch, and Levi was moving. He tipped her head back and kissed her with such conviction that it was an unspoken promise, "I'm getting you through this."

And her return kiss told him that she was right beside him in their fight for a future.

The tree was only as wide as Mojo's body, and Tess couldn't put the puzzle together in her mind. But Levi had been a SEAL for decades. She was sure that his brain processed in ways that hers could not.

Levi rolled until his hips balanced on the edge of the beam, and he lowered himself. Hanging from one arm, he swung his foot out again and again until he was a pendulum. On the next swing, Tess covered her eyes with a guttural moan.

The children were whooping and clapping, telling Tess that Levi made it.

When she pulled her hands away, Levi had a leg on either side of the trunk and the root ball at his back. He looked over his shoulder and called, "Everyone sit very still. Mojo, to me."

Mojo scrambled out from his little den. His jug attached to the handle of his vest flipped from side to side. He came to Tess first and caught her eye, checking on her.

"I'm okay, Mojo. I'll be with you in a minute. Thank you, baby." She took an extra moment to scrub behind his ears, lowering her forehead to his. "Okay, you need to go now."

Levi called out again, "Mojo, to me."

Mojo gathered himself in a tight ball, then, pressing his back paws against the beam, he leaped into Levi's outstretched arms.

The children were clapping and whooping at Mojo's success. Next, Levi commanded Mojo to go out.

Tess had seen this command the other day. Enrico showed off Mojo's skills on the obstacle course. On command, Mojo walked a thin beam and lay down in the end, waiting.

This was a tree in flood waters, hardly the same thing other than the sequence of commands.

Soon, though, Mojo was lying in place.

Tess could see that the floatation jugs could be lifesaving or deadly. What if the water rose under the bridge, the tree didn't release, and the jugs floated them to the top when they needed to dive beneath the apron? Everyone could be held in place until they drowned.

It was a balancing act in her brain as it always was in an emergency.

What did she know?

What could happen so she had a contingency plan?

The thing that terrified Tess was that her brain would freeze, like the teacher's, and she'd be unable to move and, therefore, die.

Panic kills.

Pragmatism. Forward movement. Hope.

That was her new mantra.

"First child, Tess."

Tess wrapped her hand around the child's wrist. Like Levi, the girl rolled until her hips were on the beam. Gripping with both hands, she lowered herself until she hung over the water. Tess clenched her abs and said, "Let go. I have you."

And to Tess's great surprise, she did. The weight was unexpected. And Tess was glad that her other hand had a tight grip on the rope. Leaning over and looking down, Tess could see that Levi gripped a root and leaned right as he reached out his left hand. He'd try to keep the tree from rolling with the dynamic shift.

"Let go, Tess!" he called.

The girl dropped straight for the water. Before she went completely in, Levi grabbed her arm and flung her up on the trunk. Levi instructed the girl to straddle the trunk and inch her way forward. "Move, Tess! Next, hurry!"

This was a change of plans. *He must see something I don't,* Tess concluded, as she reached for the next child to move closer to her so they were above Levi. In Tess's mind, having the children on the trunk made it less stable and upped the chance of rolling. But Tess also knew not to weigh in. Too many captains meant the ship went down.

One after the other, the children dropped, straddled, and moved forward.

Here was the girl that they pulled from the fire. She'd trust Levi.

Here was the boy that went over the edge of the roof. He'd trust Mojo.

Here was the brother from the fire. He didn't hesitate.

But now, there was the teacher. Immobile. She was deadweight.

Tess knew she didn't have the strength to help the teacher.

"Tess, what's going on?" Levi called.

"The teacher is in shock," Tess yelled back.

Levi's gaze scanned. "Here's the plan. You're not going to like it."

"I'm not leaving her!"

"No, we'll try to help. This is the best I can think of. You're going to untie the rope from the beam and throw it to me on the far side so I can lower her down. Next, you'll untie the rope from you and tie it to her waist. Last, you need to partially untie her flotation, letting the rope drop within my reach. One end still needs to be tied to her waist."

"Okay, then what?"

"Then you'll lower yourself to me."

"I'm not leaving her there."

"Only for a moment."

"You're right. I don't like it."

"Once I have you, you'll need to reach for the rope and bring it to me. I'll have a good grip on you."

"And the floatation?"

"I'm going to pull the floatation to drop her off the beam.

Then, I'll lower her with the rope. Imagine the beam acting as a component of a pully."

"Got it."

"Tess, she isn't coming out of this unscathed. But this is a chance at survival, And it is putting you in a thousand times more danger than I'm comfortable with."

"What if I did that and stayed up here to get her over?"

"I need you down here to help me with counterweight. It's most likely that she'll end up in the water, but we'll have her on the rope. And I'll need your help getting her onto the trunk. If I'm trying to save her, I can't help you, and there is no scenario where I'd let that happen."

"Levi!"

"Tess, we don't have time for this. The water's rising fast. I still have to figure out how to get us out from under the apron. Get the rope on her and get down here. Or we lose everyone, Tess. Do you understand?"

Tess's body was moving at a speed she didn't know was possible. After arranging the ropes as Levi specified, she did as the others had done. Rolling her hips onto the beam, wrapping her fingers as best she could, and stretching her arms long, she dangled over the raging waters.

Tess hadn't understood how frightening this was.

Trust Levi?

Absolutely.

Trust Mojo as backup?

Yes.

But she had been in flood waters with jugs before. She remembered swallowing the muddy water and how it filled her nose and made her gasp for air.

She remembered the terror.

"Tess, I know. And I've got you." Levi called. "Believe in me."

Those were the magic words. Eyes squeezed shut, she let go.

Sliding through the humid air, toes in the freezing cold water, as the tide dragged her body, Levi's grip tightened around her arm.

He pulled her to his chest. "Swing your leg over, Tess. Good job."

And now that she was here, Tess could see why Levi's voice, calm and steady, had the sharp edge of do-or-die.

The water was almost to the edge of the bridge.

"Lean right, Tess. Hold out your arms like you're going to dive. I'm lowering her now."

The tree, with her added weight, sank deeper into the flood waters.

For Tess, this was the reason why they shouldn't be on top of the trunk but holding hands across the trunk.

But after the current reminded Tess of its strength and how that felt as a child, Tess understood that this was a risk they needed to take.

Tess's heart wanted to mourn those who wouldn't make it. Surely, the idea of all of them getting to safety was improbable.

How many could they save?

And could they even save themselves?

A glimmer of hope; it looked like they had a reprieve.

For the moment, the rain had stopped again.

As Levi and Tess worked to lower the teacher. Mojo started barking.

The barks rang against the cement and filled their space.

Was he warning them about something they hadn't perceived yet?

Tess fought to keep her whole attention on getting the teacher situated.

They ended up laying her across Tess's lap.

While Levi freed the rope, Tess tied the jugs back onto the teacher.

Just looking at her face, Tess thought that whatever injury she had sustained when the schoolhouse flooded and she had nearly drowned was making her system deteriorate. This woman desperately needed a hospital. Even if everything had worked perfectly when this whole day had started with the lightning strike, the hospital was an hour away from where the school had been.

Mojo's barks grew more frantic and more aggressive.

It reminded Tess of a woman in labor or those who were dying when they seemed to reach out to the world beyond. Abraham said it was a call to the ancestors for help in passage.

Levi had pushed his floatation to his back and tied the rope under his armpits, then once around the trunk without any knots, handing the end to Tess.

"What's happening here?" she asked. The tree sunk until the water hit her thighs as she bent her feet backward against the current and squeezed her knees together.

Levi leaned in and spoke near her ear; so their plans were between them alone. "I'm going to move forward and get into those branches and see if I can't compress them to fit under the ledge. When I do that, I have no idea what will happen next. You must—Tess, listen to me—you must let go of the rope. I need a chance to swim away. You *must* let go of the teacher to save yourself because the children will need your help. If they float to shore, they will be hypothermic without food, water, or skills. You *will* get to shore. You *will* save the children."

Tess got it.

He was right.

"And you," she insisted. "You and Mojo will help them, too."

31

———

Levi

AS SOON AS LEVI WRANGLED HIS TWO HUNDRED POUNDS OFF the trunk, the tree rose to float higher in the water.

That was a good thing and a bad one. Soon, the water would lift them above the apron of cement. Then, the only way to get out would be to dive.

And with the floats, that would be impossible.

Without the floats, the children would drown.

Tess would drown. And he simply wouldn't allow that.

Mojo was going ballistic at the front of the tree. The sound of his barks sure sounded like he was trying to get someone's attention.

That might well be wishful thinking.

Levi wasn't going to depend on help from anyone.

It might well be that Mojo was warning away one of the animals that were struggling to keep their heads up and make it to shore—a floating lion or hippo.

The cull had been one way that the animals of Namibia

were affected, but this was a devastation to the living that could take generations to right.

Levi bent his knees to lift his feet in the swells. Moving hand over hand, he tried to slow his pace as he reached the drowning hazard of the branches. As he passed by, Mojo lowered his head and gave Levi a quick tongue bath before he went back to barking.

Here at the fork in the branches, Levi paused to assess, to test the limbs, and to imagine different scenarios.

Finally, he moved into the fork of the tree and reached his arms around to pull the limbs into a hug. As soon as he did, both the narrowing of the branches and his weight popped the tree under the apron and out into the broad expanse of fast-moving water.

"Hang on! Hang on!" he called back.

The children screamed and bent forward to clasp their arms around the trunk.

Mojo laid flat, but his barking was incessant.

They flowed southward.

But Mojo scrambled to turn and look behind them as he barked.

Looking over his shoulder, Levi saw a dump truck driving over the bridge with the window down. It was possible the driver would hear Mojo and take a look. It was also possible that the driver was wide-eyed in fear as he raced toward his family like the man in his pickup truck had earlier when all they had to do was escape a fire.

That must have been what Mojo had sensed.

The truck took a left off the bridge, driving at top speed parallel to the flow, bypassing them. They were probably trying to race away before they, too, were caught in the flash flood.

Levi was struggling in the water. Hugging the branches to

him, he'd lifted his knees to his chest to lessen his drag, but the current was intense.

The root ball turned.

Where Tess perched was swinging around until the tree was horizontal to the current.

Tess was yelling something.

All he could make out was, "Levi!" He desperately wanted to see her and make sure she was all right.

The root ball was forward now. And Levi trailed behind. It took Levi some time to twist himself around to see down the river.

Ahead, the dump truck had stopped, and there was a bustle of activity.

Could it be that someone was doing something that would help them?

Mojo had stopped barking. His focus was pinned on the shore activity. His tongue hung long as he panted.

They were close enough now that Levi could make out two men in gray tactical wear. Then he realized that Reaper and Goose had found them. His teammates must have gotten the message from Gwen or Iniquus and jumped into action. Where and how they'd acquired a dump truck would be a story he wanted to hear. But it was a genius choice.

Reaper stood on top of the dump truck cab, and just before a tree floated by, he did a surface dive with a rope attached to his waist.

Now, *that* was some major pipe-hitter shit there. *That* was a SEAL in action.

The rope momentarily crossed their path at the root ball and caught.

Reaper grabbed around the trunk as Tess helped him to tie the tree off.

Tethered as it was to the dump truck, the tree rotated

around. Now Reaper was closer to the shore, and Levi was down current.

The water did them a solid and shoved the branches closer toward land.

Goose high-stepped into the water and tied off the main branch with another rope. Reaper and Goose waded out of the water, each grabbing a line and pulling it toward solid ground. "Stay still!" Reaper called.

"Let go of my rope, Tess!" Levi yelled.

The moment the words left his mouth, Tess had complied.

Levi gathered the waterlogged rope and then held out the loose end. "Mojo, bite."

In the water, following Goose's line, Levi made it halfway to shore. where he bent in two. "Mojo jump!"

A moment later, Mojo landed on Levi's back, claws digging into his flesh as he sailed onto dry ground, rope dangling from his teeth. Reaper accepted the end and tied it to the dump truck.

Now, Levi was methodically making his way toward Tess. With an arm around the trunk, one at a time, he grabbed a child's arm and pressed the little one toward Reaper's waiting hands. One after the other, to the teacher, and then finally to Tess.

On the shore, Levi and Tess lay, clinging to each other as they caught their breath.

Reaper's hand jutted toward them, and Levi looked up as he grasped it, accepting the assist.

"Short window, man. You can rest later. We have to get back over the bridge before it falls away. There's nothing good happening north of here.

The children were all in the back of the dump truck.

The teacher was unresponsive as Goose worked on rendering aid.

"Tess, go up with Reaper in the cab. I need to stay back here and tell Goose what happened so he knows what first aid to give."

"I can—"

"Please, Tessy, do me a favor and go to the front. I need to know you're warm and safe." He put his hand on his chest. "I *need* that."

Moments later, the dump truck was retracing its path over the bridge, down the road, and toward safety in Windhoek.

As they pulled up in front of the hospital to deliver the schoolteacher and her class, Tess was back in Levi's arms with Mojo by their side.

The miracles of these last few days left Levi in awe of how quickly life could change.

This time, he'd gone into the fight and come out with a super-hero dog and the love of his life.

Worth the dangers?

Damned straight.

EPILOGUE

Tess and Levi walked hand in hand past the rows of white chairs toward the arch made of fruiting grape vines and flowers, where the officiant waited with a welcoming smile.

Adam, Mordecai, and Mojo stood on the bride's side.

Levi's SEAL buddies from Iniquus, who were instrumental in setting him on the path back to Tess, stood at his side.

And Betty had ambled in to see what was going on, bending her long, graceful neck to nibble on the arbor leaves that looked so enticing.

Everyone was casual and comfortable under the glory of a Namibian sunset.

Friends and family from the States, the school children who had gone on that wild river ride with them, their families and extended families filled the guest seats along with Enrico, Josef, and Kimba.

Surrounded by broad and joyful smiles, Tess and Levi continued up the aisle.

Reaching the officiant, Tess lifted a hand, gathering the air and rubbing it through her fingers, then turned to grasp Levi's outstretched hands.

"What do you sense, Tessy?"

"The air is vibrating with love, hope, and thanksgiving. It is the most beautiful thing I have felt in this lifetime." And with that, Tess stepped into Levi's arms, and their kiss was the seal that meant this wedding ritual was for their families.

For Tess and Levi, their hearts were already one.

As they pulled apart to make their vows, the officiant chuckled. "Usually, the kiss comes after the promises are made. But in this case and on this occasion, this is the perfect way to start your married life. Two hearts that had always been meant to find each other and then find each other again, dear ones, may you find peace in your union. And may you live happily together all the days of your lives."

Finally, Levi was where he belonged, with the woman he cherished.

When Levi looked into Tess's eyes, he felt sure that Tess's ancestors, Mama Ya, Moses, and Abraham, were all smiling down on them, blessing their union.

The Next Book in
The World of Iniquus Chronology
& Cerberus Tactical K9 Team Charlie is

Buy Shielding Instinct on Amazon

**For the complete list of The World of Iniquus books in
chronological order keep turning the pages.**

READERS

I hope you enjoyed getting to know Tess, Levi, and Mojo. If you had fun reading **Sheltering Instinct**, I'd appreciate it if you'd help others enjoy it, too.

Recommend it: A few words to your friends, book groups, and social networks would be fantastic.

Review it: Please tell your fellow readers what you liked about my book by writing a quick review.

Discuss it!: In **Fiona Quinn's SPOILER group** on Facebook. (https://www.facebook.com/groups/fionaquinnsspoilergroup/)

ACKNOWLEDGMENTS

My great appreciation-

To my publicist **Margaret Daly**

To my cover artist, **Melody Simmons**

To my editor **Rossana Tarantini**

To my Street Force, who support me and my writing with such enthusiasm and kindness.

To all the professionals who shared their knowledge of working K9s, especially the various Virginia search and rescue teams.

To all the wonderful professionals I called on to get the details right as I conducted my research, especially **M. Carlon** for her medical expertise.

To **Fermin Saez** for his kindness and companionship during my month of research in Namibia. The picture of Fermin enjoying a glass of side-adventure wine will always be the way I recall my trip to Big Daddy.

To **Mark Sedrak**, who filled my imagination with his amazing tales of world adventure. I appreciated his company as I explored my character Tess on the many real-world Namibian adventures touched upon fictionally in this novel.

Please note: This is a work of fiction, and while I always try my best to get all the details correct, there are times when it serves the story to go slightly to the left or right of perfection. Please understand that any mistakes or discrepancies are my authorial decision-making alone and sit squarely on my shoulders.

Thank you to my family for your love and support.

I send my love to my husband.

And, of course, thank *YOU* for reading my stories. I always smile joyfully as I type this sentence. I so appreciate you!

THE WORLD of INIQUUS

Chronological Order

Ubicumque, Quoties. Quidquid

Weakest Lynx (Lynx Series)

Missing Lynx (Lynx Series)

Chain Lynx (Lynx Series)

Cuff Lynx (Lynx Series)

WASP (Uncommon Enemies)

In Too DEEP (Strike Force)

Relic (Uncommon Enemies)

Mine (Kate Hamilton Mystery)

Jack Be Quick (Strike Force)

Deadlock (Uncommon Enemies)

Instigator (Strike Force)

Yours (Kate Hamilton Mystery)

Gulf Lynx (Lynx Series)

Open Secret (FBI Joint Task Force)

Thorn (Uncommon Enemies)

Ours (Kate Hamilton Mysteries)

Cold Red (FBI Joint Task Force)

Even Odds (FBI Joint Task Force)

Survival Instinct - (Cerberus Tactical K9 Team Alpha)

Protective Instinct - (Cerberus Tactical K9 Team Alpha)

Defender's Instinct - (Cerberus Tactical K9 Team Alpha)

Danger Signs - (Delta Force Echo)

Hyper Lynx - (Lynx Series)

Danger Zone - (Delta Force Echo)

Danger Close - (Delta Force Echo)

Fear the REAPER – (Strike Force)

Warrior's Instinct - (Cerberus Tactical K9 Team Bravo)

Rescue Instinct - (Cerberus Tactical K9 Team Bravo)

Heroes Instinct - (Cerberus Tactical K9 Team Bravo)

Striker (Striker Force)

Marriage Lynx (Lynx Series)

A Family of the Heart Cookbook

Guardian's Instinct - (Cerberus Tactical K9 Team Charlie)

Beowulf - (Certified Cerberus Tactical K9)

Red Line (CIA Color Code)

Sheltering Instinct (Cerberus Tactical K9 Team Charlie)

Shielding Instinct (Cerberus Tactical K9 Team Charlie)

With more Iniquus novels to follow!

For the most up to date list go to FionaQuinnBooks.com

This list was created in 2024.

ABOUT THE AUTHOR

Fiona Quinn is a USA Today bestselling author, a Kindle Scout winner, Amazon Top 40, and an Amazon All-Star.

Quinn writes suspense in her Iniquus World of books, including Lynx, Strike Force, Uncommon Enemies, Kate Hamilton Mysteries, FBI Joint Task Force, Cerberus Tactical K9 Series: Alpha, Bravo, Charlie, and Certified Cerberus Tactical K9, the Delta Force Echo series, CIA Color Code Action Adventure, and now, an Iniquus cookbook!

She writes urban fantasy as Fiona Angelica Quinn for her Elemental Witches Series.

And, just for fun, she writes the Badge Bunny Booze Mystery Collection with her dear friend, Tina Glasneck, as Quinn Glasneck.

Quinn is rooted in the Old Dominion, where she lives with her husband. There, she pops chocolates, devours books, and taps continuously on her laptop.

www.fionaquinnbooks.com